WHAT PEOPLE ARE SAYING ABOUT

THE FIREBIRD

This rollicking adventure...is re............ in tone of the Harry
Potter series and Jeanette Winterson's Tanglewreck. Packed with
literary references and cleverness, it focuses on the age-old
conflict between light and dark, good and evil, and on the power
of story. An engaging read for 9- to 14-year-olds.
Lucy Pearce, Juno Magazine on *Rise of the Shadow Stealers*

A cracking tale. This is a well-written, well-paced story. It
grabbed my attention immediately and kept me reading...plenty
of action and conflict.
Krystina Kellingley, author, and editor on *The Nemesis Charm*

A well-paced, absorbing read that will appeal to many adults as
much as it does to children...Both the premise and the writing
are reminiscent of other fantasy authors such as Terry Pratchett
and in particular, Jasper Fforde, although this is certainly unique
and interesting enough to stand firmly on its own two feet.
Confident pre-teen readers will enjoy it as an intriguing
adventure story, while older readers will enjoy reading between
the lines for a more philosophical experience.
Isobel Jokl, Dig Yorkshire on *Rise of the Shadow Stealers*

A great read, well-told story, lots of action, nicely paced, and the
dialogue and language hits the mark.
Maria Moloney, author and editor on *The Nemesis Charm*

I love the world created for this story...The writing reminded me
of that in a great picture book – the words flow, smooth and easy
to read. They are nearly lyrical. The writing is some of the best I

have read since becoming a book reviewer five years ago.
Suzanne Morris, Kids Lit Reviews on *Rise of the Shadow Stealers*

This thrilling quest is a wonderful read for all fantasy junkies...
Zyllah, Miss Literati on *Rise of the Shadow Stealers*

After both my children had devoured the book, I finally got to see what all the fuss was about, and I was instantly hooked. Fast paced and gripping, my son compares this to his favourite, Artemis Fowl, whilst my daughter declares it 'a book you can lose yourself in.
Platform Harrogate Magazine on *Rise of the Shadow Stealers*

The Firebird Chronicles:
The Nemesis Charm

The Firebird Chronicles:
The Nemesis Charm

Daniel Ingram-Brown

OUR STREET BOOKS

Winchester, UK
Washington, USA

First published by Our Street Books, 2016
Our Street Books is an imprint of John Hunt Publishing Ltd., No. 3 East St., Alresford,
Hampshire SO24 9EE, UK
office1@jhpbooks.net
www.johnhuntpublishing.com
www.ourstreet-books.com

For distributor details and how to order please visit the 'Ordering' section on our website.

Text copyright: Daniel Ingram-Brown 2015
www.danielingrambrown.co.uk
Twitter: @daningrambrown
Facebook: www.facebook.com/danielingrambrown

Map illustration copyright: Si Smith
Character illustrations copyright: Sarah Johnson

ISBN: 978 1 78535 285 0
Library of Congress Control Number: 2015952160

A CIP catalogue record for this book is available from the British Library.

Design: Stuart Davies

Printed and bound by CPI Group (UK) Ltd, Croydon, CR0 4YY, UK

We operate a distinctive and ethical publishing philosophy in all
areas of our business, from our global network of authors to
production and worldwide distribution.

CONTENTS

For Marcia, Kaine, Gracie and Leo

And to my own Nemesis, John Pearce. Thank you for your support.

Prologue

It worked, Libby thought. *My crazy plan – it really worked.*

Moments ago, two Story Characters from the world beyond the Un-Crossable Boundary had been holding Libby's hands. They'd been there in her house, with her in that very room. She could still feel their touch, the warmth of their skin on hers. They'd been as real as the chair beneath her, as real as her cat, Alphabet, brushing against her legs. But as quickly as they'd appeared, they'd vanished – whisked away, back to their own world.

The image lingered. Closing her eyes, she pictured the two Characters again. They were students from Blotting's Academy, the school to which all Story Characters go to be trained: Apprentice Adventurers from the Department of Quests. Scoop was a girl with a squiggle of black hair and Fletcher, her brother, a tall boy with sharp features.

You crossed the Boundary, she thought. *You did it. You really did it. Tonight, your world has become a bridge, a bridge to the person I love most in my world.*

As the reality of what had happened sunk in, something trembled inside her. A stream of emotion surged upwards, carrying with it hope, madness, pain; a torrent of light and dark. As it broke the surface of her mind, Libby laughed aloud.

'I *will* find you,' she said. 'I will cross this bridge and find you.'

She stared at the rivers of rain that were streaming down the window.

'Don't worry mum,' she whispered. *'I'm coming...'*

* * *

At that same moment, on the other side of the Un-crossable

1

Boundary, an explosion shook the Oceans of Rhyme.

To the west of the South Bookend Isles, a seagull flew quietly over the waters, searching for fish, when there was a distant rumble below. It seemed to come from beneath the surface. The sound was eerie. It grew, until the whole ocean vibrated with the noise. Instinctively, the seagull began to fly away.

Suddenly, behind it, the sea erupted.

A great pillar of water and steam shot upwards, punching through the waves. A circle of white surged outwards like a halo across the surface of the sea. The sound thundered through the air, knocking the seagull off course. Wings of ash plumed from the base of the pillar, as if a mighty angel was leaping from the water. And then, through the feathery cloud, columns of volcanic magma began to rise. They pushed upwards, puncturing the water and cloud, as if the body of the angel was breaking free.

Around the rock, the ocean turned red.

As the seagull fled, it looked back. Behind it, a new island rose, interrupting the horizon line. Its dark spires pointed up through the ash cloud that hung over it. Clearly visible in the tallest of the rocks was a sight that struck fear even into the seagull's un-thinking heart. Dark and brooding, staring out across the water, was a face. Its eyes were made from fissures in the rock and its mouth was a wide, black cave. From the seagull's vantage point, it looked like the face of a skull.

A cold wind blew from the cave's mouth. It swept across the ocean.

As it reached the seagull, the bird thought it heard a sound, a whisper on the wind…

I'm coming…

And then, as the breath of the cave reached the little bird, the seagull's world turned black. It fell from the sky, plummeting and twisting toward the water. It hit the ocean with a splash and sank slowly into the sea, never to be seen again.

Fletcher and Scoop

Chapter 1

The Firebird

A strong wind was blowing in from the west. It swept along the coast of Fullstop Island. Even though it was a beautiful day, the sea was choppy. Fletcher and Scoop were aboard the Storyteller's tall ship, the Firebird. They were wrapped in long macs and wore yellow sowesters on their heads. The ship was racing through the water at fifteen knots, leaving a ribbon of surf in its wake.

Scoop stared at the train of white water behind. It stretched back across the sea, dividing the blue expanse.

A year, she thought. *It's been a year since I started at the academy, a year since we were whisked away to that other world.*

That night seemed like a dream now.

In the months that had followed, the memory of it had faded. The two Apprentice Adventurers had lost themselves in their academy training. Their mentor, the Yarnbard, and their parents, the Storyteller and his Princess, had taken them to see them many of the island's sights. They had abseiled into the Creativity Craters, swum with the Fable Fish, and sailed around the islands of the Puddles of Plot. Now their *Beginning* year was over, and they were about to start their *Middle* year.

She scanned the pathway of white water that cut through the sea.

'Scoop!' a voice bellowed.

She blinked, her trance disturbed.

'Scoop!' the voice called again. 'Get here now!'

Scoop looked round. The boatswain of the Firebird was glaring at her. The rest of the crew were behind him, straining on a rope.

'What do you think you're doing, girl?'

Above them, the captain stood at the ship's wheel, his hair

4

blowing behind him, a dark look on his face. 'Quickly, they're gaining on us!' he shouted.

'SCOOP!' There was threat in the boatswain's voice. 'GET HERE NOW!'

Scoop shook herself and ran across the deck to join Fletcher and the rest of the crew. She grabbed the end of the rope and began to pull. In front of her, she could see her friends, Nib and Rufina. They leaned forward and hauled back in perfect unison. They were slackening the mainsail, part of which flapped uselessly in the wind. It had been ripped.

'Heave... Heave... Heave...' the boatswain yelled, red-faced. 'Come on – put your backs into it! We need to slacken her off, fix her up and get this ship moving again, before it's too late.'

Fletcher looked over his shoulder.

'Where have you been?' he hissed. 'They're gaining on us!'

To port, another mighty tall ship loomed into view. The fiery feathers and sharp eyes of its figurehead, a red falcon, rose and plunged through the waves. The falcon had been carved to strike fear into any ship it pursued. It did the trick. Fletcher's heart was beating fast.

The captain moved forward. 'Haul that mainsail back up, boatswain! Rip or no rip, we must keep up speed.'

The boatswain turned to a burly man who was frantically trying to patch up the rip. 'Quickly, is it fixed?'

'Done,' the man said, stepping away.

'Haul her up,' the boatswain bellowed. 'All together now – what are you men or mice?'

'Well, I'm a woman,' Scoop said under her breath.

'A girl, you mean,' Fletcher whispered.

The Falcon was almost upon them. It was closing the gap with every moment. Scoop could see the Red Hawks, the private army of the Falcon family, on the ship's deck, their scarlet coats and muskets flashing in the sun. They were a fearful sight.

'Heave... Heave... Heave...' the crew yelled as they hauled

the mainsail up again. The wind caught it and the Firebird's pace increased.

In the distance, Fletcher could hear the sound of a band playing, a brass band, and there was a crowd cheering.

'They're going to win the race!' Scoop squealed, looking to her side. The Falcon was neck and neck with the Firebird now.

'Not now our mainsail's back up,' Fletcher replied. 'The Firebird's the fastest ship on the Oceans of Rhyme. Nothing can beat it.'

The golden feathers of the Firebird's figurehead shone. The enormous bird seemed to be stretching forward, pulling the ship past the Falcon. Ahead, the finish line was marked by two small fishing boats. Beyond them, the Port of Beginnings and Endings was festooned with colour, as bunting flapped in the breeze. A brass band shone like a pearl at the end of the pier.

It was Dorian's Day on Fullstop Island, an annual holiday. Dorian was the seafarer who had discovered Dawn Rock, one of the North Bookend Isles. He had brought back its rejuvenating waters and so a festival had been named in his honour. There were all sorts of games and attractions at the port, but the main event was the Tall Ship Race. This year four ships had entered, the Falcon, the Firebird, the Wild Goose and a smaller ship called the Robin. The Wild Goose and the Robin had fallen behind in the second phase of the race. They had both taken the most direct route, sticking to the coast, but the wind had been lower there and their progress had been sluggish. The Falcon and the Firebird had both chosen to head further into open waters, where the wind was stronger. Their course had been longer, but the risk had paid off, both ships winning back distance, overtaking the Wild Goose and the Robin as they rounded Rainbow's End. Now, the race was between the two of them.

Scoop loved sailing. There was nothing quite like it – working as a team, battling the elements, telling stories when the wind was low, keeping watch under the night skies. The work was gruelling and the hours long, but she had learnt so much from being at sea. Galleon racing was one of her favourite lessons. It was that sort of thing that made Scoop glad she was an apprentice at Blotting's Academy. Life was never dull.

As the mainsail was tied off, she and Fletcher ran to the prow of the ship. From there, they could see who was in the lead. There wasn't much in it. They were so close to their rivals, they could see their faces. Arnwolf, the eldest son of Ullric Falcon, king of the Bassilica Isles, was standing proudly on the bridge of his father's ship, surrounded by an adoring group of Apprentice Snobs. Scoop could see Mythina in the huddle. Hector Pike and Nicklous Jaegar were there too. The Snobs spotted Fletcher and Scoop and glared at them.

'Ran into a little trouble, did we?' Arnwolf shouted across the water, smiling at the rip in the Firebird's sail. 'That old ship's been patched up so many times, I'm surprised it floats at all!' The rest of the Snobs laughed.

'I don't think so,' Fletcher yelled back. 'You may have a new ship, but it was designed to look like this one. There's a reason for that. Thing is, your ship *isn't* the Firebird. This is still the fastest ship on the ocean!'

'We'll see about that,' Arnwolf sneered.

'Perhaps it would help if you actually sailed the ship yourself, rather than leaving it to your lackeys.' Fletcher pointed at the Red Hawks, who were straining to tighten the Falcon's mainsail.

Arnwolf laughed. 'Well, there's the difference between you and me. I'm the eldest son of a king. I'm never quite sure who you are. Are you a son or a servant? Doesn't always seem to be a great deal of difference where the Storyteller's concerned.'

Fletcher clenched his fists. He and Scoop were the children of the Storyteller's princess, and although, long ago, a darkness had forced the Storyteller and their mother to part, Fletcher had chosen to believe that the Storyteller *was* his father. He'd staked his future on it. But there was always a doubt that lurked in the back of his mind.

Arnwolf could see he'd touched a nerve and grinned.

'Let it go,' Scoop said, tugging Fletcher's sleeve. 'He isn't worth it.'

'All hands on deck!' the boatswain of the Firebird bellowed.

Scoop tugged Fletcher's sleeve again. He glared at Arnwolf for a moment, and then turned away, dashing back with Scoop to join the rest of the Firebird's crew.

The boatswain was giving orders. 'Tighten that bough sail. All together now. This could be the difference between life and death, between success and failure. Give it all you've got!'

They hauled the rope, working as one, fighting the wind, intent on turning it from foe to friend.

The ship's musicians started to play, fiddles and accordions weaving frantic reels.

A strong gust of wind caught the foresail, making the ship tilt heavily starboard. Fletcher felt the thrill as the galleon swayed, creaking.

The finish line was just ahead now. The sound of the crowd ashore grew louder, horns and trumpets joining the throng.

The first mate rang the ship's bell.

They were about to cross the finish line. The race judges stood on the fishing boats, different coloured flags in their hands; red to signal a win for the Falcon, gold to announce triumph for the Firebird.

Both ships' crews were watching, their eyes on the judges. The musicians caught the moment, their melodies soaring.

Then, out of nowhere, a tiny, dilapidated fishing vessel appeared. It was directly in the Firebird's path. They could see a fisherman with a birds-nest beard and stormy hair on the deck, manically hoisting a flag. It was as if he were deliberately trying to sabotage the race.

'Look out!' Scoop called, pointing at the tiny boat.

The boatswain looked and, letting out an expletive, leapt back to the ship's bell. He rang it, the warning sounding loudly, clanging across the water. But the fisherman seemed oblivious to the danger; either that or he was deliberately ignoring it.

'Do something! We're going to hit him!' Scoop yelled, distressed.

Fletcher whistled. 'We'll make matchwood of that boat.'

'Hold your course!' the captain yelled, a fierce look in his eye. He focused on the Falcon, which was almost level with them.

'We have to do something,' Scoop hissed. She looked at the fisherman; there was a wild, desperate look about him.

The flag the fisherman was raising seemed to have a message scrawled on it, but Scoop couldn't see what it was.

She felt sorry for him. Something was obviously wrong. Nobody would dare block the course of the race without good cause, unless they were ill or confused. Her heart went out to him.

That boat's his livelihood. He's going to lose it.

'He must have a screw loose,' Fletcher whispered.

Scoop looked around, everyone was staring at the fishing vessel, but nobody was doing anything.

A sudden burst of anger exploded in her chest. Somebody had to do something. They couldn't just plough into the vessel, risking the man's livelihood, maybe even his life.

Some things are more important than a race!

Before she knew what she was doing, Scoop was running across the deck, past the Mainmast, towards the stern of the ship.

Out of the corner of his eye, Fletcher saw the movement. He glanced back. Scoop was leaping up the wooden steps that led to the quarterdeck, where the captain of the Firebird stood at the wheel, his eyes fixed on the finish line.

Oh no, what's she doing?

Quickly, he dashed after her, watching as she bounded across the ship. Before he could catch up with her, she'd grabbed the ship's wheel and was spinning it wildly.

The ship swayed, creaking, the rigging clanking. Below, the rudder trembled, as seawater churned past it, pushing the galleon off course. The crew looked away from the fishing vessel to see what was going on.

'What the hell do you think you're doing?' the captain yelled, as the Firebird curved away from the finish line. He looked back to see the Falcon inch into the lead. Red-faced, he grabbed the wheel and tried to spin it back, but Scoop clung to it, using her whole body to hold it down.

'Get her out of here!' the captain shouted. The first mate and the boatswain started to climb to the quarterdeck.

Fletcher was already there. 'What are you doing?' he said, grabbing her arm.

'The right thing,' she replied, giving him a sharp look. 'We can't just plough on and hope we'll miss him.'

Fletcher sighed. She was right. Scoop was always getting him into trouble with her need to do the "right thing".

The first mate was almost there now, the boatswain hot on his heels. They looked on, alarmed, as the captain tried to take back command of the ship.

'Help me,' Scoop hissed.

Fletcher grabbed one of the handles of the ship's wheel and joined Scoop, resisting the captain's efforts to correct their course.

The little fishing boat was just ahead. For a moment it looked as though the Firebird was going to collide with it. The golden figurehead plunged down, as if diving to catch prey. The boat swayed, disappearing from sight. Scoop looked on, her heart in her mouth. Had she been too late? If only she'd acted earlier. And then, all of a sudden, the fishing boat rose back into view. It was by the side of the Firebird now. It rolled dangerously in the wash of the galleon, but it was safe.

Scoop heaved a sigh of relief. They had averted the collision. She let go of the ship's wheel. The captain spun it back, hard the other way. But it was too late. There was a cheer from the shore.

Scoop looked. The race judges had their hands in the air. From them, red flags billowed in the wind. The Falcon had won the race.

The captain's face was thunderous. Scoop was scared he might blow into a tempest. He ordered the first mate to remove Fletcher and Scoop and detain them in the sergeant's quarters. As they were escorted down to the main deck, and shoved towards the hatch that led below, Scoop looked back at the little fishing boat. She could see the message that was scrawled on the flag now. It said, "Beware the sickness. Beware the sea." The wild-eyed fisherman was looking directly at her. He was holding up a net. It was full of fish, but they were black, as if they'd been burnt. The fisherman was shouting across the water. Scoop peered at him, trying to read his lips.

'Dead!' he was shouting, 'All dead! Beware the sickness. Keep away from the sea! You *must* keep away from the sea!'

Before she could see anything else, the first mate pushed her through the hatch into the belly of the Firebird, manhandling her into the sergeant's quarters. The door slammed and she heard a key turn. He had locked them in. They had lost the race and Scoop doubted the captain would ever allow them to sail the Firebird again.

'And all that for a crazy fisherman,' Fletcher said.

Scoop looked at him. He was grinning.

'You do like to get me into trouble, don't you?'

She smiled back shyly. 'We're Apprentice Adventurers. What else do you expect?'

'Nothing less, nothing less,' he said sagely. 'But we'd better brace ourselves. The captain's on his way, and I don't think he's very happy with us.'

Chapter 2

Dorian's Day

Fletcher and Scoop's mentor, the Yarnbard, was in his office at Blotting's Academy. He was deep in thought. His grey beard twitched and his yellow kaftan rustled as he stared at the hot wax he'd just dripped onto a scroll of parchment. It looked like congealing blood. He pressed the academy's sealing stamp into the viscous liquid. It oozed around it, before drying into a hard scab. The old man pulled the stamp away and held the parchment in his hands.

A strong gust of wind suddenly blew through his office, knocking his hat from his head. He leaned down to pick it up. As he rose, he glanced at a circular table in the middle of the room. On it, a black, jewel-encrusted box waited.

The Yarnbard stared from the box to the parchment, a heavy sadness weighing on his heart. Without another thought, he rose from his seat and, picking up the parchment, headed out of his office to begin the steep descent to the bottom of the tower, in which his rooms were located.

* * *

As the Yarnbard reached the bottom of the tower, two young girls, academy apprentices, sped around the corner, nearly knocking the old man over.

'Oh, sorry,' one of them said, skidding to a stop. She looked embarrassed.

'We didn't mean to… Are you okay?' the other asked, without taking a breath.

'Calm down, don't worry yourselves,' the Yarnbard said kindly. He peered at them. 'I know you two, don't I?'

One of the girls nodded. 'I'm Alfa.'

'And I'm Sparks,' the other added.

'Ah yes, Alfa and Sparks – Apprentice Spell-Shakers – new first years, if I remember correctly?'

'Yes, that's right,' Alfa replied. 'You took us into the Story Caves to meet Mr Tumnus for our taster Seasons lesson.'

'Aha, yes that's right – Winter to Spring. That Narnian winter was definitely a spell of bad weather that needed shaking, eh?'

The girls nodded.

'And, am I right in thinking that you know my apprentices, Fletcher and Scoop?'

Alfa and Sparks looked at each other and grinned.

'Yes,' Alfa said, enthusiastically, 'we do.'

'Well in that case, I'm glad I bumped into you. Or rather, I'm glad you bumped into me!'

Alfa blushed.

'In fact,' the old man continued, 'it's very fortuitous indeed. I wonder if you would do me a favour?'

Alfa nodded. 'Of course.'

The old man held out the scroll. 'Would you take this to Fletcher and Scoop?'

'We'd love to!' the girls replied in unison.

The Yarnbard smiled, sadly. 'So lovely to see such enthusiasm in new apprentices.' He paused. 'But you must look after this, girls. Guard it, won't you? And see that it is quickly delivered.'

'Of course,' Alfa said, glancing at Sparks. The message was obviously important.

'Good.' The old man handed over the scroll. 'Go quickly then.'

Wind swept along the pathway, blowing up dust.

Nodding, the two girls ran off.

'Thank you,' the Yarnbard called after them.

He stood for a moment at the bottom of the stairs and watched as they disappeared, a seed of nostalgia for the time that was passing already in his heart.

It had to be Apprentice Spell-Shakers I bumped into, he thought, with the bittersweet knowledge that coincidences were rare in his world.

* * *

It was mid-afternoon and the sun beat down through a hazy blue sky.

Fletcher and Scoop had spent the last two hours locked in the sergeant's quarters aboard the Firebird, while the galleon weighed anchor. Now, Nib and Rufina were rowing them back to shore. It was a beautiful day at the Port of Beginnings and Endings, which sheltered in the mouth of the River Word, protected from the sea wind. Behind them, the Firebird floated serenely, her sails now furled, her mast proud against the blue sky. She didn't seem to lose any of her majesty in defeat.

'So…?' Rufina said, her red hair fiery in the sun. She stared eagerly at the apprentices. 'Tell us everything! We didn't wait to row you back for nothing, you know!'

Fletcher's eyes glinted and Scoop looked coy. Their friends sat opposite them, pulling the oars of the boat. They were in no rush and the little dinghy drifted leisurely across the quiet water, sunlight glinting from the waves. The sound of the festivities floated across the harbour bay.

'What did the captain say? I bet you got quite a telling off!'

Fletcher puffed his chest out, imitating the captain. 'I am not so much angry, as disappointed…'

'What a liar,' Nib interrupted. 'He was livid. I thought you were going to end up having to walk the plank into shark infested waters.'

The four friends giggled.

'I think he felt guilty,' Scoop said.

Nib spluttered. 'What – for almost crushing a fisherman and

destroying his vessel?'

'So he should!' Rufina chipped in. 'You were magnificent, Scoop.'

Nib prodded Scoop with his foot. 'You looked like some sort of monkey clinging to that wheel.' He winked, and Scoop felt herself blush.

Fletcher had a mischievous twinkle in his eye. 'I couldn't decide whether to help you or the captain.'

Scoop punched him on the arm.

'Ouch – that hurt!'

'Good!'

'So what *was* the damage?' Nib asked.

'Not the fisherman's boat, thankfully,' Scoop replied.

Fletcher smirked. 'We've been banned from sailing for...one month.' He sounded triumphant.

'What? Is that it? You jammy beggars.'

'And,' Fletcher added, imitating the captain again, 'if we ever pull a stunt like that again, we'll be banned from the Firebird for life.'

'For life?' Rufina snorted. 'Oh yeah, I can see that – the children of the Storyteller banned from their own father's ship.'

Fletcher and Scoop grinned. There were some advantages of being the son and daughter of the Storyteller and his princess.

They were getting close to the quayside now. Nib rested his oar in the boat and pulled a flask from under his bench. 'I brought some provisions,' he said. 'Thought we should drink to our defeat.'

'And toast Scoop,' Rufina added, 'the "Fisherman's Saviour".'

'I always wondered if you had a secret ambition to be an Apprentice Hero,' Fletcher said.

Scoop punched him again.

Fletcher groaned. 'Watch it, or I'll push you in!'

'You wouldn't dare!'

'Watch me!' Leaning across he grabbed Scoop's leg. She half

laughed, half screamed. He lifted her up, trying to push her over the side of the boat.

'Hey, you two, stop it. You're rocking the boat,' Rufina yelped, trying to steady it.

But Scoop wasn't taking any of it. She fought back, tickling Fletcher, pushing him over to the other side. The little dinghy rocked back.

Nib reached over the side of the boat and flicked a handful of water over the fighting siblings. The two apprentices spun around, their mouths open.

'Oi!' they both said.

'Well, don't go ignoring my girlfriend, then.' Nib put his arm round Rufina. She rolled her eyes.

'Right, that's it…' Fletcher said. Before Nib could move, he'd splashed him in the face, soaking his hair.

Nib furrowed his brow. 'I see. Then this, my friend, is war.'

After a few minutes of shrieking and laughter, all four of them were totally drenched. The bottom of the boat was full of seawater. Scoop lifted the sleeve of her tunic. It was sodden. 'Look at me,' she said.

Nib laughed. 'We'll just have to dry out in the sun, won't we?'

'Over a tankard of Noveltwist,' Rufina suggested.

'Now, there's an idea!'

Scoop smiled. Despite losing the race and having to face the captain's wrath, she was happy. The sun was shining, her friends were with her, and they had the festival to look forward to – an evening of dancing under twinkling harbour lights.

Dorian's Day took place in the last week of the summer holiday. It was only a few days until the academy celebrated the start of the new year with an informal gathering at the Wild Guffaw. Scoop loved living on Fullstop Island. She loved being part of Blotting's Academy. What better way to celebrate the best year of her life than dancing the night away at the festival? She lay back in the boat and felt the coolness of her clothes soothe her.

'So where's that drink, then?' she said, staring at the sky. 'There's someone I want to toast.'

'Ah yes,' Nib said. He reached down and picked up the flask again. Pouring four cups, he handed one to each of them. 'This is Dorian's Delight – made with water from the North Bookend Isles.'

Scoop looked. The drink was tantalising; the purest water she had ever seen. 'I'd like to toast the Fisherman,' she said, dreamily.

Rufina frowned. 'I wonder why he wanted to disrupt the race.'

'He had a message on his flag. It said, "Beware of the Sea".'

'Nutter,' Fletcher muttered, 'a fisherman who's scared of the sea – whatever next.'

Nib raised his cup. 'To the crazy fisherman – and to Dorian's Day.'

The four friends lifted their cups. 'Cheers!'

Scoop took a sip, a feeling of freshness filling her whole body. It was as if the drink was washing her, opening her, creating space for something new.

For a new year at the academy, she thought, wondering what amazing experiences the future held.

* * *

Alfa and Sparks were making their way slowly along the harbour walls. It was hard to move amid the throngs of islanders. They weaved through the crowd, searching for Fletcher and Scoop. But they were only small, coming up to most people's waists, so it was hard to see much further than their immediate surroundings.

In the harbour, a competition was taking place. A mast had been suspended horizontally from the pier. It had been smeared with grease. A large man with a bushy moustache was sitting astride the pole, over the water. He was tentatively pushing himself further along, his tailcoat flapping either side of him.

'That's the slippery pole competition,' Alfa said to Sparks. 'They have to see how far they can get before they fall off.'

Just as she said it, there was a gasp from the audience. The man had slipped. He was now hanging upside down, his arms and legs wrapped around the pole. He looked like a sloth clinging to the branch of a tree.

Sparks stopped for a moment to watch.

The man made an attempt to push a little farther along and then, to the delight of the audience, lost his grip and fell, his arms and legs splaying as he plummeted to the water. He hit it with an enormous splosh. The islanders laughed, clapping.

'A big round of applause for Mr Bumbler there,' a tinny voice echoed across the water.

Spark's mind drifted. For some reason, she couldn't focus on the festivities. She was distracted. Out of the corner of her eye, she kept noticing strange occurrences. The little boy in front of her had just told his dad he didn't want his ice cream anymore. Shortly after, a portly man with a tankard had put on a long coat, saying he could feel a chill. And Sparks was sure she could feel the old woman next to her shivering.

She looked up. The sky was blue and the sun beat down on them. How was anyone cold? As she glanced back, she noticed the bunting overhead was flapping angrily. She looked around the harbour. The rest of the bunting hung limply in the summer heat. Only the little flags above her and Alfa moved.

That's strange, she thought.

'Come on,' Alfa said, breaking her train of thought. 'We need to keep looking. The Yarnbard said we needed to deliver this quickly. I wonder what the message is. Maybe Fletcher and Scoop will let us see it.'

Sparks nodded. Still distracted, she followed, continuing the search along the harbour wall. As she left, she glanced back. The portly man had started to take off his coat again and the bunting where they'd been standing had fallen still. It was as if the wind was following them.

Don't be silly, she said to herself. *Focus! Whatever this message is, we need to deliver it to Fletcher and Scoop like the Yarnbard asked us to.* She looked into the crowd, searching. Above her head, the bunting rustled ominously.

Chapter 3

A Bitter Wind

Fletcher, Scoop, Nib and Rufina were back on land. After the relaxed atmosphere of the rowing boat, the crowds at the harbour were stifling.

'Let's find somewhere to sit,' Rufina called ahead to Nib.

'Yeah, preferably where we can buy a tankard of Noveltwist,' Fletcher added.

'Excuse me,' Nib said, tapping an apprentice on the shoulder. The boy held a frothing tankard of cordial. 'Where did you get that?'

'Up on the green,' the apprentice replied. 'The barman's got a stall there. The Wild Guffaw's closed today.'

'Thanks.' Nib nodded. 'This way,' he called over his shoulder. Fletcher and the others followed, squeezing through the crowd towards the green, which was set back from the harbour.

Academy students sat on the grass in scattered formations, chatting, laughing and sunbathing. Groups of boys threw Punctuation Pucks across the clear blue sky. Friends shouted greetings to the apprentices as they passed.

Around the edge of the green, various stalls had been set up. A tombola, Splat the Umlaut and an Ast** isk Shy huddled under striped awnings. To one side of the green, a group of shopkeepers in long shorts were limbering up for a race. Fletcher looked at them, bemused.

'The Hyphen-Dash,' Rufina said, as she and Scoop caught them up. 'Thumbandingo usually wins it.'

'Well, he has got awfully long legs.' Fletcher grinned.

As he was speaking, a Punctuation Puck hit him on the arm. He shot round, fumbled for a moment and then lifted his fist, the puck in his hand.

'Good stop!' a lanky boy called from across the grass.

'I've been practising my Grammar Games, Alexander,' Fletcher replied. He paused and then threw the puck back.

Alexander smiled. 'We'll have you on the team next year! Bad luck on the race, by the way. You were robbed. Everyone could see the Firebird was going to win.'

'Thanks!'

'Look at you, Mr Popular,' Scoop giggled, nudging Fletcher in the ribs.

'Me? You're the one who's waved at almost every group of girls we've passed!'

It was true, Fletcher and Scoop had become very popular on Fullstop Island. Everybody knew who they were. It took them twice as long as most to travel through Bardbridge. Every few minutes they'd be stopped by someone wanting to give them the latest gossip or invite them to a party. After their return from Alethea and the great wedding banquet, the pair had acquired the nickname, "the Shadow Stealers". They were minor celebrities, the son and daughter of the Storyteller and his bride, the apprentices who had travelled to the darkest place and stolen their mother's story back for the island – for the Storyteller himself.

'Right,' Nib said, as they settled on a place to sit, in the shade of a tree. 'I'll head to the bar, then. Noveltwist all round, is it?'

Scoop nodded.

'I'll come with you,' Rufina said. 'You'll need help carrying the tankards back.'

Nib's eyes lit up. 'Okay, thanks.' Rufina clutched his arm and they headed off towards the open-air bar. Scoop watched as they disappeared, more than a little jealous.

A shrill rattle of tambourines broke her train of thought and she looked round. A bearded player dressed in a white suit emerged from behind a canvas curtain tied between two trees. He lifted his hands with a flourish. Either side of him a little huddle of musicians in rag-like costumes looked up at him in frozen poses.

'Welcome to marvellous, mesmeric, mysterious Tales from the Sea,' the man announced in a theatrically ghostly voice.

The musicians rattled their tambourines again and shifted position.

A little crowd began to gather around the players.

'Hear tales of monsters from the Minotaur Oceans, ghouls from the seas of the Undead Lands and...' The bearded man turned his head.

Scoop stepped back. For a moment she thought he was looking directly at her. She glanced over her shoulder. There was nobody behind her. She turned back. He was definitely looking at her. His eyes were intense. She felt her skin prickle.

'And hear the legends of Thresholds – caves that are doorways between worlds. Once you set foot across a Threshold, there is no coming back. No living Mortale can return to this world once they have crossed such a doorway.'

As he spoke the words, wind blew through the trees and Scoop felt a chill. She shivered. The player seemed to be holding her gaze. It was making her feel uncomfortable.

Why's he looking at me?

'Ouch!' Fletcher suddenly knocked into her, breaking her trance. She stumbled.

Another rattle of tambourines made her look back at the player, but he had turned away now and was continuing his performance.

'Who knocked into me?' Fletcher said. 'Was that you?'

'No.' Scoop replied. 'I was looking at...'

'It was us!' the voices of two girls rang out. Fletcher and Scoop looked down to see two first year apprentices beaming up at them.

'There you are,' one of them squealed.

'We've been looking for you *everywhere*!' the other said loudly.

'How was it?'

'We missed it! Did you win?'

The two girls looked like twins. Both of them had baby faces and frizzy hair, and both looked at Fletcher and Scoop as if they were their idols.

'Oh, hi, Alfa – hi, Sparks,' Scoop replied.

Alfa and Sparks were well known to her and Fletcher already, even though they had only arrived on the island for summer school. They seemed to be intent on becoming part of their friendship circle, often turning up out of the blue and trying to hang around with them. Scoop looked at Fletcher's face. He looked predictably irritable.

'So?' Alfa said, almost bouncing with excitement.

'Oh...um, no, I'm afraid the Falcon won. But thank you for asking,' Scoop replied.

Alfa's face fell. 'Oh, I'm sorry. Are you disappointed?'

'No, we're okay, girls.'

'We almost won,' Fletcher added. 'Would have done, had we not been driven off-course.' He gave Scoop a knowing look.

'That's the spirit!' Alfa said, patting his arm.

Don't patronise me. Fletcher shook her off.

'Next year, you'll win, for sure,' Sparks added. 'I just know it.'

'So...did you want something?' Fletcher asked, testily.

Alfa beamed and thrust her hand out. In it was a scroll, sealed with the academy's crest. 'We've been told to give you this.'

'What is it?' Scoop asked.

'I don't know.'

Fletcher rolled his eyes. 'Well, who gave it to you?'

'The Yarnbard. We were at the academy, doing some work in the Botanical Gardens for Mademoiselle Belle. When we came out, the Yarnbard saw us and asked us to bring this to you.'

'We ran straight here,' Sparks added.

'Well, thank you, girls,' Scoop said, taking the scroll.

As she did, a gust of wind blew through the bunting on the

stalls, making the flags flap.

The girls looked at Fletcher expectantly. He stared back. 'Was there anything else?'

Alfa shook her head. 'No. We just thought...'

Fletcher didn't wait for her to finish. 'Off you go, then,' he said, shooing them away.

The two girls hesitated, but then sloped off, looking deflated.

'There was no need to be rude,' Scoop admonished. She called after them, 'We'll let you know what's in the scroll when we see you again.'

They looked back and smiled appreciatively, and then dashed towards the Ast**isk Shy.

'I don't know why you encourage them,' Fletcher said. 'Maybe if we just ignored them, they'd leave us alone.'

Scoop shot him a reproachful look.

Fletcher grabbed the scroll. 'So, I wonder what this is.'

'Oi!' Scoop protested. But before she could say anything else, he had broken the seal and was unrolling the parchment.

He scanned the words.

'The Yarnbard wants to see us immediately,' he said, still reading.

'What, now?'

'Yes, straight away. He says it's urgent. And...' Fletcher looked up.

'What is it?'

'He wants to meet us in his office – at the academy?'

The leaves of the tree rustled, a gust of wind blowing through them.

Scoop hugged herself. 'But we're not allowed to climb the tower to his office. He usually meets us on the island somewhere.'

'I know.' Fletcher looked thoughtful. 'It must be important.'

Just then, Nib and Rufina returned carrying the tankards of Noveltwist.

'You'll have to drink ours for us,' Fletcher said, as they arrived. 'We've got to go to the academy. We've been summoned by the Yarnbard.'

'Summoned? What for?' Nib asked.

'No idea.'

'Well, don't be long,' Rufina said. 'It's no fun with just him.' She nudged Nib in the ribs.

'Oh, charming.'

'We'll be as quick as we can,' Scoop said.

Rufina frowned. 'Is it me, or has it turned chilly?'

'I'll keep you warm,' Nib said, putting his arm around her.

'Oh, well if you're going to start that, I'm definitely going,' Fletcher said. Winking, he set out across the green. 'See ya later, lover boy.'

Nib chuckled.

'We won't be long,' Scoop said apologetically. She turned to follow Fletcher. As she paced after him, she shivered again. It did feel as if a bitter wind had picked up. It had been such a nice day until then.

Why did the Yarnbard need to see them so urgently? Couldn't whatever it was wait until after the festival? She pulled her coat around her, feeling the chill of the wind on her face and followed Fletcher towards the Three Towers of the academy.

* * *

Back in his office, the Yarnbard picked up the jewelled box from the table. He held it for a moment, feeling its weight. He could sense the object inside calling. Its whisper was unrelenting. It pulled, drawing its prey towards it, drawing them closer. With a shudder, a vision flooded his thoughts.

He was in a forest, running.

The sky was dark. There was a storm.

The trees around him were moving.

This was the night he had received the box. He had replayed the nightmare many times and always the same question nagged him – had the decision he'd made been the right one? He closed his eyes and allowed himself to be pulled into the nightmare again. He had to know. He had to be sure there was no other way. Before he carried out the task he'd been given, he had to know that he'd made the right choice.

Chapter 4

The Choice

The Yarnbard hurried through the woods, dodging the dark trees. He was struggling to keep up. Ahead of him, the Storyteller leapt agilely over crooked roots.

Above, angry clouds spiralled into a vortex.

Turn back.

Around the Yarnbard, the trees tapped and creaked. It was as if they were threatening him.

Panting, the old man clutched his pointed hat, his kaftan dragging along the ground. The night was making him feel out of sorts. There was something unnatural about these woods, something that crept over him, twisting through his mind.

Why had the Storyteller brought him here? Couldn't they have stayed on Fullstop Island?

He dragged his staff behind. It bumped over the uneven ground, threatening to get caught in the low branches.

A lightning fork split the air and the trees flashed into view. Spiked branches reached forward, as if warning intruders. The Yarnbard could see gnarled faces in the trunks.

Turn around.

'Why are we here, Storyteller?' the Yarnbard wheezed, ducking under a low branch.

'All in good time,' the Storyteller called over his shoulder.

The Yarnbard was Ambassador to the Storyteller. He represented him on Fullstop Island. He had spent his whole life serving this man, a man who had the power to create and to change stories. He trusted him totally. But tonight there was a seed of doubt in his mind.

It's this place, the old man thought. *I have to get out of here.*

He stumbled, tripping on a root. As he stopped to shake

himself free, the Storyteller disappeared into the thicket ahead.

Leave now, the trees snarled.

'It's as if they're trying to block our path,' the Yarnbard muttered, 'as if they're moving.'

'They are,' the Storyteller called back. 'Just keep your eyes on me.'

The old man tugged his kaftan free from a twig. The branch snapped and he felt the forest wince with pain. He forced himself onward.

Suddenly, the trees gave way. In front, there was a wall. It appeared abruptly, stopping the Yarnbard in his tracks. The trees pressed right up to it, their branches piercing the crumbling stones, dead ivy having weakened the structure.

The Storyteller was ripping tendrils away from the wall. Underneath, the Yarnbard could see decaying wood. It was a large door, hidden by the forest.

'Help me with this,' the Storyteller said, panting.

The Yarnbard joined him, pulling foliage away with his staff.

'What is this place?' the old man asked.

'This is the Tower of Janus.'

The Yarnbard had heard the name. The Tower of Janus was a ruin that stood at the centre of Turnpoint Island. It had once been a place where great councils had met and judges had sat. But legend said that an enchanter, unhappy with one of the decisions made in the tower, had cursed it. The tower had crumbled and the army that defended it had been turned into trees.

Another flash of lightning revealed knotted eyes fixed on the old man. The trees were scared. He could hear them crying out as they ripped the vines away from the door.

Don't do it!

Do not enter this fortress of fateful choice.

The noise in the Yarnbard's head was deafening.

As soon as the Storyteller had exposed enough of the wooden entrance, he grabbed an iron ring and heaved at it. The old man joined him and together they prised the door open. When the gap was big enough, they slipped through, into the tower.

At once, the noise that had been assaulting the Yarnbard ceased. The tower was eerily silent.

The two figures moved slowly into the fortress.

They were in what once must have been the Great Hall. It was long and thin with two doors, one at either end. The outer wall was intact, but there was no roof and the floor was now a carpet of grass. There was nothing in the hall apart from a stone chair that stood in its centre. Carved into the side of the chair, a bearded face stared at the two intruders with sharp eyes.

The Yarnbard and the Storyteller edged towards it.

'What are we doing here?' the Yarnbard asked again. He felt as if the carved face was watching him.

The Storyteller spoke, his voice hushed. 'There is a sickness moving through our world.'

'A Sickness?'

'Yes,' the Storyteller sounded worried, 'a living death. Those who have been infected cannot be woken. Fullstop Island hasn't felt the full force of this scourge yet, but it's on its way, seeping slowly through the sea. I've had report from the king of the Basillica Isles. Many in his territory have already fallen. No doctor has been able to treat them. They have even had to turn the great city cathedrals into hospitals.'

By now, the Storyteller and the Yarnbard had almost reached the centre of the hall. The eyes of the face carved into the stone chair still watched them. As they moved behind it, the Yarnbard could see that there was a second face carved into the other side of the throne. It looked towards the door in the far side of the hall.

'But why did we have to come here, to Turnpoint Island? Why did we need to leave Fullstop Island for you to tell me this?'

'There is someone I want you to meet,' the Storyteller said, 'somebody who would not be welcome on Fullstop Island.'

As he spoke, a man, who had been hidden by the chair's thick stone sides, stood from the throne. He was tall, imposing, his face covered with a black, silk scarf. He wore a tricorn hat and had two pistols strapped to his belt. He held a black box. It looked rich and heavy, encrusted with jewels. Moonlight glinted from the hammers of his pistols. In the darkness, it looked as if death himself had decided to walk with them.

The Storyteller stopped, his eyes fixed on the man.

'No,' the Yarnbard stuttered, stepping backwards. He recognised this man, or at least he knew what he was. He'd seen pictures, heard tales. This was a Dark Pirate, and Dark Pirates were banned from Fullstop Island. 'What's happening here? I...I can't...' he tripped over his kaftan, almost falling.

'Desperate times call for desperate measures, Yarnbard.'

'But this...? It's forbidden.'

The Storyteller spoke calmly, his eyes still fixed on the man in black. 'I needed somebody who would be able to follow the sickness to its source and be immune to whatever curse oozes through the sea. Who else could I have sent other than a man who laughs at death, who has already stepped beyond the life of the land, and embraced the unknown of the sea?'

The man by the stone chair inclined his head.

'But Dark Pirates are...?'

'Forbidden, I know.' The Storyteller raised his voice. 'They are forbidden because they are feared. And they are feared because they do not let us hide from the path that each must ultimately take. But I will not stand idly by while this sickness takes hold of our island. Especially as...' the Storyteller's voice trailed away.

'Especially as what?' the old man asked.

The Storyteller struggled to speak. 'It's my princess, Yarnbard.' His voice was choked. 'She has already fallen under the spell of the sickness. We've only been married a year and...'

'She is asleep? She cannot be woken?'

'No.'

The Yarnbard went to open his mouth, but no sound emerged.

'The fever threatens her life. She has been visited by every doctor I know. Each has examined her, but there is no agreement as to what her treatment should be. I need to know what's happening out there.' He signalled to the Dark Pirate. 'This was the only way.'

The old man stared at the cloaked figure and then looked back to his friend. He could see lines of worry on his face. He paused for a moment and then, reluctantly, gave a shallow nod.

The Storyteller turned back to the man in black. Holding out his hand, he said, 'My friend.'

The Dark Pirate stepped forward. 'Storyteller,' he growled, grasping his hand.

Above, the sky cracked with thunder.

'So you have returned.'

'I always return.'

The pirate spoke with a thick accent.

'You sent word that your investigation had been successful, that you have located the source of the sickness?'

'I believe so. But I do not think you will be happy with what I have discovered.'

'Tell me.'

The pirate stepped forward and placed the black, jewelled chest on the ground. Crouching, he pushed open the clasps and slowly opened the lid. Inside, the box was lined with black, velvet cushioning.

The oil-like clouds slid apart, and for a moment silvery light fell on the object resting in the box.

The Yarnbard stepped backward.

The pirate watched the men's reactions. 'Do you know what this is?'

The Storyteller nodded.

'It is one of the Trésors de la Mer,' the pirate continued. 'Treasures of the Deep, created by Dark Pirates. It is known as...'

A bolt of lightning forked from the sky, hitting the ground. The pirate didn't flinch. 'It is known as a Nemesis Charm.' As he spoke, thunder rolled across the ocean, fading into the distance. 'And do you know how such an object is made?'

The Storyteller nodded again. He looked grave.

The pirate's voice was low. 'Nemesis Charms are chiselled from the rock of a Threshold – a doorway between realms, between worlds.'

The Yarnbard stuttered, 'But Thresholds are myths – legends to ward people away from dangerous waters.'

'That's what the people of the islands would have you believe. But Thresholds are no legend, old man. Dark Pirates have known of their existence for generations. Such doorways are our dominion.'

Stooping, the pirate carefully lifted the Nemesis Charm. He held it out towards the two men.

'I carved this myself, from the rock of a deep cave on an island west of the South Bookend Isles. I believe the cave to be a Threshold. And I believe that Threshold to be the source of your sickness.'

The Storyteller and Yarnbard stared at the charm.

The pirate lowered his voice. 'Listen.' The word seemed to echo along the ancient walls, as if each brick of the tower were repeating it.

'The charm is calling. Can you hear it?' The Dark Pirate stepped towards them. 'It calls, just as the cave from which it was hewn calls. It calls the one who must cross the Threshold.'

'Cross the Threshold?' the Yarnbard stammered. 'But the legends say that once a Threshold is crossed there is no return, that whoever crosses such a doorway is stepping into the mouth of death itself.'

'Indeed. Crossing a Threshold is dangerous. It is not something to be undertaken lightly. There are only two ways to pass through such a doorway. Firstly, the *dead* may pass through, those for whom life is only a memory – the wraith or fantôme, the exanimate or cadavre.'

The Yarnbard shot the Storyteller a dark look.

'The second requires preparation. Only those chosen by a Nemesis Charm can undertake the preparation. They must spend a night in the presence of the charm and allow it to do its work. It is a long night, a dark night, but if they come through it – and it is an if – but if they come through it they will be ready to enter the mouth of the cave. They will be ready to cross the Threshold. Without such preparation, no Mortale can step through such a doorway and live.'

Thunder rumbled overhead and the first big drops of rain began to fall. The pirate moved closer.

'Lay your hand on the charm. Listen to its call.'

The Storyteller reached out.

Nervously, the Yarnbard followed his lead.

As the old man's hand connected with the cold rock, his bones were pulled towards it. The charm grabbed with magnetic force.

The Yarnbard's fingers throbbed.

The tower vanished and a voice filled his thoughts. It was full of terror.

'*La Negro Horreur, oui,* follow the sound, the sound in the sea...'

I'm coming...

He saw a ship ploughing through dark waters.

He heard the ocean churn with a whisper, as if the whole sea was filled with the voice.

I'm coming...

He saw a volcanic rock, dark and craggy.

In the rock's cliff was a face. It loomed over the dark waters. It was the face of a skull.

I'm coming...

He saw men, Dark Pirates, climbing the volcanic ledges.

He saw them standing before the mouth of a cave, wide and

black, hammers and chisels in their hands.

I'm coming…

He felt them strike the rock, chisel the stone, shape the charm that his fingers now touched.

And then he felt as if he were being pulled, pulled into the darkness, drawn into the cave.

I'm coming…

The cave was calling.

It was calling someone.

It was calling them to enter the blackness.

And then, with a shudder, he heard a name…

Two names…

Fletcher…

Scoop…

The Yarnbard pulled away.

'No,' he yelled, stumbling backward. 'What is this?'

The pirate fixed the Storyteller in his sights. 'If you are to discover the source of the sickness, these two must cross the Threshold.'

The Yarnbard felt as if his legs were going to buckle.

'But,' the pirate said to the Storyteller, 'it is your choice.'

Anger flicked through the old man's eyes. 'Tell me you are not taking this seriously!'

The Storyteller didn't reply. He looked from his friend to the pirate. The choice was stark. He saw his children, the Yarnbard's apprentices. He saw them laughing, happy at the academy. Then, he watched them step into the cave, into that place of no return.

The Yarnbard stepped forward. 'You can't allow this. They are your children!'

But images of his princess, pale and sickly, flooded the Storyteller's thoughts. This island, with its skull rock, was the cause of her pain. It was the cause of so much pain in their world. So many had already fallen to the sickness. How could he allow it to continue to spread? The choice was unbearable. He closed his eyes, stilling himself.

What should I do? he asked.

He waited in silence. Rain fell, running down the deep lines of his face.

After a moment, he opened his eyes. Slowly, he turned to the Yarnbard and signalled to the charm. 'It is what must be done. Sometimes we must lose in order to find.' His voice was heavy with sadness.

The pirate began to lower the Nemesis Charm back into its box.

'The apprentices must make the journey.'

The old man turned away.

The Storyteller moved towards his friend. 'I would like your help, Yarnbard. If we are to...'

'Help?' The Yarnbard spun back. 'I cannot believe you are even asking me to consider it. They've only just settled. It's only been a year! To send them on this quest is tantamount to...to robbing them of everything...of their lives!'

The Storyteller was silent.

The Yarnbard pointed at the pirate. 'You trust this man?'

The Storyteller spoke slowly. 'I trust that this is the way we are being led. I am sure of it. I would like your help, old friend. But you have a choice, just as I do. If you wish, you may turn back and exit by the door through which we entered. You will go alone. I will not judge you. But if you choose the door ahead, we will exit together and the decision will be made.'

The old man shook his head. He had always been sure of the Storyteller, always carried out his instructions, but this...

He stared from the pirate to the black box.

'Please,' the Storyteller whispered. 'I believe this is necessary. I would not ask if it were not. We *must* find out what is through that Doorway, we *must* find out what the source of this sickness is. The lives of many in this world depend on it...the life of my princess depends on it.'

'And the lives of your children?' The old man's words cut the air.

The Storyteller stared at him.

'Do you trust me, my friend? Do you trust that I work everything for the good?'

The Yarnbard stared back, his eyes fierce. His mind rebelled. It told him to run, to leave that place and exit the way he had entered. But somehow, despite the pull he felt to leave, to wash his hands of the whole dark business, he knew his decision had already been made. He had made it the very first day he had chosen to serve the Storyteller.

Outside, the trees tapped the shattered window frames, as if clamouring to say, *I told you so. I told you so.*

Without speaking, the Yarnbard gave one sharp nod.

'Thank you,' the Storyteller whispered.

Silently, the carved face that watched the door through which they had entered closed its eyes and the second face awoke.

The Yarnbard knew what he had to do. Stepping forward, he knelt and picked up the black box. He would face the future, however dark. He *did* trust the Storyteller and there was no other decision he could make.

He lifted the box and began to carry it towards the door in the far side of the hall. He could feel the Nemesis Charm inside. It was breathing, whispering...

Fletcher... it called.

Scoop...

As he carried it, a tear rolled down the old man's face. It mixed with the rain and fell to the ground, seeping into the earth of the Tower of Janus. The choice had been made. There was no going back.

* * *

The Yarnbard opened his eyes again. He was back in his office, the box in his hands.

There is no going back, he repeated to himself. *I do trust.*

He looked down at the casket.

The seasons are changing, he thought.

Then, with a deep sigh, he moved to a cupboard in the round table, placed the box inside and locked it away. It would stay there, hidden in the darkness, until his apprentices arrived.

Chapter 5

The Raven

On the other side of the Oceans of Rhyme, in the seas west of the South Bookend Isles, a ship ploughed through bitter waters. It had the figurehead of a Raven, with eyes of ebony and a beak of flint. A flock of crows sat spectre-like on the rigging. They belonged to an old woman named Grizelda, who had cultivated a reputation for fear and terror across the Oceans of Rhyme.

As the ship cut through the icy sea, the ocean whispered. The sound soaked into a thick mist that had formed over the water in those parts. The crew hung from the ship's ropes like shadows, peering into the endless gloom. The sound in the sea engulfed them totally. It seemed to whisper from every droplet. It clung to their skin and trickled through their hair.

*I'm coming...*it whispered.

*I'm coming...*it sighed.

Suddenly, a bloodcurdling cry pierced the stillness. It came from a man who had been bound to the mainmast.

'Oh, here we go again,' Grizelda snarled. She looked up from a map she'd been hunched over. She had laid it out on one of the cargo hatches, where it was lit by the flickering glow of a lantern. Her thick, black sea-cloak swamped her tiny body. The crows stirred, ruffling their feathers. 'Put a sock in it, will yer? Can't hear meself think 'ere, can I? Quieten down, now!'

The man tied to the mast stared at the old woman, his body trembling.

'Anyone would think you didn't enjoy being our scapegoat!' she said.

It hadn't taken Grizelda long to realise the fog that hung over this ocean was poisoned. The sound in the sea was contaminating it. Each droplet of mist was laced with the heartbreak and loss that the whisper carried. Grizelda had taken to calling this ocean the Sea of Tears. She knew no ordinary crew would be able to navigate such a sea and live.

'But,' she had said to the captain of the Raven, 'such pain can be...let us say, sidestepped. Yer only need to know the secret of how to transfer such a pain to a talisman, to a scapegoat, and Bob's yer uncle; everything's just fine and dandy.'

The cries of the bound man gradually quietened to a whimper.

'That's better. There's a good scapegoat.' The old woman chuckled. She turned back to what she was doing. 'Now, according to this 'ere map, we should be close – very close.'

'You'd better work out the exact coordinates quickly, old woman,' the captain growled. 'We have to get there before our scapegoat gives up his spirit.' He glanced at the man truss to the mast. He looked like a wraith, slowly crumpling from the inside.

'What do you take me for? I thought you sailors were supposed to have a bit of guile. You didn't think I'd bring just *one* scapegoat, do you? No, I'm not taking any chances! I'm not ending up like that!' She waved her hand at the scapegoat. 'I've brought two or three – all good-for-nothing murderers or miscreants.' Grizelda pushed herself to her feet and limped across the deck to her talisman. Reaching him, she drew her face close, breathing in his stinking breath. 'Disposable,' she spat. 'Rubbish – the lot of 'em. Just the sort needed to take our place.'

The man looked into her eyes, pleading.

Grizelda grinned and bowed. 'Thank you, good sir, for doing us this kindness. So gracious of you to soak up all this heartbreak and loss, all this disappointment and grief, that we might enjoy our little cruise in relative good humour. I'm feeling quite buoyant meself, positively bloomin'.'

She turned back to the captain and pointed at the scapegoat. Skin was now beginning to flake from his face. 'Ha! You don't think I'm going through *that* for anyone, do you? This one looks like he's on the way out. You'd better have the next one brought up.'

The captain waved a gloved hand and a skeletal-looking crewman disappeared below deck.

'Now, where were we?'

The captain peered at the map. 'Couldn't you have insisted on more detail?'

'Well, that messenger from the Basillica Isles wasn't exactly predisposed to help, was he? Took a little "gentle persuasion", as I remember, just to get this.'

The map they were studying had been extracted from an envoy carrying news to the Storyteller.

'If that meddler's up to something, I wanna know what it is,' Grizelda had said. 'Maybe he's discovered some new treasure to be exploited.'

Having learned from the envoy of the Storyteller's interest in a new island in these seas, Grizelda had decided to make a little investigation of her own. She had "persuaded" the envoy to draw a map of the island's location, before dispatching him to his maker.

Suddenly there was a shriek from above. 'Land ahoy!'

As quick as a flash, the captain darted across the deck. He leapt onto the rigging and began to scale the ropes, vaulting from gallant to mast, his cloak glinting oily greens and purples in the dim light. The crows cawed, taking to the sky and flapping irritably about the ship. The captain reached the Crow's Nest and jumped over the rail. He grabbed the telescope from the boy who'd been on watch and gazed into the darkness.

After a moment, he snapped it down. 'He's right. There is land ahead'.

Grizelda scurried towards the prow of the ship, staring out.

'So, the rumours *are* true,' she said to herself. 'A new island, out here in the depths of the South Bookend Oceans – and *I've* found it.'

As she spoke, the mist thinned for a moment. Ahead, a wall of dark rock loomed into view. It towered over the ship, rising from the black sea, a turret in the lonely ocean. From the direction the ship was approaching, the face of a skull was clearly visible in the rock.

*I'm coming…*the icy air whispered…*night…*

Grizelda craned her neck, taking in the awesome sight.

'Volcanic,' she croaked. 'Looks like an island, formed by an underwater eruption. Ain't it a pretty sight, now?'

Behind her, there was a commotion. The skeletal crewman had emerged again. Behind him, a new scapegoat was being dragged by chains, struggling and cursing.

Grizelda moved towards him. He was bare-chested. She examined the tattoos that covered his torso – lurid depictions of men and women suffering the most horrible deaths.

She grinned at the captain, who had returned to deck. 'All the people he's murdered. Seems a shame to waste him really. Oh well, can't be helped. Tie him up with the other one.'

A second crew member joined the skeletal guard and together they hauled the tattooed man towards the mainmast.

'Get on with it! This one looks all but dead.'

It was true. The fellow strapped to the mast had slumped to one side. Grizelda tapped his cheek. 'Don't you worry now, Sonny Jim, it'll all be over soon. You've done a sterling job.' She slapped him on the arm and he slumped to the side. 'But it's time to pass on the baton. Get it – *pass on* the baton!' She roared with laughter. 'Right, enough chitter chatter, as pleasant as it is, tie the new one up and let's get back to business.'

'Get your filthy hands off me,' the captive suddenly roared, pulling back with such force he yanked his shackles from the guard's hands. The manacled man swung round, sending the chains flying through the air. They hit the guards, knocking them to the deck. 'You can't do this to me! Do you know who I am?'

Grizelda stepped forward. 'Well, that's not really the question now is it, my dear? The question you should *really* be asking is:

do you know who *I* am?' She moved forward again, the man fixed in her gaze. Instinctively, he backed away. Grizelda spoke slowly. 'Some say I'm a witch – the most powerful in the whole of the southern oceans.' She advanced. The murderer shuffled further back, towards the mast. 'There are rumours that I can twist a man's spleen with just a look of my eye.' The tattooed man blinked, trying to look away, but scared to let the old woman out of his sight. 'There are stories of people whose faces have been turned inside out, whose fingers have been transformed into snakes, whose tongues have become nooses for their own necks.' The captive was nearing the mast now. Still Grizelda advanced. She sneered at him as if he was a louse to be squashed, rather than the perpetrator of sixteen horrific murders.

Behind, the two crewmen had risen to their feet again, ready to subdue him.

Grizelda walked right up to the captive. He looked terrified. She leaned forward and, whispering, said, 'Thing is, them's just stories. I ain't no witch. But I do have a knife.'

With lightning speed she pulled a knife from the folds of her cloak and lunged forward. The captive screamed with pain. The old woman had stabbed him through the hand, the blade slicing clean through his flesh, imbedding itself in the mast. She twisted it.

'That'll teach you. Now, watch yer place, mister.'

The man writhed in agony, blood splattering the mainmast, flowing down the cracks in the wood. He was pinned to the ship.

Grizelda turned away and brushed herself down. 'He's all yours,' she said to the crewmen. 'Tie him up quickly before there're any more little scenes like that.'

The crewmen approached him, a thick rope in their hands.

'Wait,' the tattooed man pleaded. 'I have information – information you need to hear.'

The crewmen paused.

'What sort of information?' Grizelda asked, turning back.

'I heard it from a raider on the seas of the Furnace Isles. It's got to do with the Un-Crossable Boundary.'

Grizelda stepped closer. 'Well, spit it out, I ain't known for me patience!'

'If I tell you, will you'll set me free? Use one of the others in my place?'

'Well, let's put it this way – give me the information and you've got a chance, don't give it to me and they tie you to this mast right now and you're dead – your choice, of course.'

Grizelda turned away. The crewman advanced again with the rope.

'All right,' the captive snarled. 'I'll tell you.'

Just then, the first scapegoat, who was tied to the mast next to him, shook violently. He let out a sickening rasp and slumped forward. The captain, who had been watching from the side of the ship, crossed the deck and laid a finger on his neck.

'Dead.'

Grizelda ignored him, completely focused on the captive in front of her. 'Don't pay no attention to that little side show. Now, what's this information you've got for me?'

The captive growled. 'A year ago, at the wedding banquet of the Storyteller, the Un-Crossable Boundary was breached. It was then the eruption happened that formed this island.'

'Well, I could've guessed that meself, couldn't I?' Grizelda bluffed. She could feel the Sea of Tears beginning to have influence over the ship. Now the scapegoat was dead, pangs of discomfort were rising from the ocean. Grizelda had trained herself to resist such assaults, but she feared the rest of the crew were weaklings. This sea was powerful. She needed to get the information quickly. 'What else have you got?' she barked.

'It happened at the very moment two Apprentice Adventurers were sent across the Boundary...'

'I know! I was there, wasn't I! I even know their bleedin' names – that little runt, Fletcher and his dim-witted sister, Scoop.

Don't mention them to me again or I might blow a gasket!'

The captain moved to Grizelda's side. 'We must be quick,' he whispered. 'The invisible waves...'

'Shut it!' Grizelda cut him off.

The captain could feel the unseen waves beginning to break over the Raven's sides – waves of misery, loss, desperation and sadness. He feared this sea. He'd heard tales on the Basillica Isles. They called these waters the Wounded Waters. They said they came without mercy, pouring over a ship's deck, seeping into the skin of everyone aboard. Many vessels had been discovered, left as skeletons, floundering, their crews having torn themselves apart in desperation.

'Well, if that's all you've got... Tie him up!' Grizelda spat.

From the bow of the ship, a deep moan arose. The quarter-master had broken down, unable to contain the bitterness that seeped into him from the sea.

I'm coming...shadows...

The two crewmen with the rope moved forward again, both fighting the desire to give in to despair.

'Wait!' the captive interrupted. 'There's more.'

Grizelda waved him away. 'You've lost me interest now.'

'I know what they found on the other side of the Boundary – I know *who* they found.'

Grizelda turned back. 'Hmm...' she looked thoughtful. 'Well, I'm listening.'

'Quickly,' the captain hissed. He could hear the whisper growing, rising from the sea, soft and ghostly.

I'm coming...clouds of...

It struck fear into his soul.

Another crewman, who was stationed at the mizzenmast, let out a tortured cry.

'On the other side of the Boundary, the Storyteller's name is...'

'Wait,' Grizelda barked. 'Don't tell everyone. I want this information to meself. Whisper it in me ear, duckie.' She walked across the deck, moving deliberately slowly, as if she were enjoying the torture the delay was causing. On reaching the captive, she turned her ear towards him. Leaning forward, he whispered the name.

Grizelda pulled away. 'What?' For the first time she looked shaken. 'A girl? In that world the Storyteller's a *girl*?' She thought for a moment. 'Well, he's full of surprises, I'll give him that.'

'And,' the captive leered, 'she has a weakness, this girl.'

'Tell me, my dear,' Grizelda simpered.

'Her mother is missing.'

Grizelda's eyes glinted. 'Is that it?'

'There is something else.'

'What?'

'Release me and I'll tell you.'

'Oh, my dear, tell me and we could become friends. Grizelda always looks after her friends.'

The captive grinned, showing his gold capped teeth. 'They say the girl's mother has power. She has the same power as the Storyteller – the power to create and to change stories. She and her daughter are the only two who exist on both sides of the Boundary. And here's the tasty bit,' the captive's grin widened. 'The rumours are that this new island is a doorway – a Threshold to their world.'

The old woman sucked her teeth. She had heard rumours of a doorway that led across the Un-Crossable Boundary, but she had taken them as just that – rumours. But if they were true...well that would be more than interesting. She grinned, a plan already forming in her mind. Grizelda had a hunch about where this doorway might lead and her hunches were rarely mistaken. She eyed the captive greedily. 'And that's all you know?'

'Yeah, that's all I know.'

'Well, I must say this little conversation has been very useful, very useful indeed. Unfortunately for you, your usefulness is at an end. You've played all your cards, mister.' She stepped away and turned to the crewmen with the rope. 'Bind him!'

'But you said…'

'I said nothing.'

'You said we would be friends.'

'Friends?' the old woman screeched. 'Why would I become friends with a piece of scum like you? You're no use to anyone. Yer time is up. You might as well accept it. This is a Sea of Tears, after all – what did you expect?'

The two crewmen were now frantically binding the captive to the mast, driven by an animal instinct to transfer the pain they were feeling onto his shoulders. The captive struggled, but his impaled hand and the loss of blood had weakened him. In a matter of seconds, he was strapped and unable to move. Next to him, the dead body of the first scapegoat was already decaying.

Grizelda turned to the sea and pointed at the captive.

'Here's your new scapegoat, Sea of Tears. I command you to manifest all your tortures in this man's soul, instead of ours. Now, release this ship from your misery.'

Instantly, the crew felt the release. Their pain subsided and the moaning and wailing ceased. The ship fell still.

Suddenly, the captive let out a nightmarish cry. The pain of the sea was ripping his insides apart. But the Raven and its crew had been restored to its former state.

Grizelda turned to the captain and grinned. 'Well, it appears we know what that meddler's up to. A Threshold, eh? If he thinks he's the only one who can cross the Boundary – the only one who can steal *that* power – he's got another thing coming. Two can play at that! Sounds like the game is afoot, don't it? And I think I have a plan.'

The ship had now reached the volcanic island. The eyes of the rock skull stared ominously out to sea.

From the mast, the scapegoat wailed in agony again.

'And here we are, right on time to put my plan into action. I love it when things work out. Prepare to land!'

Chapter 6

The Eye of the Needle

Having locked the black box away, the Yarnbard walked to the narrow south window of his office and stared out. From there, he could see all the way across Bardbridge, past the Port of Beginnings and Endings, to the deep blue ocean. It was flecked today with white specks, where the wind whipped up the surf. He could see right out to where the ocean met the sky. He watched the crowds gathered at the harbour and imagined them enjoying the bright sunny day. The festivities felt more distant to him than the empty horizon. Sometimes being Ambassador of the Storyteller was a lonely business.

The Yarnbard's office was located at the very top of the Needle, one of the Three Towers that formed the heart of Blotting's Academy. The other two, the Giant and the Scythe, could be seen through the north window.

Each of the Three Towers had a spindly staircase carved into its rock, leading to a lookout post at the top. The staircases gave access to rooms and offices that had been hollowed into the stone.

The Three Towers was one of the natural wonders of Fullstop Island. Nobody quite knew how they'd been formed. On a misty day, they disappeared into the clouds, making them look like the turrets of a castle – the type you read about in fairytales. On those days, a cloak of cloud wrapped around the Yarnbard's office, cocooning it from the island. Today, however, the sky was blue and the Yarnbard's view, clear.

Between the harbour and the Three Towers, he could see two specs moving slowly along the river path towards the academy. He felt a pang of guilt. He knew his apprentices' day had been ruined, and he knew he was the cause.

* * *

Fletcher and Scoop reached the academy in silence, both preoc-
cupied by the strange summons from the Yarnbard. They headed
straight to the foot of the Needle. As they reached the crooked
staircase that led up the thinnest of the towers, Scoop paused.
High above, just below the lookout post, she could see a tiny
doorway.

'The Eye of the Needle,' she said, a sense of foreboding in her
gut. 'The Yarnbard's office.'

'Yes,' Fletcher replied. Wind whipped through the gap
between the Three Towers. Pushing against it, he stepped onto
the first stair and began to climb.

* * *

The stairs of the Needle were steep and the climb was hard, but
after nearly an hour, they had reached the final door. It was thin
and came to a point at the top. A sign on the wall next to it read,
"The Eye of the Needle: Office of the Yarnbard, Ambassador of
the Storyteller, Head of the Department of Quests, Guardian of
the River Word".

Fletcher reached for the doorknocker. It was shaped as two
crossed knitting needles. He rapped firmly on the wood.

'Come in,' a voice called from inside.

Twisting the iron handle, Fletcher pushed the door open.

Inside, the room was cone shaped, rising to a point. Four
narrow windows were positioned at the four points of the
compass, giving magnificent views across the island. In the
centre of the room was a circular table. Above it, across the
ceiling, a colourful thread weaved, passing through pegs that had
been hammered into the wall. The thread stretched in different
directions, creating an intricate web, just above their heads.

Scoop peered at the web as she entered.

'That is the Yarn,' the old man said, seeing her curiosity, 'from which I take my name.' He was holding a long, thin stick, with which he was tying off one end of the thread around a peg on the wall. 'The Yarn holds my story. Sometimes I use it to remember. Sometimes, I use it to direct my path. And sometimes, the Yarn can foretell possible futures. Foretelling is a dangerous business though, as the future isn't fixed. There...' he said, as he finished tying off the thread. He placed the stick on the floor, leaning it against the wall.

'Well, welcome, Fletcher, welcome, Scoop.'

Scoop thought she could hear weariness in the old man's voice.

The Yarnbard signalled to three armchairs by one of the windows, and they sat down.

'Thank you for coming in the midst of the festivities.'

The two apprentices gave a shallow nod.

'Yes, well...you're probably wondering why I've called you here.'

Fletcher and Scoop waited for the old man to continue. He shifted uncomfortably in his chair. 'Well...I'm not going to beat about the bush...I'm afraid I have some bad news for you.'

'Bad news?' Scoop said.

'Yes, I'm afraid so. It concerns your mother, the princess.'

'What's wrong? Is she okay?'

'I'm afraid not, Scoop.'

Scoop and Fletcher exchanged an anxious look.

'I am afraid to say that your mother is sick.'

'Sick?' Fletcher repeated. 'She's going to be all right though?'

'I hope so, Fletcher. I hope so.'

There was an uncomfortable silence.

'What's wrong with her?' Fletcher asked. 'What exactly is this illness?'

The Yarnbard paused. 'Well, I'm not going to lie. At the moment, nobody knows.' The old man shifted his body, the springs on his chair creaking. 'But,' he said, trying to give some comfort, 'she does have the very best doctors looking after her. Your father has summoned physicians from across the Oceans of Rhyme.'

Fletcher furrowed his brow. 'But none of them know how to treat her?'

'Um, no. Not as yet. But they are —'

'Then that's worse, isn't it? If the very best doctors don't know what's wrong with her, it's worse.'

'Well,' the Yarnbard said slowly, 'I wouldn't say *that* Fletcher.'

'Well, what are the symptoms of this illness? Is she in pain?'

'She's in a deep sleep,' the Yarnbard replied. 'Your mother doesn't appear to be suffering.'

'But she can't be woken?'

'No.'

Scoop suddenly sat upright. 'Beware the sickness. Beware the sea,' she said. 'The fisherman who interrupted the race – he was warning of a sickness – this is what he was talking about, isn't it?'

'Well, I'm not sure about a fisherman, Scoop, but we do believe the sickness is connected to the sea, yes.'

'Then he wasn't crazy.'

'Can we just leave the fisherman for a minute,' Fletcher snapped. 'I want to know more about mother.'

'But that's what I'm talking about,' Scoop replied defensively.

Fletcher closed his eyes for a moment, trying to stay calm. 'Yes, I know,' he said. 'I'm sorry. It's just – it's only been a year since we found her again – and now this?' His voice cracked.

The Yarnbard laid a hand on the boy's knee. 'It does seem to be a cruel twist of fate.'

'But I don't understand.' Fletcher looked at him. 'Can't father do something about it? He's the Storyteller, after all. Couldn't he just change her story – re-write the sickness, send it away?'

'It isn't that easy, Fletcher.'

'What's the point of having all that power if he can't use it for mother?'

'It's not a question of can't…'

'Really? You could have fooled me.'

'Sometimes we have to let our stories play out, Fletcher. We have to trust that there will be resolution in the end, even if it's hard to see how right now.'

Fletcher shook his head, unhappy with the answer.

Scoop had zoned out, too distracted to listen. Suddenly, she began to stand up. The others looked at her. 'We can't just sit here,' she said. 'We have to go and see her. We have to…' But as she rose, her head started to spin. She reached up and grabbed one of the threads that stretched overhead to steady herself.

As she touched the Yarn, the room vanished.

Day turned to night.

It was dark, but a faint glimmer of light spilled down from above. Scoop followed its beam. Curled up on the floor by her feet was a body. It was bleeding, unconscious. Scoop froze with fear.

It was the Yarnbard.

She let go of the thread.

The Eye of the Needle appeared again. It was bright. Scoop blinked and collapsed back into her chair.

'Scoop…' said the Yarnbard, sounding worried. He rose, and crossing the room, poured a glass of water. 'Are you all right?'

'Yes, I just…'

Returning, the Yarnbard passed her the drink. Scoop sipped it. 'You should sit for a moment. You've had quite a shock.'

Scoop stared at the old man. What had she just seen? The Yarnbard, hurt?

He's not hurt, she told herself. *He's standing right in front of you.*

'She's right, though,' Fletcher said. 'We should go and see mother. She might need us to be there.'

'I understand you both want to see her,' the Yarnbard replied, still peering at Scoop, 'but the doctors have said that nobody is allowed access until they have diagnosed her illness. It might be contagious, after all.'

Scoop's head was swimming. Her mother ill and the Yarnbard hurt?

What *was* it she'd just seen – a vision? The Yarnbard said the Yarn could foretell the future – was that what she'd glimpsed?

Fletcher leaned forward. 'But we have to do something.'

The Yarnbard hesitated. He was still deeply uncomfortable with what he was about to do. He stared at his apprentices. They were looking at him, their eyes wide. They were relying on him. They trusted him. 'Well, there is something...' The words come out of his mouth, as if he wasn't speaking them. How could he do this? How could he betray them?

'What?' Fletcher replied. 'Tell us! We'd do anything to help.'

'I know you would, Fletcher. I know you would.'

The Yarnbard rose and walked to the circular table. He felt shaky on his feet. Stooping, he unlocked a cupboard and pulled out the black box. Its diamonds shone in the sunlight. It felt even heavier than it had before. He stood, facing them, the box in his hands.

'What's that?'

'It's something the Storyteller has given to me to pass on to you, something that may bring about a transformation that could help your mother.'

'The Storyteller?'

'Yes.'

'What is it – a potion or something?'

The Yarnbard didn't reply.

Scoop tried to focus on what was going on. Her mother was sick; that was reality. The Yarnbard had said the Yarn was unreliable when foretelling the future – that the future hadn't happened yet. She pushed the vision of the old man hurt from her mind. She only had the capacity to deal with one crisis. She needed to focus on the one that was actually happening – her mother being ill.

The Yarnbard stared out the window. Behind Fletcher and Scoop, the rocks of the Scythe looked sharp and dangerous. 'This box needs to be taken to the Hermits of Hush,' he said. 'It is in their tents that the transformation will occur.'

'We'll take it,' Fletcher said, getting to his feet.

The Yarnbard looked at him sadly. 'Thank you, Fletcher. I knew I could rely on you. I knew you would want to help.'

'Of course we want to help. She's our mother, isn't she?'

'Yes.'

'So what do we do with it when we get there?'

'You will have a choice to make.'

'A choice?'

'Yes, the direction you need to take to help your mother will be made clear to you.'

'Okay,' Fletcher said, thrown by the Yarnbard's cryptic answer. 'So how do we get there – to the hermits?'

'Their camp is in the Dreamless Desert. I have already taken the liberty of asking one of the brothers to escort you to their dwellings. He will be waiting for you when you reach the bottom of the tower.'

'Well, what are we waiting for?'

Fletcher walked across to the Yarnbard. The old man signalled for him to stop. 'One thing first,' he said, 'this is important. On no account are you to open this box or look inside. If you do, you may compromise the transformation process. Do you understand?'

'Yes,' Fletcher said. He peered at the box. What was inside? Ingredients to make an ointment, perhaps. Or healing stones that needed to be infused with the correct properties. Whatever it was, he and Scoop would deliver it safely to the hermits. They would make their mother proud.

Hesitating, the Yarnbard handed the box over.

It was heavier than Fletcher had expected. As he held it, he had a strange sensation – as if he was carrying the weight of an entire life.

Mother's life, he told himself.

'Come on, Scoop,' he said, turning towards the door.

She rose, her mind still swimming.

Inside the box, the Nemesis Charm stirred. It sensed the presence of the ones it had been summoned to face. It had a job to do, and there was no way it would ever fail to achieve its mission.

Chapter 7

Skull Island

As Grizelda stepped onto the black beach of Skull Island, the boulders steamed beneath her feet.

I'm coming...shadows reach...

The whisper was louder, clearer.

She hobbled over the rocks, a cloud of ashy vapour rising around her. The Raven had dropped anchor on the sheltered side of the island. The captain and four of his most burly crew had rowed Grizelda ashore. They had just finished pulling the boat onto the beach and were now hauling a wooden crate from its hull.

'Careful with that!' Grizelda spat, as they lifted it from the vessel. 'That's precious that is. You should handle it as if it was yer own mother.' She looked at the crew and reconsidered. 'Actually, I'm betting most of you wouldn't hesitate to steal the coat from yer own mother's back. So let's put it this way – be careful, or I'll cut yer throats.'

The crewmen grunted their agreement. With the sea breaking around their legs, they carefully began to lift the box, under the direction of the captain.

Grizelda turned towards the island and looked up. Sharp turrets of rock thrust upwards, surrounding a central peak that pointed towards the grey sky. On the tallest of the rock faces, the skull was clearly visible. Now they were closer, they could see that its eyes were fissures in the crag and its mouth, a wide black cave that disappeared into nothingness.

'That's where we're headed,' Grizelda said, pointing to the cave.

The island was made of basaltic lava, which having been pushed up through the sea in violent streams, had now frozen into pillars of magma. The pillars cut off at different heights, creating flat platforms that could be used as steps up the side of the rock. Carefully, Grizelda began to pick her way across the beach, heading for the series of platforms that led towards the mouth of the cave. The crewmen followed, the crate balanced on their shoulders.

Slowly, they began to climb the rocks. At points, they had to pause while the brawniest member of the crew hauled Grizelda up the higher platforms, a rope tied around her waist. It was an undignified sight and although the old woman hated it (and threatened to dismember any of the crew who ever spoke of it again), nothing would stop her from reaching her goal. The crewman also had to pull the crate carefully up each crag, mindful of its contents amid threats of ever increasing, painful torture.

The climb was slow progress. Heat rose from the rocks, making the air quiver. Along with the midday sun, it made for an uncomfortable journey. By the time they reached the cave, their faces were raw and their clothes drenched in sweat. While the crew perched on boulders mopping their brows, Grizelda walked into the mouth of the cave. A cold wind blew from the darkness. It was harsh and dry. On it, the whisper hissed and spat.

I'm coming...clouds...night...

Grizelda reached out a bony hand. The voice sounded close enough for her to touch its source. She paused, feeling its power, and then lowered her hand again.

In the centre of the mouth of the cave, a pool of molten lava bubbled. It spat red-hot droplets onto the ground around it, which fizzed and blackened. Beyond the lava pool was impenetrable black.

'If there's a Threshold on this island,' Grizelda croaked, 'this'll be it.'

'How can we be sure?' the captain asked.

'Send over one of the crew,' Grizelda answered gleefully. 'Make it the one who was pulling me up the rocks. And bring that rope.'

'Yes Ma'am,' the captain growled. 'You,' he called, pointing at a crewman. 'Come here. And bring that with you.'

The crewman grunted and did as he was told.

'Right, tie one end of that around his waist,' the old woman said, signalling the rope.

The captain obliged.

Grizelda pointed a spindly finger. 'Now you, come here.'

The crewman walked forward, the rope tied around his waist.

'I want you to hold this,' Grizelda said. She reached into her cloak and pulled something out, cupped in both hands. The crewman saw it move.

'What is it?' he asked suspiciously.

'Oh, it's nothing to be afraid of, me dear. It's just a lovely little bird. 'Ere, look at its pretty feathers.' Grizelda held her hands up. The crewman peeked through her fingers. Sure enough he could see yellow feathers. The bird was squirming.

'Now, all I want you to do, me dear, is take this bird as far into the cave as you can and let it go. D'yer think you can do that?'

The crewman didn't look happy, but he nodded.

'There's a good lad. Here we go then.' Grizelda held out her hands and the crewman took the bird. 'Good boy, off you go then.'

The crewman peered into the darkness and then began to edge around the lava pool, the bird in his hands. As he passed the magma, an eerie glow lit him. Then, he disappeared from sight.

'And how exactly is this going to prove the cave is a Threshold?' the captain asked.

'Well, there's only two ways to cross a Threshold, see. The first takes preparation and we don't have time for that, so I've opted for the second.'

'Which is?'

'Well, the thing is – that little bird, I snapped its neck just before we landed.'

The captain's eyes widened.

'And then I injected it with Blood of the Undead.'

'Blood of the Undead?' The captain sounded shocked.

Grizelda cackled. 'Oh, my dear, you're not afraid those old superstitions are you? A big strapping man like yerself, scared of a little Undead Blood? Aww look at yer, you big pussy cat. Must be all them tales you've heard at sea.'

'We're sailors. We steer clear of the Undead Lands.'

There was a flash of anger in Grizelda's eyes. 'What? Are you more frightened of them than of me?'

The captain looked decidedly uncomfortable.

'You're probably glad I haven't told you what's in that crate then,' the old woman said, signalling to the wooden box the crewmen were sitting around.

'What? What's in there? I don't want anything to do with the Undead Lands – it's an abominable place!'

Grizelda grinned. 'Too late, my dear. You'll soon see what it is you've been transporting for me.'

'You didn't say anything about Undead Blood. It's powerful stuff you're messing with there.'

'Thing is, Captain, powerful stuff's exactly what I'm after. You know what they say about Thresholds, don't you?'

The captain's face turned white. 'That only the dead can pass through them.'

'Precisely,' the old woman said, her lips curling into a smile, 'which means if this is a doorway, my little bird with its Undead Blood will be able to pass through.'

'But what about my crewman?'

From deep within the cave there was a thud. Everyone stopped speaking. The rope by Grizelda's side pulled taut.

Grizelda reached down and gave the rope a tug. It didn't give. 'Ah, well here we are. I think this might just be the proof we need that this cave is a Threshold. Give us a hand.' The old woman began to pull on the rope. The captain joined her. 'Get the others too,' Grizelda spat. 'He was a heavy beggar this one.'

The captain barked the order and the rest of the crew joined them. Together they pulled on the rope. They could feel the weight on the other end dragging over the rocks. Every so often it got caught on a boulder and they had to give it a tug to free it. Finally a shape came into view. It was the body of the crewman.

The captain edged around the pool of lava to check him. 'Dead,' he confirmed.

'Any sign of the bird?'

'None.'

'Well there's yer proof then. The bird with its Undead Blood got through, but he didn't. The reports are true. We definitely have ourselves a Threshold here. Now to business. You two –' she pointed at two of the crewmen – 'throw that body into the lava pool – it's cluttering the place up.'

The two crewmen headed into the cave and, grabbing the body at either end, gave it a swing and threw it into the molten cauldron. It hit the viscous liquid, breaking the black crust. The pool cracked into forks of fiery red. As the body slowly sank into the inferno, the lava moulded itself around the corpse, making its outline glow. The crewmen stared at the place where the body disappeared.

Grizelda broke the silence. 'Well, don't just stand there gawpin' – bring that crate in here.'

'No, wait!' the captain interrupted.

The crew shot round, staring at him. Only a madman contradicted the old woman.

Grizelda fixed him with her beady eyes. 'If I didn't have any more use for you, you would be introducing yourself to your maker just about –' she paused – 'now. As it is, I need you to navigate that ship back from this god-forsaken island, so I will forgive that little indiscretion.' She stepped towards him, speaking slowly. 'Now, bring me that crate. Do it yourself, before I change my mind.'

The captain held her in his gaze, his eyes wide. Then, shaking himself he turned quickly away.

'You,' he said to one of the crewman as he left the cave, 'come and help me carry it.'

'No.' The old woman stopped him. 'Do it yourself. I want to know that you're fully repentant.'

The captain continued. Reaching the crate, he heaved it onto his shoulder, and then, like a criminal carrying his own cross, strode with resolve into the cave. When he reached the old woman, he stopped in front of her. With a look of pure malice, he lowered the crate and placed it before her feet.

'Good boy,' she purred. She turned to the rest of the crew. 'Right, you, open it.'

A crewman moved forward and freeing a crowbar that was strapped to the crate, pushed the point under the lid and forced it up. The crate opened with a crack. Inside, it was filled with packing hay.

Grizelda stooped down and ran her hands through the hay. She hit something solid and stopped. Burying both hands into the box she stood up. In her grasp was a large glass jar. She held it up to the light. It was filled with cloudy liquid. In the centre, suspended by the liquid, a heart glistened.

'What is *that*?' the captain said, his voice low.

'This, my dear, is a heart stolen from the Tombs of the Undead.'

There was a commotion as the crew stepped away from the jar, muttering protective hexes. Grizelda's beady eyes flickered as she examined the heart. 'It's a thing of beauty, isn't it?'

The limp muscle was still red with blood.

She lowered the jar and, snapping a metal lever up, released the lid. The jar hissed as it opened.

Nobody moved.

Then suddenly, the old woman plunged her hand into the jar and grabbed the heart.

The crew gasped with horror as she pulled it from the liquid and held it high. With a cry, she threw it into the fiery pool. It sizzled as the flesh hit the lava. The molten rock licked around it, folding it into its embrace. The glowing liquid covered the heart and it disappeared.

The old woman stepped forward, eagerly. She stared into the lava. Then, taking a deep, wheezing breath, she began to chant. Her words echoed in the darkness. Slow and dirge-like, they grew to a crescendo. 'I call you up, wraith of the half-life. Rise from this grave of fire to do my bidding. I am your mistress. I command you to arise.'

Grizelda stood before the molten cauldron, her chest heaving.

For a moment, nothing happened.

The crew shot surreptitious glances at one another, as if to say, "She's finally cracked."

But then, from deep within the lava, a movement stirred.

They turned back.

The magma shifted, restlessly, a thick bubble slowly rising.

The crew stared, their faces stricken.

The bubble broke the surface.

And then, before they had time to think about running, the lava pool exploded.

Out of the magma a body burst. It was monstrous; a naked torso of burning flesh, molten lava lapping at its chest.

The men recoiled in fear, cursing and shouting.

The smell was sickening.

With a gasp, the monster inhaled a violent gulp of air. Then, shuddering, it began to rise, moving to its feet. It trembled as it lifted its bulk from the pool. When it was on its feet, it fell still, molten liquid running down its skin in streams of fire. Its chest rose and fell with heavy breaths. It waited, naked, before its mistress, the lava moving around its waist.

'Come,' the old woman commanded.

The creature stepped forward, emerging from the pool. Its body was black and charred and its face burnt. Below its melted skin, muscle and bone were visible.

'What…what is it?' one of the crew stammered.

'This, my dear, is a wraith – a creature of the underworld. It is dead and yet it lives. I have the power to call life from base materials, to mould fire, smoke and ash to my will. All I need is a bit of grit, a sacrifice for a pool like this, and from that grit, I can create a pearl. This creature is mine and it will always serve me and do my bidding. I am, if you like, its mother. That's nice, ain't it? Always wanted a boy of me own.' She patted the monster's arm.

The captain's face contorted with disgust. 'Will it always look like that?'

'No, it will grow new skin. But for now, we need to cover it with this.'

Grizelda reached into the crate and pulled out a golden mask. It glinted in the firelight. She also took a red cloak from the box. It seemed to be made from feathers.

'Hawks feathers,' the old woman spat, seeing the look of bewilderment on the crew's faces. 'Ere, don't just stand there gawping. Help me with it. The poor boy needs covering.'

Awkwardly, Grizelda and the captain wrapped the cloak around the creature's body. Then, reaching up, Grizelda placed the mask on its face. It moulded around the monster's features, giving it a face of gold.

Grizelda stepped back, admiring him. 'Well, what do you think of that, then?'

Nobody replied.

'A work of beauty, isn't he?' she said with a mix of greed and awe. 'And he ain't no ordinary child, my boy. I ain't gonna have to wait up fretting through sleepless nights or worrying if my boy will come home to his mother. That just ain't my style. No, my boy's got a lovely little characteristic to keep his mum from having such worries, an adorable little trait that'll make me very proud. He's indestructible, aren't you, my dear? There's only one thing can bring him harm – that's seeing his own ugly face. But we don't have to worry about that now, do we? We've just seen to that with this mask.' She turned to the monster. 'Yer safe now, son. And mummy's got a special job for you. A little holiday to the other side of the Un-Crossable Boundary. I need you to do a little investigating. There's someone I want you to find, someone I want you to persuade to help us. And that's not all. Mummy has some special plans for you on this side of the Boundary too. I have a lot of ambition for my boy. I think you're gonna go far. Look at me, I'm wellin' up. Come and give yer old mother a hug.'

Reaching out, the monster put his arms awkwardly around the crone. The two of them stood in the mouth of the cave, frozen.

As the captain of the Raven watched, he knew there was no emotion in that embrace, no feeling. For the first time in his life he felt guilty. What had he done? What was this atrocity? What the consequence of this moment would be, he didn't dare think.

Chapter 8

The Long Night

Back on Fullstop Island, Fletcher and Scoop were in the back of an old hay cart. It trundled through the Dreamless Desert, jolting uncomfortably. Heat bounced from the sand, making them feel sick.

The man driving the cart hadn't spoken a word the whole journey. Like most of the Hermits of Hush, he had taken a vow of silence. His rough, brown cassock looked itchy, and the rope tied around his waist was pulled too tight. Every so often, he gave the reins a little shake, and the melancholy looking horse that was pulling the cart sped up, making the wagon creak and sway.

The Dreamless Desert was feared by the villagers of Bardbridge. The Gossipers said that if you weren't careful it would steal your mind. Fletcher looked down, the emptiness of the wilderness creeping over him. The endless horizon made him feel small.

He stared at an insect scuttling through the hay that was trapped under the black, jewelled box that had been given to them by the Yarnbard. It sat on the floor by his feet.

I wonder what's in there? he thought. He imagined leather pouches filled with powders from the Starlight Islands and bottles of potion from the depths of the Furnace Jungles. He imagined a hermit weighing Munchkin Seed on an old pair of scales and meticulously counting the right number of salt crystals from the Elfen Seas, before heating them together in a healing dish. He imagined his mother on her bed, her face pale, her eyelids like glass. He imagined gently pouring the elixir between her lips and then waiting. He felt his heart burst with joy as he watched his mother wake, seeing the smile on her face, realising that Fletcher and Scoop were sitting beside her.

But then Fletcher looked up. Sand stretched out in all directions, bare and uniform.

It swallowed the vision.

There were no landmarks. He had no idea how the hermit knew where he was going. The desert was a disorientating place.

Fletcher looked back at the black box and clenched his fists with resolution. He would sort this out; they would get their mother whatever she needed.

Scoop had been watching the sun as it slowly inched across the sky. It was beginning to sink now and had swelled to a giant, red orb that balanced on the horizon. The air in front of it quivered.

She and Fletcher were quiet. Every so often they would give one another a weak smile or gentle nod, as if to say, "Are you okay?" The other would reply with a shrug or a nod back, neither in the mood to speak.

Scoop's thoughts drifted back to how she'd felt that morning. She'd been on the deck of the Firebird, the sea breeze blowing through her hair. She'd been laughing with the rest of the crew, hopeful of a victory in the race. She remembered looking back at Rainbow's End, the sparkling light streaming into the sea, a shower of colour raining down, mingling with the water. At the time, she'd thought how beautiful the world was, how lucky she was to be alive.

Now, however, her bones ached from rattling around in the back of the cart. She was trying not to feel sick as it bumped over the rough ground. How much things could change in just a few hours.

Scoop looked ahead. In the distance, she could see a darker patch of land visible. As they drew closer, a series of mounds emerged, almost unnoticeably from the landscape. They looked like giant tortoise shells, resting on the sand. As they neared them, she realised the mounds were mud huts, covered with straw. It was the encampment of the hermits.

After a few more minutes of jolting, they arrived in the camp and the cart jerked to a stop.

Out of the nearest hut, a hermit emerged, stooping through the door. He was unnaturally tall, with wild, dark hair. He reminded Scoop of one of the feral horses that roamed the island, fierce and unpredictable, but with an amazing capacity for gentleness. As he approached the cart, Scoop was drawn to his eyes. They were intense – deep and focused. Looking into them, a strange sensation filled her. It was as if the hermit was whispering. His lips weren't moving, but words passed through the air like the sighing of the desert breeze.

So, you are here.

The hermit's eyes darkened and Scoop felt her skin prickle.

I know what you bring to our camp. You bring danger.

Danger? Scoop thought. *We're here to help our mother.*

The hermit's gaze softened.

'Hello,' Fletcher said, as the monk approached. 'Are you in charge here?' His voice sounded out of place in the wilderness.

The hermit inclined his head, acknowledging Fletcher without speaking.

'So what do we need to do with this box, then? I assume the Yarnbard told you why we're here?'

Again the hermit inclined his head, but said nothing.

Rude! Fletcher thought.

Who are you? Scoop wondered, transfixed by the hermit's energy.

As if hearing her thought, the monk turned towards her. *My name is of no importance. I am just Word.*

Reaching the cart, he turned to the driver. For a moment the two desert dwellers held each other's eyes. Then, the driver climbed down from the wagon. He walked around the side and reached across to pick up the black box.

As quick as a flash, Fletcher caught his arm, protective of the chest.

'What are you doing?' he asked aggressively.

Peace, apprentice. Allow my brother to take your load.

Scoop touched Fletcher's hand and signalled that he should let the driver take the box. Reluctantly, Fletcher released his grip and the driver picked it up.

Now, follow.

Silently, Scoop rose. Fletcher looked confused but followed her lead. He felt off-kilter. The fact nobody was speaking made him uncomfortable. He didn't know quite what to do, and his impatience to get on with helping his mother was growing.

Following the hermit and the driver, they weaved through the mud huts, the sand soft under their feet. Ahead of them, a column of grey smoke stretched into the evening sky. In the doorways of the huts, Fletcher noticed half-hidden monks watching them. As he passed, they darted back into their shelters like frightened deer.

Finally, they reached the hut from which the smoke rose. The hermit and the driver ducked inside. Fletcher and Scoop followed.

They found themselves in a bare room with mud walls. The floor was covered with weaved rugs. In the centre, a fire blazed, smoke disappearing through a hole in the roof. The hut was sweltering, making Fletcher sweat.

Walking to the other side of the fire, the driver placed the black, jewelled box on the floor. Then, without looking at the apprentices, he left.

'Where's he going?' Fletcher asked. 'Who's going to be working with the contents of the box?'

Still the hermit didn't speak.

Sit, Scoop heard him whisper.

She did as she was told, lowering herself onto the rugs and crossing her legs. Fletcher followed her lead, irritable. Why was nobody speaking?

A long beam of orange sunlight streamed through the opening of the hut, drawing out the red of the mud walls. It made the hut look like an oven. The heat from the fire did nothing to temper the image. It was intense.

The sun has almost set, the hermit said. *The transformation process will begin as the last rays sink below the horizon.*

He moved to the edge of the shelter and, stooping, picked up a handful of sand. Moving back to the fire, he threw it into the flames. They hissed, and a cloud of green smoke began to pour from the fire. The cloud swirled around the hut, making Scoop feel faint.

'What's that? What are you doing?' Fletcher asked sharply.

'It will help you sleep,' the hermit said aloud. It was the first time he'd spoken. His voice was hypnotic.

'Sleep?' Fletcher said. 'I don't want to sleep. We've got a job to do. We have to start working on whatever's in that box. You know what it's for, don't you? You know *who* it's for?'

The hermit inclined his head again, his face glowing in the flickering light.

Walking around the fire, the hermit knelt down and laid his hands on the box. He pushed open the clasps, smoke swirling around him. But he didn't open the box.

He stood again. *It is time for me to leave,* he whispered, moving towards the door.

'Where are you going?' Fletcher snapped. His head was groggy. The smell of the smoke was intoxicating. 'There's work to do. You can't leave.'

But without even looking back, the hermit ducked through the door and disappeared, leaving the apprentices alone.

Fletcher stared at the place where the hermit had exited.

'What do we do now?' he said, incredulous. He looked at the box. It sat in front of them, its clasps open. He hesitated. 'Do you think we should open it – see what's inside?'

'No,' Scoop whispered.

'But…'

'You remember what the Yarnbard told us, don't you? He told us not to open it. "On no account," he said.'

'But the hermit just unclipped it. Perhaps he wants us to look inside.'

Scoop shook her head. 'He doesn't. He would have said.'

'Said? He was hardly the talkative type, was he?'

'That's because you weren't listening, Fletcher.'

'Weren't listening? He didn't say anything. What are you talking about? '

Scoop ignored the question. 'I think we should sleep, like he said.'

Before Fletcher had a chance to reply, she turned away and stretched out, lying down. The desert sand was warm and uneven beneath her.

Sleep! I can't sleep! Fletcher thought, annoyed. *Doesn't anybody else care? Doesn't anybody think we should be getting this done as quickly as possible? What about mother?*

He watched the firelight flickering on the walls, dark images forming and dissolving in the shadows, mirroring his thoughts.

He turned to the box again. Perhaps *he* should open it, whatever Scoop said.

But his body was heavy and his mind cloudy. He didn't want to move. The heat was twisting his senses. It made his muscles ache.

Maybe if I just stretch out a bit, he thought, extending his legs across the warm rugs. He propped his head up with his arm, fighting to keep his eyes open.

I hope whoever's coming to do this work will be here soon.

He waited, the hut still.

Nobody arrived.

A few times Fletcher wondered if he should get up, find somebody. But drowsiness kept him from moving. The green smoke lingered in the air. He could taste its bitterness at the back of his throat.

Gradually, the flames of the fire dwindled.

Fletcher studied the embers as they danced, sparkles of light that blazed and then faded.

His eyelids became heavy.

Without noticing, his head lolled to the side.

He snapped up, willing himself to stay awake. He needed to be alert.

Again, the smoke swirled over him. He breathed it in, his body heavy.

The hut was dark now. He could hear Scoop breathing. Was she asleep?

The last embers of the fire cast an eerie light. He stared into them, his eyes becoming heavier.

Finally, despite his best efforts, Fletcher closed his eyes and drifted into a dreamless sleep.

* * *

The desert was silent.

Gradually, the temperature in the hut dropped. Smoke twisted from the dying fire, rising like a ghost into the cooling air.

Fletcher and Scoop lay unnaturally still, their sleep thick.

Then, behind the fire, something moved.

A thin shape crept from under the lid of the black, jewelled box. In the darkness, it looked like a snake slithering into the night. It paused for a moment, as if sensing the air, and then it started to rise, slowly lifting the lid. Moonlight spilled through the hole in the roof, catching the shape. It was a finger, mottled, black and brittle. No flesh covered it.

It was the finger of a skeleton.

Slowly, other shapes emerged from the box, a second finger, then a third, pushing the lid fully open. One by one they curled up until a whole hand was in view. The fingers stretched, silently lengthening. The hand waited, silhouetted by the firelight. Then, slowly, it curled around the rim of the black box and gripped it.

A second skeletal hand stole out from the box. It thrust upwards, slicing the air. Like its partner, it stretched, gaining length. It gripped the opposite edge of the box.

Gradually, the hands twisted, scraping against the wood as wrists and arm bones emerged. Skeletal elbows came into view, bent sharp, pointing towards the ceiling.

Then, quivering noiselessly, the arms pushed down. As they did, something began to rise from the box, something that would strike terror into even the bravest of souls. It was a black skull, chiselled from stone. Its eye sockets were empty, but it moved with purpose. It rose, emotionless, its cranium polished, so that it glinted in the moonlight. The remnants of green smoke threaded through its eye sockets, emerging from its mouth.

As Fletcher and Scoop slept, the skull ascended, its skeletal body following. It grew, spectre like, its neck bones lining up. Its spine appeared, as if charmed, rising from the box. Clavicle and scapula, sternum and rib cage emerged. It pushed itself up, its arms lengthening, bones taking their position like an army being summoned. A knee thrust up, bent towards its chest. The creature's thigh bone lifted towards its rib cage, pulling fibula and tibia behind it. A skeletal foot appeared. It flexed its toes, the bones clicking. Then, it extended its leg beyond the box, and lowered its foot to the ground. The skeleton paused, as if feeling the earth beneath its feet. It was crouched, still gripping the edge of the box, hunched over like an athlete at the start of a race. It let go of the box and, swaying slightly, pushed down on its leg, beginning to stand. It rose, dark and shadowy, gaining height. Its pelvis appeared now, pulling a second leg in its wake. The black skeleton straightened up, its bones extending. It was tall. It loomed over Fletcher and Scoop, filling the hut. As it finally reached its full height, it stepped out of the box into the fire.

Instantly, the flames reignited, licking around its feet. As they did, the sockets of the black skull sparked, and flames flickered to life where its eyes should have been. Lifting its arms, it stretched. Its fingers pressed flat onto the roof of the hut. Lowering them again, it paused. Slowly, it looked from Fletcher to Scoop, its neck cricking as it turned. Then, it opened its jaws and spoke.

'I AM HERE!'

The sound penetrated the air. It was petrifying.

Fletcher and Scoop shot up, spinning round to see the horror that stood above them.

Fletcher glanced at the black box. Its lid was open.

Dazed, he scrambled to his feet and backed away from the skeletal monster.

Scoop had pressed herself against the wall of the hut, cowering below the monstrosity that dominated the tiny space.

We've been tricked, Fletcher thought, his head spinning. This wasn't supposed to be what was in the box. It was supposed to be something to help their mother.

It was the Yarnbard who'd given them the chest, who'd told them to bring it here. Perhaps he didn't know what was inside. Perhaps he'd been deceived too.

Unless he's betrayed you, Fletcher's thoughts accused.

No! He pushed the impulse from his mind.

As Fletcher stared up at the terrible vision, he had a sickening feeling.

It knows who I am!

How can it? he told himself. But as he looked into the fiery eyes of the black skull, he had the overwhelming sense that somehow this skeleton knew every part of him. It knew him intimately. To the creature, Fletcher was an open book. The thought made him tremble.

The Nemesis Charm stood before them, as if gloating, its eyes blazing.

'I AM HERE!' it repeated.

It spoke slowly, its voice jolting, rasping, rattling.

Terrified, Scoop ran towards the door.

Instantly, the skeleton reached out. Fire shot from its fingers. The flames leapt forward, spilling around the edge of the hut, surrounding it with a wall of fire. Scoop was cut off from the door. She recoiled, lifting her arm to shield her face from the flames, the heat forcing her backwards.

Fletcher dashed across to her. He stood between her and the skeleton, his heart pounding.

'Leave her alone!' he yelled.

The skeleton let out a strange clicking noise. Slowly, it rocked its skull from side to side, its bones cricking. The fire in its eyes intensified.

Summoning all his courage, Fletcher stepped towards the monster. 'What are you?' he cried.

The skeleton turned its head directly towards him.

'I AM YOUR FUTURE.'

Chapter 9

The Hourglass Cup

Fletcher felt his skin prickle. Blood rushed to his face, his flesh burning.

'What do you mean?' he said, his voice husky.

'I AM YOUR DESTINY.'

The sound of the skeleton's voice ricocheted from the walls. The fire still circled the hut, cutting off any chance of escape.

The heat was overwhelming. Sweat poured from Fletcher's forehead. 'What do you want with us?' he croaked.

'I WANT NOTHING.

I AM WHAT IS.

I AM WHAT WILL BE.'

Fletcher stood silently before his Nemesis, fixed to the spot. There was nothing he could say. He stared into its eyes and a strange sensation gripped him. He was simultaneously repelled and attracted by the creature that threatened him.

Scoop emerged from behind Fletcher. 'Why are you here?' she said, her voice trembling.

The skeleton paused for a moment. Its eyes flickered.

'YOU MUST FACE ME.

YOU MUST CHOOSE.'

As it spoke, the skeleton reached for Fletcher and Scoop, its bony arms extending towards them. The apprentices tried to turn away, but the fire behind them singed their skin. It was no good. The Nemesis Charm grabbed them, sharp bones curling around their shoulders, digging into them.

It held them, its grip vice-like.

A force like electricity shot from the skeleton, burning Fletcher's shoulder, sending intense pain flowing through his arm. He convulsed and the room went black.

It felt as if the Nemesis Charm was dragging him away, the creature pulling him upwards, higher and higher. The air pressed in around him. The skeleton was squeezing him through a narrow gap. His head pounded and his stomach turned. Fletcher tried to resist, but the Nemesis Charm was too strong.

Finally, the air opened out. Fletcher gulped a deep breath, panting. He felt sick. He could taste salt on his tongue. He was standing on rock. It was cold beneath his feet. He opened his eyes. Scoop was still next to him, but she looked older, her face less carefree.

Below him, Fletcher could hear the sound of sea churning and surging. They were standing on cracked, volcanic rocks. He looked up. Before him, a cliff towered. He shivered. Looking down at him, carved into the face of the cliff, was a giant skull. He and Scoop were standing in front of a wide cave that disappeared into darkness. Wind poured from the cave. It was harsh, stark. On it, a whisper sounded.

I'm coming...sands shift...

Fletcher's froze. Somehow, the sound seemed to reach right to his core.

It was strange, he was in his own body, but something felt unfamiliar. There was a weight on his shoulders he didn't recognise. Memories jostled for his attention, but they were hazy. Fletcher looked at his hands. They were worn, his skin cracked with seawater. There was a scar across the back of his knuckles. He didn't have a scar. What was happening? He felt as if he was in his own body, but somehow it *wasn't* him. Who was this Fletcher? Not the person he knew himself to be. Not as he was now, anyway.

With a rush of clarity, he realised what he was seeing. The skeleton had said it. This was his future. Fletcher was inside his future self. He looked older. He felt older. This moment in front of the cave was a moment he was yet to face.

* * *

In the banquet chamber of his castle, Alethea, the Storyteller stared into a pool of silver threads. These threads carried all the stories of his world. In the pool, the Storyteller could watch the tale of any Mortale. The threads writhed and swirled. The Storyteller focused on the two apprentices, Fletcher and Scoop, as they stood before the cave.

* * *

Fletcher looked into the cave. He didn't know why, but it filled him with terror.

As the waves churned below, he remembered the words the Yarnbard had spoken to them before they had left his office.

The direction you need to take to help your mother will be made clear to you.

He could see the old man's face, his expression sad and heavy.

*This is it...*Fletcher thought, staring into the blackness. *This is what he meant.* He didn't know how, but he was sure of it. The cave was the direction they needed to take. They had to go into that darkness. They had to go through it.

'This is it,' said a voice next to him, echoing his thoughts. He looked round to see the older Scoop staring at him. There were tears in her eyes. 'This is the Threshold. We made a choice a long time ago. And now it's time.' She turned around, looking back across the sea. 'Goodbye,' she said simply.

There was so much sadness in that word, so much nostalgia.

A deep fear erupted from Fletcher's gut.

No!

The cave petrified him. Its darkness was otherworldly.

A Threshold? Where had he heard that word before?

Scoop knew exactly where she'd heard it before. The face of the actor from the festival filled her mind. He was looking directly at her again, his eyes dark and intense. His words came flooding back...

Hear the legends of Thresholds – caves that are doorways between worlds. Once you set foot across a Threshold, there is no coming back.

As Scoop looked into the cave, she knew it to be true. To enter that cave would mean to leave everything behind. That darkness threatened to strip her of the life she knew, the life she loved.

Pictures formed in her mind. She saw the Three Towers of the academy; she saw the Yarnbard dancing on the tables at Alethea; she saw her room at Scribbler's House; she saw Nib and Rufina rowing them back for the festival; she saw the Hall of Heroes, the House of Wisdom, Rainbow's End. And, although she couldn't yet see it, she had a sense of all the time between who she was now and the moment she would become that older Scoop, standing in front of the cave – all the adventures and experiences that were yet to be.

She clenched her fists, a surge of stubbornness and anger welling up inside her. She didn't want to leave behind everything she loved, every*one* she loved. She was happy as she was. This wasn't fair! Why had the Storyteller brought them here? Surely he didn't expect them to do this, to enter the cave and abandon everything they had worked for, everything they would become?

She wouldn't do it. She couldn't.

I'm coming...where the...wind blows...from the shadow's reach.

By now, Fletcher too had remembered where he'd heard of Thresholds. He too remembered the player at the festival. Fletcher recalled his words with a shudder, *No living Mortale can return to this world once they have crossed such a doorway.*

Fletcher had thought he was ready for anything, that he was ready to do whatever it took to help his mother. He wanted to see her healed more than anything. But this? This couldn't be right. The Yarnbard had to be mistaken. The Storyteller wouldn't ask them to do such a thing. It was too much.

There has to be another way!

But then, in one awful moment, Fletcher saw the truth. The Yarnbard hadn't been lying. He hadn't been mistaken. There *was* something in the box that could bring about a transformation to help their mother. But it was not what was *in* the box that would be transformed; what was in the box was intended to bring about *their* transformation – a change in him and Scoop.

The skeleton had said it, hadn't it?

"YOU MUST CHOOSE."

The Yarnbard had said it too – they would have a choice to make.

This was it. This was the choice. They could either accept the future the Nemesis Charm was showing them, a future where they would step into that cave, fully trusting the Storyteller that it would bring healing to their mother, or they could turn back and walk away, protecting themselves and the life they loved.

The choice was horrific. But it was a choice.

Suddenly, Scoop felt her older self begin to move, to step forward into the mouth of the cave.

Fletcher felt it too.

This was the moment.

A sharp pain flowed from Scoop's shoulder, down through her body. All of a sudden, the cave vanished. She became aware of the skeleton's grip again. It was pulling her back through the narrow opening, back to her own time. Her bones squeezed and stretched, her stomach turned, and then, with a thump, her feet hit solid ground.

The skeleton released its grip and Scoop felt her body attune once more to its natural age, as if shedding a skin.

Her eyes stung as she opened them. She looked around. She was back in the hermit's hut. Fletcher was next to her, his face pale. There was sweat on his forehead.

The Nemesis Charm stood before them, its eyes glowing.

In its bony hands was a large goblet. It was carved from reddish stone and resembled an hourglass.

The skeleton reached forward, clicking and cracking as it moved. "DRINK," it said. The word sent a chill down Scoop's spine. She knew to drink from the cup would be to accept the future she'd just seen. She didn't know how long it would be until she'd have to stand in front of that cave, until she'd have to turn and say goodbye to all she loved, but she knew that if she drank from the cup right now, sooner or later that time would come. To drink would be to accept the quest, to set in motion the series of events that would ultimately lead them to the Threshold.

She stepped backwards, tears streaming down her face.

I can't, she thought. *I just can't.*

For a moment, nobody moved. It was stalemate. The skeleton stood fixed, its hands outstretched, offering the hourglass cup to the apprentices.

Fletcher felt defeated. He couldn't take the cup either. He couldn't do what the Storyteller was asking. He didn't have what it took to help his mother.

Then, in the gloom, the embers of the dead fire spat and crackled. The skeleton, who was standing in the pile of ashes, looked down, surprised. As it did, the fire leapt to life again.

The flames were bright.

Fletcher and Scoop stepped back, shielding their eyes.

The blaze rose higher, a plume of light shooting up through the hut. The skeleton pulled away, raising a bony arm to shield its face. It swung the cup back to keep it safe. Slowly from the plume of fire, flaming wings spread out. Above them, a fiery creature appeared. It filled the hut.

Scoop looked up at the bird that blazed over her. It was beautiful and terrifying.

From its pinions, bright drops of light began to fall, blazing like stars. Fletcher and Scoop instinctively ducked but soon realised the shower of light wasn't burning them. Instead, as the brilliant drops landed on their skin, they felt strengthened.

They recognised what was hovering above them. They had

seen it once before at the wedding banquet of the Storyteller, the evening that their mother had been reborn.

It was a Firebird.

They looked up in awe. And as the light streamed down, making their faces glow, they heard a voice.

Trust me. In losing you will find. I know you fully, your strengths and your weaknesses, your light and your dark. I have chosen you. You are not alone. You have one another. And you have me. Walk forward in the knowledge that you are loved with a love that can never be lost, a love that is stronger than death.

Fletcher felt a familiar sensation rising inside him. It was something he'd often felt while travelling with the Storyteller and his mother – courage.

We can do this, he whispered.

As if hearing him, the Firebird pulsed. Scoop's heart leapt. And then, glowing brightly, the Firebird dissolved into a thousand sparks of light. They drifted down through the air, sprinkling Fletcher and Scoop, before sinking into the floor. As the last droplet extinguished, the hut fell back into darkness.

A heavy sense of peace hung in the air. The hut was so still that Fletcher hardly dared to breathe.

But in the stillness, there was a movement. A black hand was slicing silently through the darkness. Slowly, the skeleton turned back to Fletcher and Scoop and, as if it had all the time in the world, it reached out again, the cup still in its hands.

"DRINK," the Nemesis Charm said.

Fletcher looked at Scoop. 'Together?' he whispered.

She nodded slowly. And then, as one, they stepped forward.

Fletcher took the cup from the skeleton, surprised by how steady his hands were.

In turn, they raised the red stone goblet to their lips, and drank.

Chapter 10

The Sandman Comes

The Storyteller fell back, exhausted. He sank to the floor of the Great Hall of Alethea and stared into space. At his feet, the silver pool bubbled and churned, story threads weaving around each other, knotting and slipping, swirling into complex patterns. He had been watching Fletcher and Scoop in the pool.

And then, through their eyes he had seen it.

The cave.

That cave was the source of his princess's sickness.

It was the source of his misery.

It was strange. He had heard the whisper.

I'm coming...

But he had heard more than that, more than Fletcher and Scoop had heard, more words, buried deep within those words, carried on the wind that blew though the cave.

He closed his eyes. He could feel the chill on his face. He could feel it flow through his hair.

The words swam through his thoughts, tangling his senses.

He focused, allowing his mind to descend deeper, deeper into the whisper, into the very heart of the words.

A sudden sadness filled him.

I'm coming on the clouds of night...

It was as if the whisper was calling something deep within him.

I'm coming from the shadow's reach...

Something from long ago, something half-remembered.

I'm coming where the dream wind blows...

An exquisite pain flooded his body.

I'm coming where the time sands shift...

It was as if a dam had been breached, a dam that had been

protecting him from these words, from the memories they held.

The Sandman comes, the Sandman sings,
And sleep's the gift the Sandman brings.

The Storyteller began to hum a tune. It was distant, as if from another life. He began to sing, softly, joining the whisper from the cave.

I'm coming on the clouds of night.
I'm coming from the shadow's reach.
I'm coming where the dream winds blow.
I'm coming where the time sands shift.
The Sandman comes, the Sandman sings,
And sleep's the gift the Sandman brings.
I'm coming...

* * *

On the other side of the Un-Crossable boundary, Libby Joyner looked up from her laptop. She knew those words. She knew that rhyme. It was a song her mother used to sing to her, long ago, when she was a child.

She looked out of the window. The familiar sight of red brick houses, of the old mill chimneys on the other side of the valley, of the mobile phone mast on the horizon, told her she was back in her world, back in what people liked to call the *real world*.

She looked at the clock. It was nearly seven. She had been in the World of Mortales for the past three hours. The shock of hearing the rhyme had jolted her from it.

She sat frozen, feeling the movement of her legs against the soft mattress beneath. Her eyes darted, half-taking in her surroundings. She was sitting crossed-legged on her bed, her laptop open in front of her. Her eyes were bleary, as if she wasn't quite in her own body yet, as if this was someone else's life and she was just watching.

It was always strange leaping between worlds.

Leaping between worlds, she repeated to herself, her head still hazy. She knew other people would call that melodramatic language – *leaping.* "You're just writing," they would say. But Libby knew it was more than that. When she entered the World of Mortales, she became somebody else. She went from being Libby Joyner – schoolgirl, half-decent violin player and loyal, slightly quirky friend – to being a man who could direct the destiny of a whole world, who could spin the stories of that world into beautiful patterns, intricate threads.

She became the Storyteller.

It was through him she inhabited the World of Mortales. She didn't know how. She didn't know why that was the body she took on, but she knew it was more than "just writing". She saw through his eyes. She leapt into his flesh.

They were separate, but they were one – connected across an Un-Crossable boundary.

I'm coming on the clouds of night.

I'm coming from the shadow's reach.

The words of the rhyme rang through Libby's mind.

She tried to hover between the two worlds, not losing focus on either.

She hadn't heard that song in years. Why was it being whispered across the sea of that other world? How had it got there?

Memories that had been deeply buried rose like bubbles pushing through the sea. She could almost feel her mother next to her, her voice fragile as Libby lay on her lap. She closed her eyes and tried to imagine her mum stroking her hair, singing the song.

The Sandman comes, the Sandman sings,

And sleep's the gift the Sandman brings.

Her mother used to sing it at night, as Libby drifted off to sleep.

The bubbles burst the surface of the water. With them, the

unbearable ache Libby carried. She laid her hand on her chest and massaged her skin. She could never settle while that ache was in her. It was an ache that had entered her heart a year and a half ago, the day her mother had gone missing. Libby hadn't seen her mum since. Perhaps she would never see her again.

Her desktop image appeared, silently on the screen. It was a picture of Alsmcliff Crag – a rocky outcrop in the valley just to the north of Leeds, the city where she lived.

She had picked the crag as her desktop picture because of a particular memory. One time, when she'd been driving with her mum to visit her gran in Knaresborough, she'd asked about the crag. Uncharacteristically, her mother had decided to shelve their plans for the afternoon and take her daughter to see it.

They had turned off the main road, parked near the bottom of the hill and spent the afternoon climbing the rocks. It had been a perfect day. The sky had been blue and the sun, hazy. They'd watched a Red Kite soar on the air currents. Libby remembered gazing across the valley, seeing the long red viaduct and the meandering river. She'd felt as though she was on top of the world.

It wasn't long after that her mum went missing. Libby always wondered if her mother had known what was going to happen, if she had planned it, if that's why she'd taken her to the crag that day.

She reached forward and moved the mouse. Almscliffe Crag vanished and Fletcher and Scoop's story appeared again.

There was a knock on her bedroom door. Libby jumped.

Her heart pounded. Why did she feel guilty?

Without waiting for a reply, her dad pushed in.

'Dad!' she complained, quickly closing the laptop. 'You can't just push in here like that.'

'Why not?' her dad asked, looking at her suspiciously. 'What are you up to?'

'Nothing,' Libby said. 'It's none of your business anyway.'

'It is my business.' Her dad looked at the laptop. He pointed at it. 'This daydreaming – it's no good for you...'

Libby went to interrupt. 'But my counsellor says...'

Her dad raised his hand. 'I don't care what your counsellor says. As far as I'm concerned, you're getting too caught up in your own imagination. I'm your dad. You're losing the ability to tell fact from fiction. If you ask me, you need to get out more, do some exercise or something.'

'I'm not daydreaming, Dad. I'm writing.'

'What's that?' He pointed to a book on her bed, his voice suddenly cold. It lay open, next to her laptop.

Libby groaned. It was her mother's writing journal. She'd left it out. Usually, she kept it hidden. The journal was a great source of contention in the Joyner household.

'I've told you, I don't want you looking at that,' he snapped. 'You saw what it did to your mother.'

Libby's dad blamed the journal for her mother's disappearance. It was where she used to write, where she used to create her own worlds. He said she'd got lost in her own imagination. He said that's why she'd gone missing.

Libby saw it differently.

Her dad glared at her.

'All right, all right, I'll put it away!' Libby snapped. She picked up the book and thumped to her desk. Opening the drawer, she buried it inside and slammed the drawer shut.

Just like Mum, she thought. *That's why she went missing, because she wasn't able to express herself – because you wouldn't let her. She had to hide her creativity. She had to hide this journal from you – a piece of her soul!*

Libby had found the journal hidden behind a chest of drawers in the spare room a month after her mum had gone missing. She'd no idea her mum had been writing – none of them had. It had been her mother's secret.

It was in her mother's writing journal that Libby had first

learned of Fullstop Island. The World of Mortales was her mother's creation. Those pages held Libby's first encounters with Fletcher and Scoop. She'd fallen in love with them instantly. Her mother's journal was full of Mortale characters and half-finished stories from that world.

Since her mother's disappearance, Libby had taken to continuing her mum's stories. She planned to finish them; it had become quite an obsession. Somehow she felt closer to her mother when she was working on them.

What would her dad do if he knew why the book was out? What would he do if he knew she'd been continuing to write her mum's stories?

She knew the answer. He'd take the book and burn it. He'd take her laptop too.

She wasn't going to let that happen, especially now.

For a while, Libby had entertained an irrational thought. It lurked at the back of her mind.

The World of Mortales is full of clues, she would find herself thinking. *And all I need to do is follow them.* And although she never fully admitted it, the end of the thought was always the same – that if she followed the clues, they would lead to her, they would lead to her mum. By following those clues, Libby would find her, and they would be reunited again.

She knew it was a ridiculous thought. But even though she told herself so, it still lingered in her mind as a hope, as an unspoken plan.

And now, with the whisper from the cave, the plan felt even stronger. It felt even more powerful. This was the biggest clue so far.

There's no way he's taking that away from me.

Her dad interrupted her thoughts. 'And don't you think it's time you took those down?'

He was pointing at a bunch of newspaper clippings she'd tacked to the wall. The top headline read, "SEARCH FOR

MISSING WOMAN CALLED OFF". 'It's not healthy having them there as a reminder the whole time. She's gone, Libby. We have to accept it. We have to get on with our lives.'

Libby didn't reply.

Her dad sighed. 'Look, I've not come up here to argue. I just wanted to let you know that I have a friend coming over later.' He looked awkward. 'A female friend.'

Libby blushed. She didn't want to hear this, not now.

'It's okay, Dad – it's your house.'

'I just wanted to let you know. Okay?'

'Yeah, okay.'

Her dad left the room, pulling the door closed behind him.

Libby sat for a moment, not wanting to move. Her dad had given up. He'd given up hope of finding her mother. He was "moving on". Her lips curled into a sneer. How could anyone move on? How could he forget? Libby hadn't forgotten. One thought dominated her mind: finding her mother. She needed to follow that whisper. She needed to find out what was beyond the skull cave.

Without waiting, she flipped open her laptop again and pressed the power button. A dull glow spread across the screen, washing Libby's face with ghostly light. She clicked the icon in the centre of the screen and leaned forward to type her password.

F1R3B1RD

The document she'd been working on opened up. She leaned forward, excitement rising. It was time to leap again. Putting her hands on the keyboard, she began to type. The words appeared easily on the screen, as if she were not the one typing them, as if she were merely participating in some great drama that existed beyond her. Before she knew it, she was in his body again.

* * *

The Storyteller moved back to the silver pool and stared into it.

He could see Fletcher and Scoop. They were asleep in the camp of the Hermits of Hush. They looked so peaceful. He studied them closely. There was something different about them, a sort of freshness he couldn't place. They looked almost like newborn babies. He reached out towards them and Fletcher stirred.

Chapter 11

Completion

It was morning. Bright light poured through the hole in the roof of the hut. The two apprentices lay in the shade, comfortable on the warm rugs. The smoke had gone now and the air was clear. Fletcher opened his eyes and scanned the mud walls, slowly remembering where he was. The hut looked different in the morning light, simple and peaceful. The intensity of the night before had vanished. His eyes fell on the remains of the fire. Scattered among the ashes, the bones of the Nemesis Charm lay, the black skull at an angle, half-buried.

Fletcher closed his eyes.

With a flash, a vision of the previous night hit him. He was standing, the skeleton towering over him, its eyes blazing. The cup was at his lips. He felt his pulse rise, his body torn between fear and resolve. Before he could change his mind, he tipped the goblet back, gulping down the drink. As the cold liquid slid down his throat, he winced. He was drinking his own destruction. It was an odd sensation, bitter and painful. The liquid hit his stomach and a wave of icy cold swept through him, freezing every muscle, penetrating his bones. Tears leaked from his eyes. But as quickly as the ice had filled him, it transformed, turning into fire. Fletcher's body exploded, as though his flesh was blazing, as though the fire that shone in the skeleton's eyes was inside him.

It was amazing.

In that moment, Fletcher felt he had the strength to fight an army, to leap through the roof and fly into the sky. He had never felt such power, never known such freedom. It was as though his old body was burning away and, from inside, a new body was shining out, bright and vibrant; a body that had been hidden to him but that felt more fully *him* than anything he had ever known. Next to him, Scoop was undergoing a similar experience. Her face glowed. All of her self-doubt, her lack of confidence, her reliance on others, her need for appreciation, was being stripped away. It was as if she were naked before the black skull, as if she were a newborn child.

And then, as the two apprentices stood silent before their future, the Nemesis Charm quivered.

'THE CHOICE IS MADE,' it said, triumphant.

The light in its eyes flickered and went out. Then, as if in slow motion, its bones buckled. They fell from one another, tumbling down, clattering to a heap on the ashes of the fire.

Released from the power of the Nemesis Charm, a wave of exhaustion crashed over Fletcher and Scoop. They practically fell to the floor. Before they knew it, they were covered by a deep and dreamless sleep.

Fletcher opened his eyes again.

He looked back at the bones that lay in the ashes. They didn't look half as terrifying now. They lay, unmoving, robbed of their power. The skull just looked old, a reminder that things pass. But somehow even in that passing – maybe *because* of it – Fletcher had experienced a fire. That fire blazed inside him now; a fire he knew was stronger than death.

The hermit who had welcomed them entered the hut, carrying a loaf of bread and a jug of water. Fletcher propped himself up on his elbow. He felt as if he'd slept for a hundred years.

Good morning, the hermit whispered.

Scoop stirred, waking. Sitting up, she stretched. She looked different, as if she'd grown. Her eyes looked deeper, her face kinder. Fletcher also felt different. He was aware of a new sense of confidence; not brash and arrogant but quiet and still, as if he didn't have to hide. The hermit set the bread and the jug on the floor. *Eat and drink,* he said. *You have had a long night. You need to restore your energy.*

Fletcher was hungry and the bread looked good. *Thank you,* he replied. He looked into the hermit's eyes, realising he'd understood the monk, even though the hermit hadn't spoken.

So that's what Scoop meant, he thought.

The hermit smiled, his eyes wrinkling, and Fletcher knew the desert dweller understood what he was feeling. The hermit laid a hand on Fletcher's shoulder.

So you accepted the invitation. You drank from the cup.

How do you know? Fletcher replied.

It is written on your face – the mark of a selfless choice.

'So,' Scoop said, yawning. 'What do we do now?'

'Rest a little,' the hermit replied, 'and then my brother will take you back to Bardbridge. The Yarnbard has sent word that he will meet you at the inn for the gathering that marks the start of the new year at Blotting's Academy.'

'But,' Fletcher interrupted, 'we have a job to do. The skeleton told us—'

The hermit raised his hand, signalling for Fletcher to stop. 'Whatever you heard in the presence of the Nemesis Charm is knowledge for you and you alone. Do not be quick to share it, apprentices, even with friends.' The hermit looked into Fletcher's eyes. *Knowledge changes when shared. This revelation is meant for you. Treat it gently. Hold it. Digest it.*

Fletcher nodded. Reaching forward, he picked up the bread and ripped off a chunk. Despite everything, he felt calm. He wasn't afraid. He bit into the bread, enjoying the taste on his tongue.

'So how do we move things forward?' Scoop asked.

The hermit smiled. 'Do you think you can hold the future back?'

She thought for a moment and then shook her head.

'The future will be upon you sooner than you know. Go back to Bardbridge. Meet with your mentor. For now, that is all you need to do. You have made the choice – *that* is the important thing.'

Fletcher turned back to the black skull. The jewelled box stood open behind it. So much had changed since it had sat by his feet in the cart. A pang of sadness touched him. At the time he'd thought the box contained something for his mother. He'd hoped that by now they would be riding to her, carrying medicine that would save her life.

It looks like this is going to take a lot longer than I'd hoped, he thought.

'What about those?' he said, pointing to the bones.

'I will ensure the Nemesis Charm is returned to its rightful owner,' the hermit replied. The monk turned towards the door of the hut. 'Now, I must leave. Rest and eat. My brother will call you when it is time to go.' Just as he was about to stoop under the doorway, he turned back.

There was something in his eyes. Concern, maybe? Respect? *Peace go with you, apprentices,* they heard him say. With that, he ducked under the door and disappeared into the Dreamless Desert.

Chapter 12

Over the Threshold

After witnessing the unnatural birth of the monster from the lava pool, the crew of the Raven had retreated to their ship, muttering discontent. Grizelda had instantly vanished into her cabin, taking the monster with her. They hadn't been seen since.

It had been a long night, the Raven lurching listlessly on the squally sea. The crew barely slept, scared of the horror that dwelt below.

As the captain awoke, bleary-eyed, he had the vague hope that the events of the previous day had been a bad dream. But as he looked out at the scar on the ocean, the skull staring at him, he knew the night had only been a brief pause in a waking nightmare that was rolling on without mercy.

Before they knew it, the crew were on the island again. Without breakfast in their bellies, they were tramping back to the cave. In contrast to the monotonous trudge of the crew, Grizelda had a spring in her step. She looked unnaturally excited.

What's she up to, the captain thought. He didn't trust the old woman. He looked around. The monster wasn't with them.

'Where is he?' he asked.

Grizelda grinned wickedly. 'All in good time, me dear, all in good time.'

As they climbed, the sun fought to pierce the lingering mist, every so often tingeing the volcanic rocks orange. The mouth of the cave gaped above them. It looked hungry. As they got closer, the old woman's strength seemed to increase. She didn't need to be pulled up half as many of the rocks.

Before long, they reached the mouth of the cave, and Grizelda shooed the crew to the boulders that framed its entrance, telling them to sit down. She fussed around, lining them up, as if they were on a trip to the theatre.

'Right, there we are. Move over, dear, I want everyone to be able to see. I got somethin' to show you.'

Turning, she lifted her fingers to her lips and whistled. The shrill sound echoed from the rocks.

She spun back. 'Right, you bunch of morons, I'd like to present the man of the moment – a man who is goin' to make us very powerful, very powerful indeed. Well, I say "us", o'course, meanin' me. But I'll remember you when I'm rich and famous. Grizelda don't forget her friends.' She grinned. 'This is a moment of history in the makin' 'ere. I hope you appreciate it!'

The crew peered into the darkness. Through the gloom, they could see a shape coming towards them – a tall shadow. Gradually, it neared the light.

Grizelda glanced back at the motley gang. *No, this ain't right.*

'Be upstandin'!' she yelled, 'Come on, get up, show some respect.'

As the crew began to stand, a voice echoed from the cave. 'Don't fuss, mother.' Its tone was deep and calm, its English precise. Whoever was speaking, sounded like a gentleman, a man of standing. The crew glanced at each other, confused. Who was it? This wasn't what they were expecting.

Grizelda huffed.

'Let them sit down,' the voice said. The shape had almost reached the glow of the lava pool. As it stepped into its fiery light, the crew froze, half-standing, half-sitting. They stared in disbelief. The figure in the cave was tall and broad. He still wore the cloak made of hawks' feathers, but he was now handsome, maybe fifty or sixty years of age. His skin was olive and his complexion perfect. He had wavy, silver hair, combed meticulously into place. It was only outshone by his electric smile. He walked confidently past the lava pool, emerging into the light.

'Please be seated, gentlemen,' he said again.

Not taking their eyes off the man, they lowered themselves

onto the boulders.

Grizelda looked embarrassed. 'Oi, you lot, it's rude to stare! I'm sorry, me dear, they have no manners.'

'It's fine, mother. There's no need to fuss.'

The captain was still standing. 'The monster?' he said, pointing at the man.

'Watch your tongue! This is Mr Victor Falk – my son.' She grinned at Victor, and he smiled back.

'But,' the captain stuttered, 'he is…transformed.'

'Yes.' Grizelda licked her thin lips with delight. 'I told you, didn't I, fresh skin would grow.'

'But the mask?'

'Shh!' Grizelda lifted her hand. She looked at Victor. 'Would you be so kind as to cover your ears, Dear, just for a moment. Yer old mum needs to tell the captain 'ere somethin', somethin' that's just between me and him…and this lot,' she said, signalling to the crew.

Without a word, Victor did as he was told.

Grizelda lowered her voice. 'He doesn't know nothin' about the mask. He doesn't know what he is. And he's not goin' to neither.' She looked menacingly at the crew. 'The mask is still there, under his skin, protecting him, hiding his real face. But no one needs to know that, do they? And if I find out that anyone – and I mean anyone – has let it slip, they will regret the day their mother gave birth to 'em. Do I make myself clear?'

The crew nodded slowly.

'But how did he learn to speak so quickly, to carry himself – he seems so…articulate.'

Grizelda's eyes twinkled. 'Yes, he is, ain't' he? I had a Life Draught given to me by Ullric Falcon. That pompous prig keeps the stories of his dead ancestors distilled, just in case he needs to bring 'em back.' Grizelda cackled. 'One of 'em was Mr Victor Falk. I fed my boy that draught and hey presto, I have meself a fully formed gentleman. The looks and personality of Falk mixed with the undead heart. And I've thrown in a little of me own history for luck. I still control his story. He's mine to do my bidding.'

Grizelda walked back to Victor and touched his arm. He lowered his hands from his ears.

'Brushes up well, my lad, don't he?' Grizelda said, looking at him proudly. 'But now, to business. There's a little trip we need you to make, Victor. This cave's what's known as a Threshold, a doorway to the world beyond the Un-Crossable Boundary. I need you to go through it, Son. Do you think you could do that for me?'

Victor nodded obediently. 'And what am I to do when I reach the other side?' he asked.

'You need to find a particular woman. This woman has the same power as the Storyteller. It's a power she's not used since the creation of this world. I have a hunch this Threshold will open somewhere close to where she's to be found, and Mummy's hunches are rarely wrong. You're to find her and convince her to take up her rightful title again. But we want her to use her power for us, do you understand?'

Victor nodded.

'We need her to work *against* the Storyteller. That'll make for a fairer game now, won't it? We must act quickly, though. He knows about the Threshold and he's bound to be making his own plans to cross it or recruiting someone else to do his dirty work for him. He can never keep his hands off this sort of thing. But she's scared, Victor – she's run away and she won't want to be found – least of all by him. Play on that fear.'

'How will I know who she is?'

'Oh, you'll know. You'll be able to see it in her, in the air around her. You're connected to her. We all are. She's the one who first dreamed up this world. Just follow yer gut. Now go, and don't let me down.'

'I won't, Mother.'

'There's a good boy.'

With that, the monster, Victor Falk, turned and headed into the cave. The firelight licked at his cloak, making the hawks' feathers glow. He looked infernal, disappearing into the darkness. Gradually, the red shape faded and Victor Falk disappeared from sight. The gathered crowd waited, hardly daring to breathe. After a while, Grizelda turned, her eyes alert. 'So, it's done,' she whispered. 'My boy is about to cross the Threshold. Luckily, with his undead heart, Mummy here will have him back soon enough. Only the dead can come and go through a Threshold as they please. But at least for a while, Mr Victor Falk will no longer be of *this* world.'

* * *

As Victor moved through the darkness, he was ill at ease. Something was nagging him, something he couldn't put his finger on – a strange dullness, a sort of numbness at his core. The hawk-feather cloak weighed heavily on his shoulders, as if he were wearing the wrong clothes.

No, that's not it, he thought to himself. *It's as if...*he searched for the right words, but he couldn't find them. It frustrated him. Victor was an educated man. He was good with words. He had spent long hours in the great libraries of his home on the Basillica Isles. *No*, he thought. *The clothes I'm wearing are mine – they're right. That's not it, it's...* He paused again, trying to put a finger on what was nagging him. An unnerving thought occurred to him.

It's my body that's wrong.

Yes, that was it. Somehow he felt at odds with his own flesh.

Don't be ridiculous, he scolded himself. *You are Victor Falk of the Falcon Household. You are a man of standing. You sailed here with your mother...*

Again, the nagging feeling tugged at him.

You sailed here with your mother, he repeated, resolutely.

He pictured the old woman. She was harsh, yes, and perhaps not as good-looking as she once had been, but she was his mother.

He tried to look around. It was no wonder he was feeling unnerved. The blackness of the cave was all encompassing. It was as though the world had vanished altogether.

As he continued through the darkness, he realised he was still turning things over in his mind. He was trying to remember moments from his childhood – his mother cooking tea for him; being tutored; the house they had lived in. Nothing came to him.

He stopped and clenched his fists. *Pull yourself together, Victor. You have a job to do. A Falk is never shaken, never shows weakness, is never diverted,* he said to himself, repeating his family's motto. *Now, focus!* He repeated his family motto again and again, pushing the nagging thoughts from his head, until they were as deeply buried as the cold, un-beating heart within his chest.

I need to pay full attention to the task at hand, he told himself. *I need to navigate this cave and cross the Threshold.*

Robbed of sight, he used his other senses to orientate himself. He could hear his breathing echoing from the rock. The air was cold and damp. He was obviously still in the cave, still on his side of the Threshold.

Suddenly, he stopped. There was something in front of him. He could sense it. He reached out. Sure enough, his fingers connected with a soft material.

What…?

It felt like a film of water, suspended vertically across the cave. Slowly, he moved his hand forward, pushing into the membrane. It wobbled, bowing where he pressed it. He pushed a little harder and, to his surprise, the jelly-like material swallowed his hand, moulding around it. The barrier must have been thin, because before he knew it, his hand had emerged on the other side. Beyond the membrane, the air was warmer and drier. Victor's hand felt different. For the first time, he was aware of hairs on the back of it and the gentle prickling of his skin. It was as if he could feel each cell. Somehow his hand felt more...

Real, he thought, quickly pulling his arm back. He stood for a moment, thinking.

This must be it.

He touched his hand. It was dry. Whatever the Threshold was made of, it wasn't water.

What was on the other side?

Well, there's only one way to find out.

Taking a deep breath, Victor stepped forward. His body pressed into the gelatinous material. For a moment it resisted him. But then it split, moulding around him perfectly. For a brief instant, he couldn't breathe. He pushed forward, about to panic, but before he knew it, he'd emerged on the other side. He breathed in, coughing. He felt knocked off-balance, as if something deep within him had shifted. It was subtle, but whatever had happened had affected his very core. After a moment, the dizziness wore off and his head cleared.

He waited.

He was aware of the coolness of the air on his tongue as he drew it in through his mouth. He was aware of the hardness of the floor beneath his feet. He was aware of a draft brushing his skin.

I've never been this aware before, he thought, trying to take it in. *I've never been fully aware. Not in this way.*

Although he was just standing still, although nothing was happening, there was too much to take in.

Although nothing's happening, he thought, realising that in his world something was always happening; things never stood still, they were always moving forward.

There were so many new sensations to take in. This other world had a completely different quality to it. It was slower. Victor was aware of every moment. In the world he had come from, time seemed to jump forwards. There were no in-betweens. And where the jumps happened, there were gaps. In his world, if something hadn't been spoken, it didn't exist. Here, he existed independently from words. He was…physical.

Outside the realm of the Storyteller, he thought to himself, a sense of power growing. For a moment, he felt elated.

I still need to focus, he thought, pulling himself back to the job he had to do. He still had to find the woman who had power equal to the Storyteller's. He waited a moment longer, adjusting to his new reality more quickly than he'd expected.

He tried to take in his new surroundings. He was still inside, still in the dark, but he could hear the sound of wind. And just ahead, he could see light glimmering through what looked like gaps in a series of slats.

A wall? he thought.

The air in this place was musty. He could have been mistaken, but he thought he could detect the smell of cooked food, lingering.

He breathed in deeply.

Fish and vegetables.

Unlike the cave, he was aware that the floor beneath his feet was flat. Gently he stamped, listening for a clue as to where he was. The sound reverberated with a dull thud.

Wood, he said to himself, *hollow underneath.* From the sound, he guessed the room he was in was small. The wind was making the structure creak.

His eyes were adjusting now. From the thin beams of light that seeped through the slats, he could see shapes beginning to appear. Just in front of him was a circular object.

A table?

Beyond it, he could see what looked like a row of low cupboards.

What is this place?

Feeling his way forward, he edged around the table, towards

the wall made of slats. When he reached it, he laid his hand on the surface. It was rough.

Wood again.

Slowly, he ran his hand along the wall.

He stopped, coming to something that protruded and ran his fingers across it.

Metal...Rusted...

The metal jutted out. He ran his fingers over it and suddenly realised what it was.

A latch. This must be a door.

Gripping the latch, he paused for a moment and then lifted it. Before he could stop it, a thin wooden door had swung open, pushed by the wind. Victor raised his hand to cover his eyes. Light poured through the opening. After the dark of the cave, it caught him off guard. The door swung on its hinges, creaking and banging against the wall.

Sea, Victor thought, smelling salt in the air. He lowered his hand and blinked, his eyes still adjusting. In front of him, grey ocean spread out, white surf whipped up by the strong wind. A low bank of cloud clung to the horizon. He was on a beach, standing in the doorway of a wooden hut. Just in front of him, waves clawed the shingle, as if reaching out to him.

Victor looked up. It was a cold, unwelcoming day. The light in this place was different. He couldn't put his finger on it, but the colours were somehow less vivid. Everything was tinged with grey.

He stepped out of the door and peered along the beach. The hut he'd emerged from was one of a long row of brightly painted, wooden beach cabins. Some had decking with garden chairs propped up, waiting for better weather. Others had upturned boats in front of them. He looked back at the hut from which he'd emerged. It was less well kept than the others, white paint peeling from its shutters, which were pulled closed.

He stepped back inside, leaving the door open for light. It

clattered in the wind. The hut was a single room. It was simply furnished, but somebody obviously lived there. An old camp bed was pushed into the corner, partitioned by some makeshift curtains. Through a gap, he could see it was unmade. The cupboards he'd picked out in the darkness formed a small kitchen area. An old kettle sat on the hob, a plate of half-finished food next to it.

Fish and vegetables. I was right.

In the corner of the room, next to a shuttered window, was an armchair. The only other piece of furniture was the table, a wooden chair pushed under it. A battered gas lamp hung above.

Victor walked across to the table. There was a box of paint tubes on it. A couple of brushes stuck out of a glass of murky water. Next to them, a half-decorated plate rested on the surface. Victor examined it. The picture that was being painted was of the sea, a black Tall Ship cutting through the waters.

A dark sea, he thought, *tempestuous.*

Around the edge of the plate, someone had painted words in neat calligraphy. Victor picked it up. Turning it in his hands, he read what was written:

I'm coming on the clouds of night.

I'm coming from the shadow's reach.

Quickly, he put the plate down and stepped back. The words had a strange effect on him. They made him feel cold. He looked back at the plate. A dark aura surrounded it.

This is it, he thought, *the place where she lives. I can feel it. Mother said I would recognise it.* He stared at words circling the plate again and knew, without doubt, he was in the right place.

This is the home of the one with power equal to the Storyteller's?

He was surprised. He was expecting a great hall, a throne, riches and soldiers.

But this – an old wooden hut?

A feeling of disdain came over him.

Whoever lives here doesn't deserve such power. I'm glad I am here to steal it.

He walked across to examine the kitchen area. The food was still warm.

Not long since she was here.

Deciding what to do, he walked back to the door and closed it. The sound of the wind quietened, and the hut descended into darkness. Slowly, he crossed to the armchair in the corner and sat down.

I will wait here until she returns, and then we will talk.

Chapter 13

The Silver Pen

Ms Speller limped painfully across the shingle towards her beach hut. She was carrying a bag of shopping and leaned heavily on a walking stick that sunk into the sand. Although she was in her late forties, she looked older than her years.

She'd just returned by ferry from Mudeford Quay. It was only a short journey across the small straight of water called The Run, but to Ms Speller, it was a world away. She tried not to make the journey to the mainland more than once a week, only going when she needed food provisions or gas for the hob. The sandbank this side of the Run was her safe space, the place that she'd chosen to make her home. It was a spit formed by longshore drift, which carried sand and shingle around Hengistbury Head. As she looked from the grey sea to the stones beneath her feet, she muttered, 'Drifters, drifters, just like me, swept across the stormy sea.' It was a ritual she often repeated. She had never felt fully at home in the world, but this place of lost debris was the closest she'd come.

Above, the gulls shrieked at her. It sounded as if they were laughing.

'Shut up!' she muttered. But secretly she found their cries comforting.

Hobbling up to the wooden door, she passed her walking stick to her other hand and fumbled for her keys. Pulling them from her pocket, she lifted them awkwardly to the lock and turning the key, pushed the door open with her shoulder. As she entered, she twisted her body and pushed the door closed with her walking stick.

'Must finish it,' she mumbled. 'Finish the work.'

Not looking up, she limped across the wooden floor to the

kitchen units and dumped the bag on the surface. Then, grabbing the kettle, she filled it with water and put it on the hob. Picking up a box of matches, she struck one and lit a flame under the kettle. As she always did, she moved to the table, struck another match and lit the gas lamp. It hissed, swinging above her head. Then, pulling the wooden chair out from the table, she collapsed into it, panting.

She paused for a moment, waiting for her breath to settle. Once it had, she reached forward and rummaged through the box of paint. Pulling out a tube, she squinted at it.

'Red,' she muttered, 'too bright.'

She put it down on the edge of the table and turned back to find a darker colour. As she did, there was a sharp crack, as if someone had thrown a stone at the hut. Her head shot up, anger in her eyes. Kids were always throwing stones at her hut, tormenting her. She cursed under her breath and started to push herself up from the table. Another crack sounded, sending a spasm through her body. She lurched forward, her arm slipping across the table. It knocked the plate onto the floor, sending it clattering down, the tube of red paint falling with it, splattering the wooden floor, bright drops landing on the plate.

Ms Speller let out an anguished cry. 'Damn and blast!' She reached down to pick up the plate, but then changed her mind.

'No, I'll get you this time!'

Grabbing her walking stick, she hauled her body from the chair and struggled towards the door, still muttering under her breath. Her bad leg refused to bend and she swung it out angrily, her stick pressing against it as she jerked across the room.

'Damn kids – when I get hold of you...'

She took a big breath, ready to give her tormentors an earful. Flinging the door open, she stared out, wheezing. She listened for sounds of running or giggling, her stick raised, ready for a confrontation. But there was no movement outside, just the constant rhythm of the waves beating the shore. Ms Speller pulled closed the door.

'I'll get you,' she muttered, moving back, her leg scuffing the floor. She clattered to the other side of the hut and pushed open the window shutters. Leaning on the frame, she stared out across the sand, the dark sea beyond.

'Do they come to disturb your peace often?' a deep voice said, behind her.

She spun round. On her armchair, in the corner of her room, a man sat, his legs outstretched and his feet crossed. His silver hair was well groomed. An earthen red cloak was wrapped around his broad shoulders. It was made from feathers of some sort. Their barbs made the cloak rough, out of keeping with the man's meticulous grooming, as if his preening hid an under-current of wildness.

Ms Speller staggered back, bumping into the kitchen units. Wheezing heavily, she reached behind her and grabbed a frying pan. She held it up, threatening the man.

'Get out!' she screamed. 'Get out of here or I'll…'

'Come, come,' the man interrupted, quietly. 'Don't you recognise me? Recognise my kind? I'm no ordinary visitor. I've travelled a long way to find you. I've travelled across worlds. My name is Victor, Mr Victor Falk.'

Ms Speller stared at him. Suddenly, a look of recognition flashed across her face. Her muscles went limp and her arm fell to her side, her fingers loosening. The pan clattered to the floor. She stared at Victor, open-mouthed.

'No,' she whispered. 'No, it can't be. You're a…'

'Mortale,' Victor finished her sentence. 'Yes – from beyond the Un-Crossable Boundary.'

She gaped at him. But then, gradually, a look of resolve crept across her face. Her lips pressed tightly together, her mouth wrinkling like a used tea bag. Her features hardened and she averted her gaze.

'No,' she said harshly. 'I won't…I won't even…' She hobbled

back to the table, waving a hand as if she was trying to bat away a fly.

Above her head, the gas lamp hissed at the intruder.

The kettle, which had been heating on the hob, began to whistle. Ms Speller seemed oblivious to the shrill noise. She reached down and picked up the fallen plate.

'You can't ignore me forever,' Victor said smoothly.

'I'm not ignoring...you're not even there,' Ms Speller half replied, 'just a figment...not even listening.' She picked up an old rag from the sink and, getting to her knees, began to scrub the wooden floor, aggressively trying to clean the paint away, but it just spread across the wood in streaks.

Still the kettle whistled.

Victor leaned forwards on the chair. 'They're coming, you know – those who want to find you. The Storyteller...'

At his name, Ms Speller stopped cleaning. 'Shut up!' she spat.

Victor ignored the interruption. 'The Storyteller is planning to cross the boundary, or to send someone across for him. No doubt he's already making preparations for the journey. You must know – you've been painting it yourself.' He pointed at the plate and repeated the words:

I'm coming on the clouds of night.

I'm coming from the shadow's reach.

He's coming for you, and so are his allies. And they won't stop until they've found you.'

Ms Speller threw the rag on the floor and rocked slightly on her knees. She wiped her forehead in distress.

'But luckily for you, I got here first. You need to protect yourself. I'm assuming you don't you want to be found?'

'I'm not...I'm not even...'

'Aren't you going to turn that off?' Victor signalled the kettle. Its whine was piercing.

'What's it to you?'

'It's loud.'

She turned to face him, jabbing her thumb into her chest. 'This is my house.'

'I know. I just thought...'

'You're not even here!'

'And yet, I can hear the kettle. There won't be any water left soon.'

'Pah,' Ms Speller waved him away. But after a slight hesitation, she limped to the hob and turned off the gas.

The beach hut fell still.

'So...' Victor said, staring at her. 'You know why I'm here, don't you?'

Ms Speller turned away again, searching desperately for something to do, something to distract her from the figment that sat on her armchair. 'He's not here,' she said to herself, sternly. 'It's just me, alone – how I like it.'

'The Un-crossable Boundary has been breached. That's why I'm here. The Storyteller...'

She cut him off. 'Just a figment...piece of cheese...brain function...ignore him...it.'

Victor continued, unperturbed. 'The Storyteller helped two Apprentice Adventurers to cross the boundary between my world and yours at his wedding feast.'

'I'm not listening,' Ms Speller almost wailed, suddenly breaking down. She covered her ears, shaking her head, erratically.

'And now another doorway has opened up and it leads here, directly to you. And I'm telling you, he intends to use it. You need to listen. They're coming, and they plan to find you.'

'No!' Ms Speller cried.

'But that's why I'm here. I can help you.'

Victor stood up and walked across to the table. 'We can protect you. All you have to do is pick it up again.' He tapped a drawer in the table.

Ms Speller darted across the room and pushed herself between Victor and the drawer. Turning her back on it, she held it closed. She looked up at him, her face contorted with fear. He towered over her.

Victor laughed. 'I know it's in there. I can feel its power.'

'I won't. I can't!' Ms Speller croaked. 'They take control – your type. Look what they did to me.' She stretched out her hands. She looked like a crucified Christ, her eyes pale and watery. She allowed Victor to take in her twisted body. 'I came here to get away, to find some peace…' her voice trailed away.

'Well, I'm afraid you can't. They're coming and they will find you, just as I have. But if you let us, we can help – help keep things…under control.'

Ms Speller turned, collapsing onto the wooden chair.

'Open the drawer,' Victor commanded.

'But it's been two years since I used it.'

'Then it's time.'

Neither one moved.

'I can wait,' Victor said. 'I can wait as long as it takes.'

Ms Speller looked up, meeting his gaze.

'You can protect me?'

'Yes.'

'You can stop him from finding me?'

'Yes.'

Slowly, she reached forward and slid the drawer open. Inside, it was empty, apart from a single object – a silver pen. She stared it, her eyes wide.

'Pick it up,' Victor coaxed.

A voice inside Ms Speller's head warned her, *Don't touch it. Don't listen. Whatever you do, do not pick it up.*

As if her body wasn't connected to her mind, she reached into the drawer and wrapped her fingers around the silver pen. She closed her eyes, feeling the cold metal between her fingers.

'That's right,' Victor smiled. He leant over her, his mouth almost touching her ear, 'And now,' he whispered, 'it's time to get to work.'

Chapter 14

The Princess Awakes

In a room at the top of the tallest tower of Alethea, the Storyteller sat beside his princess. She lay paralysed by the sleeping sickness on a four-poster bed, surrounded by curtains embroidered with fiery feathers. She looked like a statue in a mausoleum, her body perfectly straight, her feet together, and her arms by her sides. Her breathing was so shallow that her chest barely moved. Her pale eyelids were shut, making her look oddly serene.

The Storyteller spoke softly to her. 'Everything is going to be made right, my love. We are going to find out what is causing this sickness. We have found its source and are making an investigation. You will be healed, I promise.'

A bowl of warm water steamed on a small side table by the window. Every so often, the Storyteller would go over to it, pull a cloth from the water and return to mop her brow.

The Storyteller's castle had fallen into a tense silence since news of the princess's illness had been announced. No longer did it ring with the sound of musicians playing fiddles or harps at the great feasts. Instead, the only sound that echoed through its empty corridors was the footsteps of doctors making their way up the spiral staircase to the princess's bedroom.

The Storyteller rose and wandered to the window. Fullstop Island stretched out below him, the snow-capped peaks of the Mysterious Mountains descending to the fertile flood plain of the River Word. Bardbridge nestled in the curve of the river, just before it opened out to the sea. He loved this island, but while his princess lay sick, he could find no joy in it.

He lowered his head and turned back to the bowl. Dipping his hands in, he pulled out the cloth. The sound of the water soothed him. He wrung it out and turned back to the bed.

As he did, he froze.

Surrounded by her fiery feather curtains, his princess sat, bolt upright.

The Storyteller dropped the cloth. 'You're awake,' he whispered. For a moment, he didn't know what to do.

Then, with a wave of excitement, he dashed across to her.

'You're awake!'

But his princess didn't move. She didn't turn towards him. She sat, her body tense, her head fixed, facing forward.

Reaching her, the Storyteller flung his arms around her tiny body. She was so fragile. He pulled her close, holding her. Her body tilted towards him, but still she didn't move.

'What...?' the Storyteller said, releasing her. She sprang back, sitting upright again. He looked at her face. Her eyes were still closed.

As quickly as his excitement had erupted, it dissipated.

He studied her face. There was no movement, no sign of life. 'You're still asleep,' he whispered. 'But you sat up. That's something.'

Standing, he rushed to a thick wooden door and pulled it open. It was the top of a spiral staircase. He called down, 'Doctors, come quickly. I need you.'

Almost immediately, the sound of footsteps ascending the stairs echoed along the stone walls. A few moments later, two doctors appeared, panting.

'She sat up,' the Storyteller exclaimed.

'Awake?' one of the doctors replied, tiny eyes blinking through small round spectacles. His neatly trimmed beard twitched.

'No,' the Storyteller replied.

The doctors looked at each other gravely and entered the room.

'But she's still sitting?' the second doctor said in a thick accent. He was larger than the first doctor, with bushy white hair circling his bald head and a long square beard.

'Yes.'

Immediately, the two physicians strode to the bed. The smaller of the doctors began to examine the princess, picking her wrist up and measuring her pulse against a gold pocket watch.

'No change,' he said.

The second doctor scribbled notes.

After pushing open her eyelids, swaying a torch in front of her face, and listening to her heart through a stethoscope, the two doctors moved to the side of the room and began to talk in hushed tones.

The Storyteller stared at his princess, filled with sadness. For a moment, he'd thought she had woken.

All of a sudden, he reached out, pointing. 'Look!' he whispered.

The doctors ignored him, deep in conversation.

'Look,' he said again, raising his voice.

The physicians turned. Seeing him point, they looked at the princess.

'Her eyes...'

The smaller doctor stepped forward. The princess's eyes were open. She was staring straight ahead.

Then, before he could move to examine her more closely, she opened her mouth.

'Drifters, drifters,' she said, unnaturally slowly, her mouth wide. The words rang around the room. She seemed to roll the sound before it left her mouth. Her voice was disturbing, low and resonant. It didn't sound like the princess at all.

'What's happening?' the Storyteller asked, alarmed.

The doctors looked at each other, worried.

The princess began to speak again, the movements of her mouth exaggerated. 'Drifters, drifters, just like me...'

The doctor with the notepad started to jot down what she'd said.

The princess's mouth opened again. For a moment she sat stock still, her lips wide. But no sound emerged. Then a low moan began to pour from her lips. It seemed to come from deep within her.

'Make it stop!' the Storyteller shouted.

The doctors stared, paralysed.

Gradually, the moan turned into words. 'Drifters, drifters, just like me,' she repeated, 'carried by the stormy sea.' As she finished, her head dropped, as if she were exhausted.

The doctor with the spectacles stepped towards her again, but before he could reach the bed, the princess began to whisper.

'I'm coming on the clouds of night. I'm coming from the shadow's reach.' Slowly, she lifted her head, a malignancy in her eyes. 'I'm coming where the dream winds blow. I'm coming where the time sands shift.' Her words echoed around the chamber. They struck fear into the Storyteller.

'The rhyme,' he said, starting towards her, 'the rhyme coming through the cave.'

The princess continued to chant, her voice rising. 'I'm coming on the clouds of night. I'm coming from the shadow's reach.'

A mist descended on the Storyteller. He felt drowsy, numb.

'I'm coming where the dream winds blow. I'm coming where the time sands shift.'

He had almost reached the bed, but it was as if something was dragging him down, a strange heaviness in his soul.

And then the princess stared straight at him. The look in her eyes sent coldness running through his veins.

'The Sandman comes,' she hissed, 'the Sandman sings…'

The two doctors sank to the floor. They lay slouched against each other, their eyes closed.

The Storyteller reached the bed, lifting his hand towards the princess. But it was too late. She opened her mouth to speak the last line of the rhyme.

'And sleep's the gift the Sandman brings.'

A disabling blankness swept over the Storyteller. He staggered a little further forward and then collapsed on the bed behind her, his body sprawled across the sheets. His eyes flickered and then the light vanished.

The sickness had taken hold of him.

The princess was still on the bed, her body tense. Then, after a moment, she too collapsed backwards, her body falling across the Storyteller's. She lay on him, her arm dangling from the side of the bed.

With that, the Storyteller's bedroom in Alethea fell still.

* * *

On the other side of the Un-Crossable Boundary, Ms Speller looked at the pen she was holding. Then she stared at the words she'd just written. They were the first words she'd written for two whole years. She felt drained. She read them again.

I'm coming on the clouds of night.
I'm coming from the shadow's reach.
I'm coming where the dream winds blow.
I'm coming where the time sands shift.
The Sandman comes, the Sandman sings,
And sleep's the gift the Sandman brings.

They were the words of a rhyme she used to sing to her daughter, a daughter she had left a year and a half ago, a daughter she believed was better off without her.

Chapter 15

Shut Out

Two hundred and fifty miles to the north of Mudeford Quay, Libby stopped typing. Her fingers froze, hovering over her laptop. She stared at her hands, as if she were looking at the hands of a ghost.

She looked up, confused.

I'm in my room.

She turned to the clock. It was a quarter past eight.

What's happening?

A moment ago, she'd been on Fullstop Island, she'd been in the Storyteller's body, in the princess's bedroom.

Where's it gone?

Usually, when she came back from a leap, it felt as though she were falling, her consciousness tumbling back to her own realm, before resurfacing in familiar surroundings.

This had been different. It was as if somebody had flicked a switch. One moment she'd been there, the next she was back in her room.

Libby became aware that her nerves were on edge. Her skin was hot.

She lowered her head and moved back to the keypad again. Words would come, they always did.

Just wait.

She tried to focus on the screen.

In the background, she could hear the clock ticking, loudly.

I wish it would stop!

She waited a moment longer. Still no words came.

'Infernal thing!' she said, leaping off her bed. She marched across and grabbed the clock from the wall. Pulling out the battery, she slammed it face down on her desk.

There! Now maybe I can focus.

Going back to her bed, she sat down again. She wriggled around, trying to get comfortable. Her stomach rumbled.

Oh, come on! she said to herself, frustrated. *I need to get back to Fullstop Island! I need to get back to the Storyteller.*

Reaching forward, she typed a word.

No, that's not right.

She deleted it.

The familiar ache in her chest was back again. She massaged it.

My mind's blank, she said to herself. *My mind's never blank when I'm writing.*

For a while now, Libby had been having panic attacks. They happened without warning, but usually in crowded places where she felt overwhelmed or out of control.

She knew the signs: trembling hands, chest pain, sweating, racing heart, feeling as if she was going to choke.

Calm down! she told herself.

She closed her eyes and tried to regulate her breathing, counting slowly as she did.

'One...two...three...four. One...two...three...four.'

She opened her eyes again and glanced around the room. It was a mess. Across the floor, piles of paper were scattered, hiding half-finished notes and scribbled paragraphs. Layers of post-it notes clung to the wall, their corners curling. Old cups of half-finished tea perched wherever they could find a bare surface, and Alphabet was sleeping on a heap of dirty washing in the corner of the room.

Perhaps it's this place, Libby thought. *Perhaps that's what's stopping me leap.*

In the beginning, when she had first started leaping, she had discovered that she was able to make the leap more easily in certain places and at certain times of day. After a while, she had realised what the connection was – they were all times or places where one thing met another: the seaside, rivers, dawn or twilight – all borderlands, all connection points.

Making a decision, she leapt from the bed. She grabbed a canvas bag from the floor and, closing her laptop, stuffed it inside. Crossing to her desk, she took out her mother's writing journal and put it in the bag with her laptop.

She glanced at the mirror. She was still in her school uniform. Quickly, she changed, pulling on some skinny jeans and a t-shirt. Then, picking up the canvas bag, she threw it over her shoulder.

If I can't leap here, I'll go somewhere else.

Libby left her bedroom and tiptoed down the stairs towards the front door. She crept along the hallway, the sound of the TV blaring from the front room. Her dad was watching the football. She didn't want to disturb him. Quietly, she reached for the door handle.

'Where d'ya think you're going?' her dad called from the lounge.

How was he able to hear even the slightest noise?

'Just out!'

The last thing Libby wanted was another argument.

She waited. But there were no more questions. In fact, it sounded as if her dad had turned the TV up louder. There was a roar of, 'Foul! Come on, Ref!' and she pulled the door open and slipped quietly onto the cold, grey street.

The Joyners lived on an unremarkable road in the north of Leeds. The red brick houses clung to each other, as if shielding themselves from a future that couldn't remember why they'd been built.

Outside, it was a chilly evening, twilight slipping into dusk.

The sky was dark and threatened rain. Setting off down the hill, Libby hugged the walls of the front yards. She felt like a shadow, unnoticed by the world.

How different to the World of Mortales, she thought to herself, picturing the different body she inhabited there and the name she bore.

She felt herself beginning to panic again.

I have to get back!

In front of her, on the other side of the valley, she could see the chimneys of the old mills poking up between the trees, now gated communities for students. She scuttled around a corner, her feet hardly touching the ground. The grey outline of an abbey came into view. It looked like a broken tooth in the gum of the valley. Behind it, a river bubbled.

I'll be able to leap there, she thought. *My secret place.*

Realising she was almost running down the hill, Libby slowed herself to a walk and took some deep breaths.

Before long, she reached the busy A-road that separated her housing estate from the abbey grounds. The exhaust fumes of the cars and lorries made her cough. This road always felt like a desert, dusty and arid. But on the other side, her sanctuary waited.

She crossed the road and slipped through the shadowy gates. She glanced around furtively. The abbey grounds were practically empty. A dog walker in a waterproof coat was being pulled along the riverbank, from tree to tree. A homeless person sheltered under one of the ruined outbuildings. Other than that, there was nobody in sight. The ancient site felt out of keeping with the city that had grown up around it. It was an oasis in a world that had forgotten its roots, existing somewhere between the past and present.

An ideal place to leap, Libby thought, heading quickly towards the river. She weaved through the maze of strange shapes that scattered the grass, remnants of walls, which had once supported the thriving abbey. To her left, the ancient tower rose, hauntingly beautiful, a shadow of its former glory.

Reaching the river, she sat on a bench. It had been drizzling, and the air was still damp and fresh. She could hear the river rushing past.

Perfect, she thought, trying to reassure herself, *just the right atmosphere.*

But despite her best efforts, Libby's mind was racing. *Why did I find myself back in this world? What happened? What if I can't get back?*

Somewhere at the back of her mind, a thought jostled for attention.

You've been thrown out. You've been rejected.

She pushed it from her mind.

Stilling herself for a moment, Libby watched the water flow. It headed towards the weir, where it disappeared in a band of white water. She often came here to calm herself, especially since her mum went missing. The river was hypnotic. It seemed to soothe her, to wash her anxieties away.

After a moment, she slipped the canvas bag from her shoulder and opened it. Inside, her laptop and the writing journal waited. She paused. Which to use? They felt different. Sometimes she found it easier to make the leap when writing directly in the journal. Perhaps it was the physical connection that helped, both to the paper and to her mother. She made a decision. She would write with pen first and then move to her laptop. Her heart rate increasing, she pulled the journal from her bag and unclipped the pen she kept with it. It had been her mother's, discovered along with the journal. There was a little sticker of a golden feather on it. She ran her fingers over the sticker, feeling the embossed image on her skin. Then she opened the book.

A raindrop fell from the tree above and splattered the paper, darkening the page like a bullet wound.

Lowering the pen, Libby held the nib against the page.

She closed her eyes and imagined falling, falling into the watery wound left by the raindrop, falling through to the other side, to the World of Mortales. She imagined the pen moving over the paper, marking it, shaping the stories of that world. She imagined the Storyteller kneeling by his silver pool, stirring the threads, making them swirl into different patterns.

She opened her eyes.

The river seemed to be louder than before, as if it were mocking her. Behind, the ancient tower peered over her shoulder, dark and stern.

She was still in the abbey grounds. The leap had failed.

She closed her eyes again, squeezing them shut. She was aware that she was gripping the pen tightly. It hurt her fingers. After a moment, she moved it erratically across the paper, pressing down hard.

She opened her eyes again. There was a black mark scrawled across the page. It ripped into it.

Libby realised her shoulders were shaking.

Why had her mum left her? Why had she walked out on her? What had Libby ever done to deserve that?

She suddenly let out a cry and threw the pen. It hit a tree stump by the riverbank, bounced from it and fell into the water.

'No!' Libby cried, springing to her feet. The writing journal slipped to the floor, pages spilling onto the path, mud smearing them.

She ran to the river and peered into the churning water, her eyes darting.

That pen had been her mother's. With it, her mum had written about Fullstop Island, about Fletcher and Scoop. It was a connection to her, a bridge.

Libby fell to her knees, the mud seeping into her jeans. Plunging her hand into the water, she ran it through the silt. The pen wasn't there.

'No!' she cried again, angry with herself.

She'd lost it. She'd lost her mother's pen.

'I'm sorry!' she said, as she knelt by the water. 'I'm sorry…I'm sorry…I'm sorry…'

And then, her hands dirty and her trousers muddy and wet, she began to cry.

What had she done? What had she been thinking?

But as she knelt by the river, she had a sudden sense of clarity. She knew. She knew without a shadow of a doubt. She *had* been shut out. She didn't know why, but she was sure of it. She had been shut out of the World of Mortales and she couldn't go back.

Thoughts flooded her mind. She would never feel the power of the Storyteller again. She would never see Fletcher and Scoop. And her plan to find her mother – it was in tatters. If she couldn't leap into the World of Mortales, she couldn't follow the clues. And if she couldn't follow the clues, she was finally cut off.

'I'll never find her. I'll never see her again,' she cried.

As dusk faded to night, Libby Joyner knelt by the river and sobbed. She had to accept the reality. Her mother had gone, she had gone and Libby would never see her again.

Chapter 16

The Raven's Return

A cackle of delight sounded across the waters of the South Bookend seas. It was harsh, like the cawing of a crow. The flock of birds resting on the Raven's rigging took to the air, mimicking the laugh with cries and squawks. They formed a cloud that followed the ship as it headed away from Skull Island. There was the noise of a table being thumped below deck, followed by another great burst of laughter. The crew of the Raven glanced at one another, as silent as condemned men.

In the belly of the ship, Grizelda was in her quarters. Victor Falk sat at her table, his hawk-feather cloak hanging round him like a king. A carafe of wine and a rich banquet was set before him.

The old woman was excitable and couldn't settle. She strutted and twirled around the cabin, every so often glancing through the portholes at her crows or touching trinkets that lined the walls of her quarters. Routinely, she would return to Victor and grin at him or pat his shoulder.

She tried to pour him some more wine, but he covered his goblet.

'Tell me again, my boy. Tell yer old mum what you told her to do.'

Victor rolled his eyes. 'I told her to pick up the pen, Mother.'

'And she did?' Grizelda said greedily.

'Yes. I've already told you.'

'I know, me dear, but yer old mum wants to hear it again. She's been waiting for something like this her whole life, see?' She stroked the feathers of his cloak. 'And she's so proud of her boy.'

'Very well – just to humour you.'

'That's right, humour me, me dear.' There was a manic look in the old woman's eyes. 'And after she picked up the pen, she started to use it?'

'She did.'

Grizelda cackled again and twirled across the room. She turned back. 'And then you gave her some instructions?'

'I did.'

'About how she might "protect" herself.'

'That's right.' Victor looked impatient. 'What is the purpose of me repeating this, Mother?'

Grizelda momentarily raised her voice, 'The purpose, Victor...' but then she caught herself shouting and twisted her face into a smile. 'The purpose, *Son*, is that I might enjoy just how *brilliant* my boy is. I mean, I knew you would be brilliant, Victor, but you've exceeded yer old mum's expectations. So be a good boy and tell me *exactly* what you said to her.'

Victor sighed, studying his fingernails. 'I told her that if she wanted to protect herself, she needed to take control. I told her the island needed firm leadership. I told her that it needed to be guarded, that its borders needed to be secured.'

'Very good,' the old woman purred. 'What else?'

'I told her that to do that, an army was needed.'

Grizelda all but screeched. 'An army all of me own!' Victor raised his eyebrows and she corrected herself, 'All of *our* own, Dear. Well, I never. Who'd have thought?'

'Indeed. Do calm down, Mother, you're making a scene.'

Grizelda ignored him, continuing to almost dance around the room. 'And what else? What else did you say?'

'I suggested that perhaps a change of leadership at the academy was needed. I proposed that somebody be introduced who could take care of the situation, somebody uncompromising, somebody commanding.'

'And the person you suggested was...?'

'You know full well, Mother.'

'Just tell me!' the old woman snapped.

'Very well, very well,' Victor sighed. 'I suggested that perhaps *I* was the man for the job.'

Grizelda yelped with glee. 'And she agreed.'

'She had little choice in the matter.'

The crone thumped the table with delight.

'Be careful, Mother, you'll spill the wine.'

'Victor, you make yer old mother proud. There's more than just a little of *me* in you, you know, if I do say so meself. You, in charge of the academy. I can't wait to see the look on that meddler's face when he finds out. We're sailing back to our rightful prize, Victor! It's about time the story went my way.' She looked at Victor. 'So, how's it going to happen, then?'

Victor picked up an envelope and waved it nonchalantly at his mother. 'I've already received an invitation from Headmaster Grammatax. Apparently, he is establishing a research team to investigate the sickness. He's heard report of my good name and has invited me to join the academy's staff as head of this new faculty for research – the Synitorium.'

'Perfect,' Grizelda purred. 'Perfect.'

'I am to meet him at the Wild Guffaw. There's a celebration to mark the start of the new term. He has requested that I accompany him so that he might introduce me to the gathered staff, apprentices and villagers.'

'Then we had better hope for a fair wind, Victor. We are still a long way from Fullstop Island.'

'There is no need for something as insubstantial as hope, Mother. Don't forget we have *her* under our control now. Nothing can stop us.' Victor looked skyward, as if speaking to someone. 'I am sure a fair wind will arise for us very soon.' He spoke slowly and pointedly.

No sooner had the words left his mouth than there was a cry from the deck above. A northerly wind had picked up – just what the Raven needed.

They would arrive at Fullstop Island within days. And when they arrived, they would find the island in a very different state to when Grizelda had left.

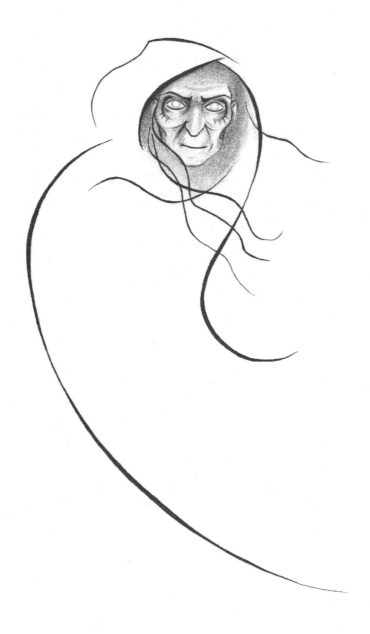

Chapter 17

Roadblock

Fletcher and Scoop rested for a few days in the camp of the Hermits of Hush, before making their way back to Bardbridge. When the time came, they climbed into the same hay cart that had brought them to the Dreamless Desert, ready for the journey back.

It seems like years since we were in Bardbridge, Fletcher thought to himself. *Everything feels different.*

The two apprentices were packed in with produce for Bardbridge Market. They sat among large alabaster urns stuffed with rolls of parchment; clay bowls and cups, baked in the hermits' ovens; weaved rugs; and pots of Desert Sand used to restore reality to those lost in delusions.

They sat quietly, the silence of the desert having become familiar. There was peace to the journey, and although questions did rise in Scoop's mind, *(I wonder what will happen next? Will we really be able to do this? Will we really be able to cross the Threshold?),* and although every so often the wide, black cave dominated Fletcher's thoughts, both apprentices felt calm and still.

Fletcher was still getting used to the new sense of awareness he had. The world seemed somehow crisper and brighter. His mind was clearer, helping him observe tiny details he would have never noticed before. He watched the driver. Where before, he had seen a sort of austere weariness in the man, Fletcher now glimpsed wisdom. His grey hair, and the way he guided the cart, gave him a quiet authority.

Fletcher looked to his left. The Creativity Craters rose, puffing their colourful smoke, and ahead, he could see Bardbridge. The village nestled in the curve of the river. A high wall surrounded it: four gates allowing access to the town, a watch post stationed above each. Every night, these gates were closed to keep the village safe from wild animals. From their vantage point, Fletcher could see a jumble of black and white buildings, narrow alleyways and small cobbled streets, all jostling for space. The Three Towers of the academy crowned the centre of the village.

Fletcher felt a pang of sorrow. He and Scoop would have to leave this all behind. They would have to leave their home.

He stopped that train of thought and directed his mind to his mother. He recalled the words they had heard in the hut: *"In losing you will find."* He didn't know exactly what they meant, but they reassured him.

We have to trust, he told himself.

Ahead, a wagon was pulled across the road. It was blocking the path. Beside it, wooden crates had been placed in a series of stacks, lining the lane. There was a streak of bright red on one of the stacks. As they drew closer, Fletcher could see it was a man wearing a long scarlet coat. He was sitting on one of the boxes. There were glimpses of other red-coated men among the stacks and inside the wagon too.

Scoop had also seen the blockage. 'An accident?' she suggested.

'I don't think so,' Fletcher replied, studying the formation of crates. 'Those crates don't look like they've fallen. It looks to me as if they've been placed there.'

Sure enough, as the cart rumbled on, it became clear that the crates formed a corridor in the road, the wagon at the end acting as a barrier or roadblock. As they approached the corridor, the man perched on the stack of crates climbed down. He called two of his companions, and the three red-coated figures approached the cart.

'Red Hawks?' Scoop said, as they approached.

'Yes, looks like it.'

'What are they doing here?'

'I don't know.'

The three men were impeccably dressed. The gold buttons on their long scarlet coats flashed in the sun, and the braiding on their uniforms sparkled. Silver swords glinted against their black trousers, and polished muskets rested in their hands.

The leader of the three, a sergeant, stepped in front of the cart. 'Halt!' he commanded, raising his hand. The two other soldiers flanked him. Scoop could see the outstretched wings of the Red Hawk crest on their helmets. The hermit pulled the cart to a stop.

'What is your business here?' the sergeant barked.

The hermit didn't reply.

The Red Hawk commander stepped forward. 'I said, what is your business?'

Still the hermit didn't respond.

'Right, we don't have time to mess about. Search the cart,' he said, turning to the other soldiers.

They stepped forward, one of them heading to the back of the cart, the other crossing to the hermit. The first guard grabbed a rug and pulled it down from the hay wain. It caught one of the Alabaster urns, which fell from its place, shattering on the ground. Rolls of parchment spilled out.

'What are you doing?' Fletcher said, getting to his feet. 'These things aren't yours! Get off!'

The guard glared at him and deliberately stepped on the parchments, his heavy boots tearing them under his feet.

Fletcher moved towards him. 'Watch it!' he said, trying to get the soldier to back away. 'Do you know how long those scrolls take to make?'

The Red Hawk ignored him. Instead, he reached forward and began to root through the contents of the cart, pulling out rugs and searching through pots.

Meanwhile, the second guard had grabbed the driver by the cassock and was pulling him down from the cart. Distressed, the hermit was trying to hold his cassock down as the guard manhandled him from his seat.

'Speak when you're spoken to!' the guard was saying. 'I don't like insolence!'

Scoops face flushed with anger. 'He can't speak! He's taken a vow of silence!'

'I don't care if his tongue has been cut out. We're here on important business. He needs to answer my questions.' He hauled the desert dweller roughly to the ground.

'Stop it!' Scoop yelled. 'This is outrageous! What important business are you on?'

The sergeant joined the commotion. 'You should sit down, miss. We've been charged to search every vehicle coming into or out of Bardbridge.'

'Search? Why? Who's told you to do that?'

'We're on the Sickness Squad.'

'Sickness Squad?'

'That's right, looking for signs of infection and removing anyone suspected of having the sickness – taking them to quarantine.'

'Infection? What do you mean?'

'I don't know how long you've been away from Bardbridge, but a sickness has broken out. A temporary hospital has been set up in the Botanical Gardens, and we're to take all the infected there.'

Fletcher and Scoop looked at each other, concerned.

Fletcher moved back to join the conversation. 'What do you mean, infected?'

'Thirty cases recorded so far and more breaking out all the time.'

'What sickness?'

'A sleeping sickness, sir. Now, I suggest you sit down and let us do our work.'

'But why are you in charge? Who's given you authority? You're not even from Fullstop Island.'

'Orders are straight from Alethea. See for yourself.' The

sergeant handed over a notice. Fletcher scanned it and then passed it to Scoop to read:

By order of Alethea: Authority is hereby given to the Red Hawk army to patrol all routes into and out of Bardbridge, including the Port of Beginnings and Endings. Red Hawk patrols are permitted to use all reasonable force to ensure the security of the village, and to remove those showing any sign of infection to immediate quarantine. Alethea would like to express its thanks to the King of the Basillica Isles for his assistance in this matter in these troubling times.

At the end, the notice was stamped with the Alethean seal.

'It's genuine,' Fletcher said to Scoop.

She nodded, but looked confused. Why would the Storyteller treat people in this way when his own princess was suffering with the sickness? It didn't make sense. 'But...' she said, about to mention her thoughts. But Fletcher shook his head. He obviously thought speaking of their mother's sickness in front of the Red Hawks was a bad idea.

Just then, behind them, the guard who was searching the cart smashed a large clay pot with the butt of his musket. The hermit flinched, and Desert Sand spilled onto the road.

'Nothing here but a few pots and old rugs,' the guard barked.

'Right you are,' the sergeant replied. He turned to the hermit. 'Looks like you're lucky this time. You're free to move on. But you'd better watch your attitude. We might not be so forgiving next time.'

The hermit scrambled around the cart, picking up the rugs and pieces of pot that scattered the ground. Fletcher and Scoop climbed down to help. When everything that could be salvaged had been restored to the cart, the driver climbed back up. The sergeant signalled to the wagon and it moved forward, clearing the track.

The hermit gave the reins a shake, and the cart jolted forward, continuing its journey.

'I'm sorry,' Scoop said to the hermit as they pulled away from the roadblock. 'I know how long these things take to make.' The hermit nodded, appreciatively.

Before long, they reached the gate into Bardbridge. Either side of the large wooden doorway were signs showing a Red Hawk soldier with the words, "BE VIGILANT" emblazoned underneath. "If you see any sign of infection, report it immediately," the signs read. Fletcher stared into the sharp eyes of the face on the poster. Why had the Storyteller given authority to the Red Hawks to patrol Bardbridge? It was well known that Fullstop Island had no army. The island's Guardians prided themselves on the fact they did things differently, that they rejected the use of force. Why had this changed? And why was it those suspected of being infected with the disease were being removed by soldiers – that was no way to treat the sick. It didn't make sense. As they rumbled down the cobbled street towards the Wild Guffaw and the gathering that marked the start of the academy's New Year, Fletcher felt the calmness of the desert slipping away. Something was badly wrong.

* * *

At the moment the hermit's cart entered the village, a tall, handsome man wearing a cloak made of hawks feathers ducked under the doorway of the Wild Guffaw. He paused, scanning the gathered crowd. He was here to take his rightful place as head of the Synitorium, the academy's new faculty for research into the sickness.

I'll soon bring some order to this filthy little backwater, he thought with a sneer.

'Ah, hello!' a voice boomed. 'We've been expecting you. Welcome!'

Victor looked towards the bar. A stocky, red-faced man was coming towards him, flushed and beaming.

'Ah, headmaster,' Victor said, switching on an electric smile. He held out his hand. 'It's a pleasure to be here, a real pleasure.'

Chapter 18

At the Wild Guffaw

'What will you have, dear fellow – a tankard of Noveltwist?'

Mr Grammatax was standing at the bar of the Wild Guffaw, looking admiringly into the face of his guest, Victor Falk. Victor was a whole head taller than Mr Grammatax, and the headmaster's nose was being tickled by the rough hawk-feather cloak he wore.

'Not for me, headmaster, I find the taste of Noveltwist too sickly.'

'Then what can I get for you, Victor? We must toast your arrival!'

'That's very kind of you, headmaster. I'll have a glass of Tonguetwister.'

'Water?'

'No, just as it comes. I find the snap exhilarating.'

'Tonguetwister it is, then. We have to keep our spirits up in these difficult times.'

'Indeed.'

Mr Grammatax turned to the barman, who had been waiting for the order. 'Well, you heard the man – glass of Tonguetwister.'

'Right you are, sir. Veeerry good!' the barman replied, pouring a dark red spirit and handing it over.

Victor wrapped his unusually large fingers around the glass and turned round, holding it high to avoid the throng of people clamouring for his attention.

Mr Bumbler pushed through the crowd and grasped Victor's hand. 'Just like to add my congratulations,' he growled. 'Dreadful times, dreadful times – but we're expecting good things from you, Mr Falk, good things – great things!'

'Well, you're very kind Mr...'

'Bumbler,' Grammatax interrupted, introducing his monocled friend. 'Mr Bumbler is the island's historian. You may have heard of his seminal work, Bumbler's Guide to Bardbridge?'

Victor inclined his head. 'Oh, indeed I have. Your reputation precedes you, Mr Bumbler.'

'Why thank you, sir,' Mr Bumbler flushed. 'Would you like another?' he signalled to Falk's drink.

'Very kind, but I think I'm well stocked for now.'

'Very good. Maybe another time then?'

'Most definitely.'

* * *

As academy staff swarmed around Victor Falk, Fletcher and Scoop arrived outside the inn. They climbed down from the old hay cart and said goodbye to the driver, who hugged them both. Then they turned to face the Wild Guffaw. It seemed to be grinning at them.

'Well,' Fletcher said. 'We'd better go and find the Yarnbard, hadn't we?'

'I suppose so,' Scoop replied.

For a moment, neither of them moved. Usually, they all but ran into the inn. It was one of their favourite places and held many happy memories. But today, it was as if an invisible thread held them back. It was a strange feeling, a sort of foreboding.

Fletcher walked forward, breaking the thread. Scoop followed, ducking under the door. The Wild Guffaw was packed to bursting. Scribes, shopkeepers and villagers perched on the barrels and lined benches. Scoop caught sight of the entire crew of the Firebird squeezed around a little table, clanking tankards and singing sea shanties. Despite the sickness, the inn was still as boisterous as ever. In a way, Scoop was glad to see things continuing as normal. She breathed in the atmosphere and felt her body relax.

Looking around, Fletcher caught sight of Nib and Rufina in the corner.

'Over there,' he shouted to Scoop, above the racket.

The pair began to push their way through the crowd towards their friends.

Fletcher squeezed passed Miss Dotty, the academy secretary. 'Terrible business,' she was saying to Mademoiselle Belle.

'Oui,' the Seasons Mistress replied. 'I have heard Monsieur Scriven has been taken by the illness.'

'Oh my, oh my. And Jacob Twain too?'

'Oui.'

'It makes one wonder who will be next!'

Fletcher pushed passed them to find himself pressed against Nicolas Jageur, who was in a huddle of Apprentice Snobs, listening to Arnwolf make a speech.

'It's about time, of course,' Arnwolf was saying. 'Fullstop Island has needed a militia for a long time. Without the Milice Basillica, father says the Basillica Peninsula would have been overrun by raiders from the Furnace Isles years ago. The Red Hawks are quality as well. They aren't just bandits and brigands. They're trained by the Malice Basillica itself.'

'The do look awfully strong,' Mythina said with a simper.

'They are. Only the best for Fullstop Island. This place has been allowed to descend into anarchy for too long. It needs a firm hand.'

As Fletcher shoved his way past, he elbowed Nicolas Jageur, making him spill his drink on Arnwolf.

'Careful!' Arnwolf snapped at Nicolas, brushing himself down.

Fletcher smirked.

The names of those suspected of being taken by the sickness buzzed around the inn, and opinions about the presence of the Red Hawks were being expressed in loud voices.

A great burst of laughter suddenly rang from the seafarers'

table.

'They don't seem to be too bothered by the sickness,' Fletcher said, catching up to Scoop. 'It's as if nothing's wrong at all.'

'Well, this is the Wild Guffaw,' Scoop replied. 'But have you noticed,' she asked, nodding at a small round table next to the bar, 'only one of the Quill sisters is here? I've never seen them apart.'

Fletcher looked across to where Mr Jocular sat, gesticulating wildly at Mr Snooze. Scoop was right, only the taller Quill sister was there, squashed between them. She sat upright, her face pinched and stony.

'Yes, you're right,' Fletcher said, watching her, as her eyes darted intermittently towards the door. The jolly atmosphere couldn't hide the fact that something was wrong.

Reaching Nib and Rufina, Fletcher and Scoop squeezed onto a window seat next to them.

'Ah, there you are!' Nib said, beaming. 'We've been wondering where you'd got to. Where have you been since the festival? What did the Yarnbard want?'

'Oh, nothing important,' Fletcher replied, glancing at Scoop. 'He just wanted to talk through some plans he has to take us to Posyshire, to visit the Green Guardian.'

Rufina looked surprised. 'What, in the holidays? '

'Well, you know what he's like,' Scoop added. 'He never seems to take a holiday – always up to something.'

'True. For an old man, he does have an incredible amount of energy. But you'd think he'd let his apprentices take a break, particularly during the festival.'

'Have you seen him, by the way?' Fletcher asked, looking around.

'Who?'

'The Yarnbard.'

'No. I'm surprised he's not here, to be honest.'

'So am I,' Fletcher muttered.

Scoop scanned the inn. The old man was nowhere to be seen. He was meant to be meeting them there. They were relying on him to tell them what to do next. Where was he?

Just then, something pushed past Fletcher's legs. He looked down to see two faces gazing up at him from under the table.

'What in the name of...'

'*We've* seen him!' one of the faces squealed. It was Alfa. Sparks was next to her. They beamed at Fletcher, their faces red and dusty.

'You've seen him?' Scoop asked.

Fletcher glared at them. 'Why are you under the table? What are you *doing* down there?'

'Well, there have to be some advantages to being small,' Alfa replied, pushing herself up next to Fletcher and Scoop, and squeezing onto the seat between them.

Sparks followed her. 'It's hard work getting through a crowd when you're little.' She jammed herself onto the seat on the other side of Fletcher. 'So we decided to squeeze between people's legs...'

'...And get here under the table,' Alfa finished.

'Did you say you'd seen him, the Yarnbard?' Scoop asked, again.

Fletcher ignored her. 'But why are you *here*? I mean, what are you *doing*? Have you been *following* us? Have you been *listening* in on our conversation?'

'No,' Sparks said defensively.

'Well...' Alfa added, 'maybe just a little.'

Sparks nodded. 'Yes, maybe just a little – but only to the last bit.'

'That's right – to the bit about the Yarnbard.'

Scoop leaned across the three of them. 'And you say you've seen him?' she said firmly.

'Yes,' Alfa replied. 'He told us to give to you this.' She took an envelope from her pocket and held it in front of Fletcher's face.

'What are you, the Yarnbard's mailmen or something?'

'Mailgirls,' Scoop corrected him.

'Whatever.'

'We do seem to bump into him when he has a message to deliver, don't we?' Sparks grinned.

Fletcher grabbed the envelope, looking decidedly uncomfortable squashed between the two first year apprentices.

But before he could open it, there was a loud clinking sound from the bar. He looked up to see Mr Grammatax taping his tankard. A couple of the other tutors joined in a little too enthusiastically, and the inn quietened down. Standing next to the headmaster was a large man with silver hair, swept back in waves. Scoop didn't recognise him.

'Who's that?' she whispered.

'Don't you know?' Nib replied. 'He's been brought in especially to research the sickness. His name's Vincent or Virgil or something. Everyone seems to be very excited about his arrival.'

Mr Grammatax started to speak, 'Well, thank you for coming to this little gathering to mark the start—'

The academy headmaster disappeared behind a wall of heads. 'Can't see you,' a sailor from the School of Seafarers shouted.

'Or hear you!' the boatswain of the Firebird boomed.

'Okay, okay,' Mr Grammatax grumbled. The crowd parted and he emerged again, looking flustered. 'As I was saying, thank you for coming to this little gathering to welcome—'

'On second thoughts,' the sailor interrupted again, 'it was better when we couldn't see you.'

'Or hear you,' the boatswain added, to the great hilarity of the inn.

'Yes, thank you, thank you,' Mr Grammatax said, flushing. 'I should have known better than to try and make a speech here.'

'You should have known better than to try and make a speech anywhere!' the sailor heckled. The seafarers roared with laughter;

it was infectious and the rest of the inn collapsed into hysterics, banging the tables and wiping tears from their eyes.

'Have you *quite* finished?' Mr Grammatax yelled over the noise.

'Not quite! Have you?' the boatswain replied.

'That was a very short speech!' the sailor quipped.

'Just the way we like them!' the seafarers roared in unison.

It took a good ten minutes before the inn quietened down again, in which time Mr Grammatax knocked back a couple of shots of Tension Builder. With newfound energy, he suddenly turned and boomed across the bar, 'Ladies and gentlemen, seafarers and rapscallions, I give you Mr Victor Falk – wielder of The Knife, honorary member of the Scissor Society and new head of the academy's Synitorium.' He turned towards his guest, looking at him with admiration. 'Victor, would you like to say a few words?'

'It would be my pleasure, headmaster.' Victor Falk stepped forward. He spoke quietly, but the inn instantly hushed.

Scoop raised her eyebrows. She scanned the crowd. All eyes were fixed on Victor Falk. The islanders seemed to have fallen into a sort of communal trance. Only Molly Quill was distracted, her eyes darting towards the door at regular intervals.

Impressive, Scoop thought.

Victor breathed in deeply. 'It is a great honour to accept the newly created role as head of the academy's Synitorium. My thanks goes to Mr Grammatax, and to the academy staff, who have so kindly welcomed me to the island.' Victor turned to Mr Grammatax and inclined his head. The academy's headmaster flushed and sputtered, waving a hand, as if brushing away the compliment. Victor turned back to the expectant crowd, a grave look on his face. 'We have a long road ahead of us and the challenge is stark. As many of you know, the sickness that plagues this land has already claimed many victims from across the Oceans of Rhyme. Recently, it has reached the shores of this little island, this diamond in the sea. Our thoughts go out to all affected by this terrible plight.' The crowed nodded, in solemn agreement. 'At this time, we must be vigilant. We must pull together as a community. I know many of you will feel disquiet at the presence of Red Hawk patrols on these streets, but without their protection, the sterling work being undertaken by the volunteers helping at the temporary hospital would be in vein. I would like to pay tribute to all those who have committed their time to the care of the sick.' A murmur of agreement rippled through the inn. 'I am, however, pleased to announce that a new home has been found for the care for the sick, a home more conducive to the research needed to combat this plague. The academy's headmaster has been kind enough to offer the Scythe as a permanent hospital and research facility. This will be the base of the new Synitorium, and as such, care for the suffering will rightly be placed at the heart of the academy.'

Scoop glanced at Fletcher. The Scythe had always housed the Faculty of Edits, a rather bureaucratic department, with which apprentices had little contact. She had always seen the faculty as rather grey and remote, the sharp rocks of the Scythe acting as a deterrent to unwelcome visitors.

'Headmaster Grammatax,' Victor continued, 'has also been kind enough to lay at my disposal two of the finest minds from the Faculty of Edits, who will be working alongside me in my research.' He signalled to two stony-faced men in long white coats standing in the corner of the inn. 'On orders I sent ahead of my arrival, Mr Snip and Mr Splice have already begun the work of developing a new antidote to the sickness…but more about that later. For now, let us raise our glasses to those who even now lay, unmoving, in the hospital, and to toast the precious treasure with which each of us is entrusted – our life and our story.'

In unison the whole pub raised their tankards, but just as they were about to put them to their lips, the door burst open. Framed in it was the tall, broad figure of Cadmus Reed. In his arms, a limp body dangled.

Cadmus scanned the tavern. Seeing Molly Quill, he stopped and stared at her, his eyes wide. Then he held out the body towards her. The person dangling from his arms was dishevelled, her bobbed hair tangled and windswept, her face white as a sheet. As Molly saw who it was, she rose to her feet, letting out a strangled gasp. The sound of the chair scraping the floor set Scoop's teeth on edge.

'Mabel,' Molly exclaimed, her voice hoarse.

'I'm sorry,' Cadmus said, stepping towards her.

'Mabel!'

Cadmus moved to a table. The villagers shuffled up to make space, and he set Mabel Quill's body down on it. She lay there, unmoving, as if she were a corpse on a mortuary table.

And then, as if waking up, Molly began to scramble across the inn, catching tables and tripping over feet as she ran. She reached the place where Mabel had been laid out and threw herself onto her sister's body.

'Mabel, wake up. Wake up! You have to wake up!'

Cadmus laid a hand on her shoulder, trying to comfort her. 'I'm sorry, Molly,' he said, 'I'm sorry. I found her on my way here. She's resting now. She will be looked after. She will be made comfortable.' Gently, he pulled her away from her sister. Molly turned towards him, her face pressed into his chest. She held onto him, her arms around his neck, and sobbed.

For what seemed like an age, the only sound that could be heard in the Wild Guffaw was Molly Quill sobbing. The villagers looked on, feeling powerless.

Finally, Victor Falk broke the silence. He stepped towards the place where Mabel had been laid. 'If I might make a suggestion, Miss Quill...' His voice was smooth and comforting. Mabel looked round to him, her cheeks streaked with tears. He moved towards her, seeming to glide around the obstacles in his way, totally focused on Molly. 'I would like to take your sister into my care, if I may. We are beginning our research into the sickness immediately. If you will allow it, I will take her to the new hospital in the Scythe. She will have the very best treatment. I think we can help her – protect her.'

'You can protect her?' Molly asked. She looked so fragile.

'Yes. I am confident that we can bring about a full recovery.'

Molly let go of Cadmus and stared at Victor Falk.

'Yes,' she said, her voice calm. 'You may take her. Thank you. You will look after her, won't you?'

'Of course,' Victor replied. 'She will receive the very best of care. Headmaster,' he said, turning to Mr Grammatax, 'Miss Quill is obviously extremely shaken. May I suggest she is taken back to her home and made comfortable there?'

'Yes...of course...sounds like a good idea,' Mr Grammatax stuttered.

Cadmus stepped forward. 'I'll take her.'

'Thank you,' Victor replied, smiling. But Cadmus didn't return the smile. He held Victor's gaze for a moment and then turned away. 'Come now, Molly.' He took her by the arm and began to lead her, shaking and pale, towards the door. The villagers moved to clear a path.

Victor turned and nodded to Mr Snip and Mr Splice, who walked over to where Mabel Quill lay and, taking her by the feet and arms, picked her up and followed Cadmus and Molly out of the inn. Victor turned and bowed to the watching crowd. Then, with a swish of his cloak, he left after them.

The patrons sat, staring at the door.

After a moment, they began to turn back to their tables, a buzz of noise returning to the inn. But the party atmosphere had been well and truly broken. Slowly, people made their excuses and began to filter away, dispersing back across Bardbridge to their homes, leaving the Wild Guffaw as subdued as Scoop had ever seen it.

'Poor Molly,' Nib said, staring at the place where Mabel had been.

Rufina put her hand on his. 'I know. It's horrible, isn't it? I wish there was something we could do.'

'Well, there's not a lot we can do by sitting around here,' Fletcher said, getting to his feet. 'We'd better be going.' He shot Scoop a look. She frowned at him. Ignoring her, he started to push his way out from the window seat.

'Aren't you going to stay for one more drink?' Rufina said, 'It would be good to catch up. We haven't seen you for ages and it's at times like these you realise how important your friends are.'

'No,' Fletcher said bluntly. 'It's the start of term tomorrow. We should all be getting back to bed – especially these two.' He signalled at Alfa and Sparks.

Rufina looked at the two first years. They looked tired and dejected. 'I suppose you're right,' she said, reluctantly. 'But we must find some time to talk soon. We miss you when we don't see you.'

'Yes, yes, sure,' Fletcher said dismissively. 'We'll be off then. See you later.' He grabbed Scoop's sleeve and almost dragged her from her chair.

'What are you doing?' she asked, annoyed, as they headed towards the door, leaving Nib, Rufina, Alfa and Sparks behind. 'I really don't understand you sometimes, Fletcher. You can be so rude.'

'Have you forgotten?' he replied irritably. 'We need to read this.' He pulled the Yarnbard's envelope from his pocket. 'I've waited long enough to look at it.'

'Oh,' Scoop said, as they ducked out of the inn. 'Yes, of course.'

'You'd forgotten about it, hadn't you?'

'Well, there was so much going on, Fletcher. It's a lot to take it.'

'You're telling me. That's why I need to see what it says. The Yarnbard was supposed to meet us here. He's supposed to be telling us what to do after the Nemesis Charm. And now he's not here. I can't hang around. I need to know what it says.'

'Yes, of course.'

They stopped just outside a window. It was dark, but the light spilling from the inn was enough to read by. Fletcher ripped open the envelope and pulled out a letter.

'What does it say?' Scoop asked.

Fletcher paused, reading. 'It says the Yarnbard has had to go away on important business. He says he'll be back soon. He says we're to go back to Scribblers House, pack and be ready to leave. But until he returns, we're to start the term as normal – carry on as if nothing's wrong.'

'That's it?'

'Yes, that's it,' Fletcher said, looking up. 'How frustrating!'

'Yes,' Scoop agreed. 'It is. Hopefully he'll be back soon, though.'

'He'd better be. Mother's ill and the sickness is spreading. We need to start the journey to this cave, wherever it is. I can't hang around forever.'

'But what else can we do?'

'I don't know,' Fletcher said, stuffing the letter back into his pocket. 'But if he thinks I'm just going to hang around waiting, he's got another thing coming. Come on. We have some packing to do.'

Chapter 19

Waiting

'If he thinks I'm going to hang around one more day, he's got another thing coming,' Fletcher whispered angrily, grabbing a pile of branches he'd been clearing from a patch of earth in the Botanical Gardens. They were tidying up after pruning the fruit trees, which now stood bare and skeletal in the dim afternoon.

Scoop looked exasperated. 'You've been saying that for three weeks, Fletcher. Give it a rest!' This was the same argument they'd had every day since receiving the Yarnbard's note. It was getting on her nerves.

'Well, I mean it this time!' Fletcher's breath swirled angrily in the frosty air. 'Where is he? I mean, what's he up to? Mother's lying sick and we're doing nothing!'

'I know!'

'We should be doing something – anything's better than this waiting!'

Scoop glared at him. 'But what? What exactly do you suggest we do?'

'I don't know!' he hissed, throwing the pile of sticks back onto the ground.

The other apprentices working in the garden looked round, peering at them from under long coats and woolly hats.

'Now, now, my little petals,' Mademoiselle Belle said, floating across to Fletcher and Scoop. Even in this bitter weather, she looked like a summer flower, wisps of bright blue hair falling across her delicate skin. 'I understand how you feel. The work of growth is hardest in winter, but we must not be discouraged. Under the surface, the first notes of a symphony are already beginning to sound. Life waits, ready to burst forth again. That is the secret every plant in these gardens keeps. There is a time for us to enjoy the scents and pleasures of summer, and there is a time to wait in the darkness. Both are necessary.'

'It's not even winter yet,' Fletcher said sullenly.

It was true. It had only been a few weeks since the end of summer. Autumn winds had started to blow from the South, sending the leaves spinning from the trees. With them, the atmosphere on the island had begun to change. Fear of the sickness lingered over Bardbridge like fog. The streets were quieter than usual: villagers choosing to stay protected in the warmth of their homes. Mutterings and rumours circled the village, and mistrust seeped through the cobbles.

But within the walls of the Botanical Gardens, seasons were less fixed. One day you could step into that little magical acre and find it alive with the songs of swallows and warblers, redstarts and wagtails, cuckoos and turtle doves; another day, you might find the ground hard with frost, and the trees stark and bare. This was one such day.

'That is true,' Mademoiselle Belle replied. 'Outside it is not winter yet. But these gardens are sensitive to the times, Fletcher – sometimes more sensitive than the island itself. You would do well to listen to them. But, no matter, it is the end of your lesson for today.' She turned to the rest of the class. 'Come, come – time to pack up. Gloves, saws, hedge clippers and lopping shears back in the apothecary please. Good work, my little petals. The ground is much clearer.' She clapped lightly. 'Back to your houses, now.'

Sluggishly, the apprentices filed into the apothecary (which was connected to the gardens) to return their tools, before heading back onto the streets of Bardbridge.

As Fletcher returned his gloves, his mind drifted back to the morning after Victor Falk had arrived at the Wild Guffaw. He had woken to discover a new timetable pinned to the notice board of Scribbler's House. Lessons, which usually took place across the island, had been limited to a handful of places in Bardbridge. There had been a notice, which read:

**No student is allowed to leave the village limits.
Lessons may only take place in the following designated
venues:
The Wordsmith's Yard - The Department for
Overcoming Monsters
Quills' Quenching Tea Rooms - The Department
of Underdogs
The Botanical Gardens - Department of Seasons
Twain's Undertakers - The Department of
Tragic Turnarounds
The Wild Guffaw Inn - Department of Lovers and Comics
And Mr Snooze's Bedtime Story Slumber Shop - Department
of Dreams**

'What about the Department of Quests?' Fletcher asked the
warden of Scribbler's House. Lessons for his and Scoop's
department often began at the Port of Beginnings and Endings,
taking apprentices out to the seas surrounding the island. But it
wasn't mentioned.

'Lessons for the Department of Quests have been postponed
until further notice,' the warden answered. 'The Port of
Beginnings and Endings is off limits. It's being patrolled by Red
Hawks.'

'But how are we supposed to learn? We're supposed to learn
by being *in* stories. That means we *have* to leave the village –
whatever department we're in.'

It was true. Although the activities of the different depart-
ments did tend to did orbit around the establishments named on
the notice, lessons were rarely restricted to these places. Instead,
these venues acted as springboards to the rest of the island,
catapulting apprentices into the various stories that waited for
them beyond the village.

'Not my rules,' the warden replied. 'Instructions from Mr
Grammatax – on direct orders from Alethea.'

Alethea? Fletcher thought? *That can't be right. Why would the Storyteller restrict travel to the island?*

'It'll be this way until the sickness is brought under control.'

'And what's this about the First Word Welcome?' Fletcher asked, examining the notice more closely.

'It's been postponed until "safer times".'

'But the First Word Welcome is the official start of term.'

The warden sighed. He had been answering the same questions all morning. 'Well, term is officially starting now, without the First Word Welcome – like I said, not my rules.'

Despite Fletcher's protestations, Scoop had convinced him not to make a scene. He had bitten his lip, attending each of the scheduled lessons. But every day Scoop had had to put up with some sort of outburst against the Yarnbard. Fletcher insisted they should be doing something. Scoop kept telling him to wait, that the Yarnbard would be there soon. For three weeks she had woken with the hope that the old man would finally arrive. But at the end of each day she had climbed into bed, tired and disappointed, her travel chest and knapsack still waiting in the corner. Each night, as she stared at them in the dark, they had begun to look more and more like a bundle of fallen twigs waiting to be turned into a bonfire. To be honest, after three weeks waiting, Scoop was beginning to lose patience too.

* * *

Fletcher and Scoop wandered silently along the empty street away from the Botanical Gardens. They were heading back towards Scribbler's House.

A mottled green wagon rumbled by, carrying a patrol of Red Hawks. They glared at the apprentices. The patrols, which had continued to blockade the village gates, had become increasingly visible on the streets of Bardbridge.

Rounding a corner, the Three Towers came into view. Scoop

looked up. In the windows of the Scythe, lights flickered. Two Red Hawk soldiers had been posted at the bottom of the steps.

'I wonder what's actually going on up there,' she said, half to herself.

After Victor had taken Mabel Quill from the Wild Guffaw, all those suffering with the sickness had been moved to the Scythe. The volunteers who'd been working at the temporary hospital had been thanked for their efforts and dismissed. Only those who had been personally vetted by Falk were now allowed access to the sick, and the Synitorium was guarded around the clock.

'I don't know,' Fletcher replied to Scoop. 'But whatever it is, Mr Falk seems to be flavour of the month. I overheard the barman talking to Romulus Twain at the Wild Guffaw yesterday. He was saying that Mr Falk was the only hope we have of ridding the island of the sickness. Rumour has it he's trialling an experimental cure.'

'Well, I don't like him,' Scoop said as they neared the bottom of the tower. 'I can't put my finger on it. Somehow he's almost...too perfect.'

One of the Red Hawks guarding the tower stepped towards the two apprentices. 'No loitering,' he barked. 'Move along now.'

'We're not loitering. We're on our way home!' Fletcher snapped. 'We're allowed to walk through the village, you know!'

'I don't care what you're doing or where you're going – speed up and move along!' The guard lifted the butt of his musket. 'We don't want apprentices around here.'

'Around the academy, you mean? You do know what an academy is for, don't you?'

The guard stepped forward again. He didn't look in the mood to argue.

'Come on,' Scoop whispered, pulling Fletcher's sleeve. 'We don't want any trouble.'

Fletcher held the guard's gaze for a moment and then turned

and began to walk away, his head held high. Scoop sped up, but Fletcher walked deliberately slowly, falling behind her.

As they navigated around the base of the Needle, away from the Scythe, they heard shouts behind them. Fletcher turned to see one of the mottled green wagons roll up at the steps of the Scythe. A group of Red Hawks leapt out of the back and, under the instruction of one of the soldiers guarding the steps, pulled a body from the back of the vehicle. It looked rigid and heavy. It was covered with a white sheet. The Red Hawks lifted it onto their shoulders and began to carry it slowly up the narrow steps of the Scythe.

'Another one,' Scoop said from behind him. She was watching too. 'That's why he wanted us out of the way.'

'Yes,' Fletcher said, his voice subdued, his mind turning to their mother lying sick.

The guards marched slowly up the tower, the body on their shoulders. A wooden door opened. Fletcher glimpsed the shadowy figures of Mr Snip and Mr Splice behind it. The guards walked through, carrying the body, and disappeared inside.

For a moment, Fletcher stood in silence, staring up at the Scythe.

'You're right, you know,' Scoop said suddenly. 'We should be doing something.'

Fletcher looked at her. 'I know I'm right!'

'Yes, but you haven't suggested anything we can actually do, have you? You've just moaned.'

'I know, but—'

'I have an idea,' Scoop interrupted.

Fletcher looked thrown. 'An idea? What? What idea?'

'I think we should ask the talking animals for help. Get word to the other Guardians that the Yarnbard hasn't been seen for weeks. Ask their advice.'

Fletcher thought for a moment and then nodded. 'Yes,' he said, 'you're right. One of them must know something. Someone must have heard from him.' He clenched his fists. 'We can finally do something!' He paused, thinking again. 'But how will we get a message to a talking animal? They're notoriously shy. They don't come out for anyone.'

'True. But you remember what we learnt in our Anthropomorphism lessons?'

Fletcher thought again. 'They're all around us,' he replied slowly.

'Exactly – if you only know how to call them.'

'But—'

Scoop interrupted again. 'I have some ideas.'

Fletcher raised an eyebrow. 'You have been busy, haven't you?'

'Well, I've been thinking instead of just moaning, Fletcher.' She winked at him.

Fletcher grinned. 'All right, all right.'

'Come on, we have work to do.'

* * *

As they walked through the door of Scribbler's House, a commotion met them. A knot of apprentices were huddled around the notice board.

'What's going on?' Fletcher asked, as an orphan boy from the Department of Underdogs emerged from between the legs of the crowd.

'It's the First Word Welcome,' the boy replied. 'It's been rescheduled.'

'Rescheduled? When for?'

'Tomorrow.'

Fletcher looked surprised. 'Tomorrow?'

'Yes,' the orphan called over his shoulder as he sped along the corridor. 'Apparently there's going to be a big announcement.'

Fletcher looked at Scoop. 'It looks like things are finally

starting to move forward.'

'Yes,' Scoop replied. 'We'd better hurry up and get this message out. Who knows what this big announcement is. Probably more restrictions. Come on, I need some things from my room.'

* * *

On reaching her bedroom, Scoop began to scurry around, opening drawers, rifling through her knapsack and rooting through the piles of parchment on her desk.

'What are you doing?' Fletcher asked, standing awkwardly in the doorway.

'Looking for the right things. Don't just stand there. Come in.'

'The right things?'

'Yes,' she said. 'Come here. We need to write five letters.' She signalled to the desk. 'You can do that.'

'Of course,' Fletcher said, glad to be of help. 'What do they need to say?'

'Something like, "To the one who finds this message…"'

'Hang on.' Fletcher sat down and pulled out a quill. He dipped it into a pot of ink on Scoop's desk. 'Okay, go ahead.'

'To the one who finds this message, your help is needed.'

The quill scratched the parchment as Fletcher wrote.

Scoop continued, 'The Yarnbard has always been a friend to the talking animals and to the Council of the Undergrowth. He is missing – not seen for three weeks. We need your help. Please send word to the other Guardians of Fullstop Island. Has anybody seen him? Does anyone know where he might be found? Please return any news to Scribbler's House. Receive this gift in good faith for your service. Yours in hope, the Shadow Stealers.'

Fletcher scribbled the last few words and the quill came to rest. 'Got it,' he said, blowing the ink dry.

'Good. Four more of those and then we need envelopes that

say, "Read Me!"'

'I'm on it,' Fletcher said, beginning the next letter.

As he scratched out the words, Scoop continued to busy herself around the room, creating a little pile of objects in the centre of the floor.

When Fletcher had finished, he looked up. Scoop was standing over the small pile of objects. She nodded and then looked up at him.

'What have you got there?'

'Gifts fit for talking animals.'

Fletcher walked across to the pile.

He picked one of the objects up. 'Isn't this...'

'...The pocket watch given to us by Mr Snooze for our Dreaming sessions.'

'But why—' Fletcher began.

'Oh my ears and whiskers,' Scoop interrupted. She held her hands up to her mouth and wiggled her fingers.

Fletcher's eyes widened. 'Oh, of course – I'm late, I'm late,' he said, mimicking her.

'Precisely,' Scoop said, her eyes twinkling.

Fletcher put down the pocket watch and picked up a yellowish cake of bread wrapped in a leaf.

'Lembas bread,' Scoop said. 'The Yarnbard gave it to us on our journey to the Cliffs of Uncertainty.'

'And this is for...?'

'...Talking birds.'

'Okay,' Fletcher nodded. He looked through the rest of the pile. There was a brightly painted toy car and a small parcel that Scoop had wrapped in shiny paper and tied with a ribbon.

'What's this for?' Fletcher asked, picking up a thimble.

'We can fill it with honey –' Scoop grinned – 'and leave it at the foot of a tree.'

'Ah!' Fletcher said. 'Chubby little cubby all stuffed with fluff.'

'That's the one. Now all we need to do is put each of the gifts in the right place along with one of the letters.'

'And then we hope.'

'Yes.'

Scoop knelt down and gathered up the objects. Before Fletcher knew what she was doing, she had dashed out of the room.

'Come on,' she said, poking her head back round the doorframe. 'What are you waiting for?' Fletcher shrugged and then dashed after her. He followed her down the stairs, through the kitchen (where she filled the thimble with honey) and out of Scribbler's House. It was getting dark. He watched as she placed the thimble on top of one of the letters and put it at the bottom of a tree. She then scanned the ground and darted away. As Fletcher caught up with her, he could see that she was placing the pocket watch and a letter by the side of a rabbit hole. Then, without speaking, she ran towards the lane that led into the village. By one of the lampposts she left the parcel, a letter slipped under its ribbon. Lastly, he followed her to the river, where she placed the toy car on a luxurious clump of grass.

'Poop poop,' she whispered as she put it down. Then she turned and ran away.

Fletcher stared at the car for a moment. He furrowed his brow. And then, widening his eyes, he said, 'Of course – Toad!' He laughed aloud, and then turning, ran after Scoop.

They headed back to Scribbler's House and up to Scoop's bedroom again. As soon as they got there, she pushed open a window, broke off a piece of Lembas bread, ground it in her fingers and sprinkled the crumbs along the sill. Carefully, she closed the window, leaving the last letter trapped under the sash.

Then she turned to look at Fletcher, a hopeful look in her eye.

'So what do we do now?' he asked.

'Now, we wait.'

Fletcher sighed. 'I'd hoped the waiting was over.'

'Just a little longer. Hopefully in a day's time we'll have news of the Yarnbard. Until then, we sleep. It's the First Word Welcome tomorrow. I want to be fresh and awake to hear what this big announcement is. I have a bad feeling about it, Fletcher, a bad feeling.'

Fletcher nodded. He shared Scoop's fear.

* * *

As he climbed into bed that night, Fletcher looked at his packed chest and let out a heavy sigh. It was as if the Nemesis Charm was squatting in the corner of his room, biding its time. He turned onto his side, his back to the chest, and drifted unnoticeably to sleep.

A wide, black cave disturbed his dreams. No matter where he turned, the cave would always appear in front of him. He ran, sweat pouring from him. But there was no escape. The cave was greedy. It was coming to swallow him, and there was absolutely nothing Fletcher could do to stop it.

Chapter 20

The First Word Welcome

The next morning, Fletcher and Scoop waited among the crowd of apprentices ready to file into the Hall of Heroes for the First Word Welcome. The biggest of the Three Towers, the Giant, which housed the hall, loomed over them. The atmosphere was subdued. The confident shouts of third years, the darting games of orphans, the nervous buzz of new apprentices – these were all missing. Instead, the students waited in melancholy silence. The number of villagers who'd made the trip to the academy was greatly diminished, perhaps less than a quarter of those who usually attended the event were there.

When it was their turn, Fletcher and Scoop walked through the dark doorway and looked around the hall. Many of the stone seats chiselled into the side of the chamber were empty. The Hall of Heroes was usually packed for the First Word Welcome. Today it felt cold and sad.

'It really hits you, doesn't it?' Scoop said.

'What?'

'The scale of what's going on. I don't think I'd really taken it in. Not properly. But we're being decimated, Fletcher. The island's being decimated.'

Fletcher gave a shallow nod, still taking in the scene. 'Yes. We are.'

At the front of the hall, a podium and lectern had been set up. Behind it, Mr Grammatax sat. His face, usually flushed and friendly, was pale, and there were dark rings under his eyes. He looked old. To one side of him was an empty chair. Scoop saw him glance at it, pull a handkerchief from his pocket and dab his eyes.

'Miss Merrilore gone as well?' she whispered to Fletcher.

'Looks like it.'

The Deputy Headmistress usually led the First Word Welcome with Mr Grammatax. They were a legendary double act, Mr Grammatax with his stern bluster and love of order, and Miss Merrilore with her unrestrained enthusiasm and flights of fancy. Their speech was usually the highlight of the First Word Welcome. The older apprentices laid bets on how long it would take Miss Merrilore to wind Mr Grammatax up to the point where he exploded. As Scoop stared at the empty chair, a lump formed in her throat. This was too sad. So much was changing. So much was being lost.

On the other side of Mr Grammatax sat Victor Falk. His red cloak made him look regal. In contrast to everyone else, he seemed to be composed and calm. Scoop watched him. He was quietly scanning the hall, taking in the scene.

I don't trust him at all, she thought, but then stopped herself. *Perhaps I'm being unfair.* What had he done? He was caring for the sick. Why didn't she trust him? She couldn't put her finger on it, but inside a voice told her to beware. It told her that he was dangerous.

When everyone had taken their seats, Mr Grammatax stood up. He looked weary. He moved to the lectern and tapped it hesitantly with his stick.

'Settle down, settle down...' his voice trailed off. The hall was already quiet. 'Yes, well,' he continued, apologetically. 'It seems you're already settled.' He paused and coughed, trying to compose himself. 'So...welcome to this year's First Word Welcome, later than usual, but here we are. Usually, Miss Merrilore and I...' his voice trailed away again. There was an uncomfortable pause as he pulled out his handkerchief and blew his nose. The sound echoed around the hall. 'Yes well, I'm afraid, like so many others who should be here, Miss Merrilore has been taken by...' His voice cracked and he turned away, clearly upset.

Victor Falk rose and walked across to Mr Grammatax. He laid

a hand on the academy headmaster's shoulder and said something quietly to him. Mr Grammatax nodded and turned back to the lectern.

'Well, I think without further ado I shall introduce Mr Falk. He has an announcement to make.'

Mr Grammatax returned to his seat and sat down, hunching forward to wipe his eyes.

Victor Falk stepped up to the lectern and looked out at the crowd. In comparison to the academy's headmaster, he was a giant. He waited, all eyes focused on him. After a moment, he took a deep breath.

'Thank you, Mr Grammatax,' he said, acknowledging the headmaster. Mr Grammatax blew his nose loudly again. 'This is a difficult time for us all. There is not one among us who has not been affected in some way by the sickness. There is nobody here who doesn't have a friend or loved one lying in the Synitorium at this very moment, enslaved by this deathly sleep. There is no one here who does not fear being its next victim. But this morning, I have an announcement to make. I asked Mr Grammatax to call us together for this purpose.' Falk paused again. 'This is not the time for words or long speeches. You, like I, want to see action.' Victor held up a clenched fist. 'And so, instead of speaking, I will show you why I have called us together.'

He suddenly clapped his hands, twice in quick succession. The sound resonated from the rock, making the crowd flinch. Then, behind Scoop, there was a gasp and a yelp of surprise. The crowed shuffled as people turned to see what was happening. A collective wave of shock rolled through the chamber.

There, standing at the back of the Hall of Heroes, dressed in black, was Mabel Quill. She stood stock still, her face fixed and blank. But she was awake.

'Mabel!' There was a commotion at the front. Mabel's sister, Molly, was pushing her way through the seated apprentices. 'Mabel! Is that you?'

'It is,' Victor announced, triumph in his voice.

Mr Grammatax had risen to his feet, his mouth open.

He obviously didn't know what this announcement was then, Scoop thought.

Victor continued, 'May I introduce Miss Mabel Quill, awake and restored to health. Come, Mabel.' At his word, Mabel began to walk forward. The crowd cleared a path for her, students beginning to break out in applause as she passed them, with whispers of 'She's awake' and 'She's okay.'

The two sisters met in the middle of the hall. Molly flung her arms around her sister, tears on her cheeks. Mabel acknowledged her calmly but continued to walk forwards, never taking her eyes from Victor Falk. Molly, almost hanging from her sister's neck, walked with her. They moved together, the applause growing to a cheer. It filled the hall; all the fear and sadness the sickness had caused was being transformed into hope.

'Mabel is the first,' Victor called above the noise. 'Others will follow. I will return your loved ones to you one by one. I will reverse this sickness. It will be defeated.'

Molly and Mabel reached the podium and climbed up next to Victor. Molly flung her arms around him. 'Thank you,' she sobbed. 'Thank you. How can I ever repay you?'

'I ask for no payment,' Victor said, patting Molly's arm. 'It is merely my duty – indeed my pleasure.'

Mabel looked out at the expectant crowd.

'Would you like to say a few words, Mabel?' Victor asked.

'Yes. I would like to say a few words,' Mabel repeated quietly.

Victor turned to the crowd and lifted his hands for silence. Instantly, the hall hushed.

'I give you Miss Mabel Quill, the first to be returned to us.'

Mabel glanced at Victor. He gave a small nod.

'I would like to thank Mr Falk,' she said.

Scoop looked at Fletcher. There was something strange about Mabel's voice, something cold and detached. But Fletcher was entranced.

'I would like to thank Mr Falk for bringing me back to full health,' Mabel said. 'I would like to thank him for all he has done for me.'

'Thank you, Mabel,' Victor replied.

There was a ripple of applause again.

Victor turned to Molly and spoke quietly. 'Would you like to take your sister home, Miss Quill? She is still weary from her ordeal. She will need to rest.'

'Of course, Mr Falk,' Molly replied. 'Thank you again. Thank you.' Taking her sister by the arm, she led her carefully down the stairs and back through the crowd. Everyone watched as the two women moved slowly through the hall. It must have taken them a full five minutes to reach the door, but the picture of the two women, reunited, was mesmerising, and nobody dared break the silence. Finally, the Quill sisters left, leaving apprentices staring at the empty doorway, still trying to take in what they had seen.

Victor gazed over the gathered audience, his face chiselled and grave. 'Although we have this good news,' he said, breaking the silence. There was a moment of shuffling as the apprentices turned back to the front. 'Although we have had this good news,' he repeated, 'although we have reached this turning point, there is a long way still to go. Each of those affected by the sickness needs personal care. Each responds to the treatment differently. I am confident that all will be returned to full health, but it will take time. And...' Victor looked down for a moment, pausing. He shook his head, as if unsure whether to continue. The apprentices glanced at one another, unnerved by what appeared to be a moment of doubt. Slowly, Victor raised his head and looked out. 'I have a piece of news that many of you will find disturbing, shocking even. I have withheld it from you until we had proof that the sickness could be reversed. But I am going to tell you now. I urge you to remain calm. Remember what you have just seen,' he pointed at the doorway and then, lowering his voice almost to a whisper, said, 'and trust me.' The crowd waited, holding its breath. What could this news be? What was so bad that even Victor Falk was unsure whether to voice it? 'I will be direct with you,' Falk said, as if making a decision. He raised his voice again. 'Both the Storyteller and his princess have been taken by the sickness.'

A murmur of dismay, of shock, echoed through the hall. Apprentices turned to each other to ask if they'd heard rightly.

Fletcher looked at Scoop, his mouth open. 'The Storyteller?' He shook his head. 'No... No, it can't be. It doesn't make sense. The whole of this world is dependent on him. Without him, none of us even exist. Nothing in this world exists.'

'I know.' Scoop nodded, looking equally incredulous. She opened her hands to him. 'But we're still here, aren't we?'

'How?'

'I don't know.' She looked back at Falk. 'The Storyteller sick? This is bigger than anything we've seen, isn't it?'

'Yes,' Fletcher whispered. 'Yes, it is.'

There was the sound of a stick striking the lectern. The students quietened down and turned back to see Falk holding Mr Grammatax's cane in his hand. He struck the lectern again.

'You are not to panic,' he said, his voice commanding. 'We have things under control. The Storyteller and his princess are being kept safely at Alethea, protected by Red Hawks. I am personally taking care of their treatment and they will also be returned to health.' He hesitated. 'And...'

He knows how to hold a crowd, Scoop thought, *I'll give him that. He's a showman, if ever I saw one.*

'And,' Falk continued, 'I am able to communicate with the Storyteller.'

Again a murmur of shock spilled through the crowd.

Scoop glanced at Fletcher.

'He communicates with me through a simple squeeze of the hand,' Falk said. 'At the moment, he communicates only with *me*.

But I am able to ask questions and you have my word that I will pass on all his responses to you and to the island. You must not fear. We are not without leadership. Trust me. I want you to remember what you've just seen. I want you to remember Mabel Quill. She is a symbol of the beginning of the end of this plague. You must hold faith. You must not doubt.'

Scoop watched as most of the students nodded in agreement. *I don't like this. I don't like this at all.*

'Now, it is time for you to return to your houses. Your lessons will continue as usual this afternoon. Continue to work hard, apprentices. Make your Storyteller and his princess proud. Do not be distracted. Do not be drawn into pointless gossip or specu-lation. In fact, if you hear any such speculation, you are to report it directly to me. Remember the importance of your work here at Blotting's Academy. Work hard, listen to those of us who wish to keep you safe – keep your heads down, and Blotting's Academy will come through this. Now, file out quietly. Back to your houses, please.'

As Victor finished speaking, two or three tutors began to direct apprentices to leave, row by row. The atmosphere in the hall was subdued again, the momentary joy of seeing Mabel awake dispelled by news of the Storyteller's sickness.

Without waiting for the tutors who were directing appren-tices, Fletcher stood up.

'What are you doing?' Scoop whispered. 'It's not our turn yet.'

'I need to speak to Falk,' he said.

'What? Why? What do you need to speak to him about?'

'What do you think? He can cure the disease. He can help mother.'

'What?' Scoop said, her voice unintentionally loud. The apprentices around them turned to look. She reached up and grabbed Fletcher's sleeve. 'Sit down,' she hissed.

'No. Let go.' Fletcher pulled away. 'I want to catch him before he leaves.'

The tutors in charge reached Fletcher and Scoop's row and everyone stood up.

'You can't,' Scoop said, getting to her feet. 'You mustn't speak to him.'

'Why not,' Fletcher said, not taking his eyes off the podium at the front.

'I don't know. I just don't trust him.'

'What's your reason?'

Scoop paused, searching for one. Other apprentices began to push past them, making their way towards the door. Fletcher and Scoop didn't move.

'I don't know,' Scoop said. 'There's just something about him.'

'Well, that's not good enough.' Fletcher shoved past a student and began to walk forward.

Scoop caught his sleeve again, getting in the way of another apprentice, who jostled past them.

'Let me go!' Fletcher said, struggling to free himself.

'No!'

'I need to speak to Falk!'

'I won't let you!'

'You can't stop me.'

'You mustn't. He's dangerous. He's…'

Fletcher spun round and glared at Scoop. 'Don't you see? He can cure the sickness. He can cure mother and the Storyteller. And he can do it without *us* having to go on a wild goose chase to some cave. He can do it without us having to leave the island at all.' Fletcher pulled his sleeve free. 'Don't you see? He can cure them without *us* having to lose *anything*. Isn't that worth speaking to him about?'

Scoop froze, taken off-guard. She hadn't thought of it like that. Perhaps they didn't need to leave the island. Perhaps they didn't need to enter the skull cave. Perhaps they could see their mother and the Storyteller restored without having to leave behind everything they loved.

She turned to look at Falk, who was still on the podium speaking to Mr Grammatax. The hall was almost empty now, the last few rows of apprentices just filing out.

'No,' she said, quietly. 'No, it's not right. It was the Yarnbard who gave us the Nemesis Charm. He knew what it meant for us.'

'And where is he now?' Fletcher spat.

'I know... But it was the Storyteller who asked him to give the charm to us. He must want us to travel to the cave.'

'That could have been a trick. Who knows? But I do know that Falk has cured Mabel. I've seen it with my own eyes. And if he can cure her, he can cure mother.'

'But did you hear Mabel's voice? There was something wrong with it – it didn't sound like her somehow. It sounded...cold.'

'She was awake, wasn't she?'

'Yes,' Scoop said, thinking. 'But it's all too perfect.' She stared at Falk. 'Everyone's fallen under his spell too quickly. Look, he's practically in charge of the place. *He* led this meeting, not Mr Grammatax. And where's he come from? And now he speaks for the Storyteller as well? I don't like it.' She paused for a moment, studying Falk. 'I bet the Red Hawks are here because of him.' As she said it, she knew it was true. The Red Hawks, the restrictions, it wasn't like the Storyteller. Why would he make such decisions? It had to be Falk. But how? A knot tightened in her stomach. If it was true, Victor Falk was far more dangerous than she'd first thought. In a matter of weeks he'd basically usurped the Storyteller and taken over running the academy. And nobody had raised an eyebrow. Nobody seemed to have anything bad to say about him. In fact, he seemed to be loved universally. Scoop shuddered. Had even Fletcher been taken in by him?

'You mustn't go to him, Fletcher,' she whispered. 'He's dangerous.'

At the front of the hall, Falk and Grammatax had finished speaking. Falk picked up some notes and began to climb down from the podium.

'I don't care,' Fletcher said, shaking his head. 'If there's a chance to save mother, I'm taking it.' Turning, he began to walk away.

'But, Fletcher...' Scoop called after him.

But it was no good. Fletcher wasn't listening to her. He strode towards Victor Falk, who was heading to a side door in the Hall of Heroes. Scoop was left standing alone in the middle of the empty chamber, a sick, powerless feeling deep in her gut.

* * *

'Mr Falk,' Fletcher called, catching up to Victor, who was about to leave the chamber. Victor turned. On seeing Fletcher, a broad smile spread across his face. His teeth were perfect white. They almost gleamed.

'Ah, Fletcher, I believe.' Victor's voice was deep and warm. He held out his hand.

Fletcher reached forward and grasped it. As their skin touched an electric shock snapped between them.

'Ouch!' Fletcher said, automatically trying to withdraw his hand. But Victor closed his fingers around it, holding Fletcher tight.

'It's just a small shock, my boy,' the head of the Synitorium said. 'Static electricity – nothing to worry about, Fletcher.' Falk smiled again.

'You know my name?' Fletcher said, composing himself.

'Of course I know your name, dear boy. You're quite famous here at the academy. Even beyond Fullstop Island, many have heard the story of how you and your sister rescued the Storyteller's princess from the darkness, restoring her to us. Such bravery!' Victor paused. 'I should really have mentioned your mother's and the Storyteller's sickness to you before announcing it today. That was thoughtless of me. I apologise.' Fletcher nodded in acceptance. Victor smiled. 'It's a pleasure to meet you, a real pleasure. How may I be of service to you?'

Victor let go of Fletcher's hand.

'Well, I wanted to talk to you about mother and the Storyteller, actually.'

'Ah, of course. I am so sorry to be the bearer of bad news. You and your sister must be extremely worried for them.'

'Yes, we are. And with what you've done for Mabel, I wondered...'

'...You wondered how your parent's treatment is going. Of course you did. You're wondering if they've shown any sign of responding.'

'Well, yes.'

'It's early days, Fletcher, but as I say, I have confidence they will make a full recovery. Now I must—'

'It's just that we've been told – by the Storyteller and the Yarnbard – we've been told we have to go on a journey.'

Falk turned back. 'A journey?'

'Yes – to a cave. Apparently, we have to go through the cave in order to heal mother's illness.' Fletcher felt silly as he said it. 'But if we don't need to—'

'A cave?' Victor raised his eyebrows.

'Yes. It's a long story, but we've been told we have to travel to the cave and go through it. It's a sort of doorway. We've been told that it's the only way to heal mother. We're waiting for the Yarnbard, but...'

Victor laughed. 'Ah, I see. Well, of course there are different ways of dealing with a phenomenon like the sickness we face. In the absence of any tried and tested cure, there are all sorts of superstitions and stories that people turn to in an attempt to help their loved ones. It's only natural. The Yarnbard and the Storyteller are both experienced and intelligent people. No doubt they have heard news of some cure to be found in a cave – something worth exploring perhaps, but in the end who can say where such stories really lead? I don't know. Do you?'

'I've no idea.'

'Well, I'm sure the Storyteller knows what he's doing. I think in the absence of a reliable treatment, such…risks…well, they may well be worth exploring. But now we have something solid, Fletcher, a treatment we can trust. You've seen it with your own eyes.' Victor sighed. 'Unfortunately, neither the Yarnbard nor the Storyteller are here to see my breakthrough. No doubt if they were, they would call off such…such a foolish exploration, in favour of something more reliable, something more under our control.'

Fletcher nodded. 'Yes,' he said, 'you're probably right.'

'There's no probably about it, my boy. Neither the Yarnbard nor the Storyteller would choose to endanger you with such a quest if they knew there was no reason to do so.'

Fletcher looked down. Part of him was relieved to hear that he didn't need to make the journey to the cave, that he could avoid the sacrifice the Nemesis Charm had demanded. But another part of him felt disappointed. The thought that there was something he could do to help – that there was some way for him to contribute had given him a sense of purpose; it had made him feel valuable. It was a feeling that had all but drained away over the past few weeks of waiting, but it was still there – that spark, the memory of the fire that had burned in him.

Victor Falk laid a hand on the boy's shoulder. 'I know what you're thinking, Fletcher. It's admirable that you want to help your mother.' He paused for a moment. 'You know…perhaps there is still a way you can help her.'

Fletcher looked up at him.

'But I don't know,' Falk said, shaking his head.

'I want to help, Mr Falk. I want to do something.'

'Well, I'll tell you what, you should come along to the Scythe tonight. Come after dark. Tell the Red Hawks guarding the steps that I've sent for you. There is perhaps a way you can help with your mother's treatment. Come tonight and I will tell you about it.'

'Thank you, sir.'

'That's quite all right, Fletcher. I can see that you want to help. You're a good boy. It will be an honour to have you on board with the Synitorium's work. Now, I'm afraid I have some important business to attend to. But I will see you tonight at the Scythe. Remember, come after dark. Let nobody see you – we wouldn't want to stir any jealousies, would we?'

'No sir. Thank you, sir.'

Victor smiled at Fletcher and then turned to leave. As he disappeared through the door, Fletcher looked back. Scoop had gone. Why hadn't she come with him to see Falk? She was so annoying sometimes. She always thought she was right. It served her right that she wouldn't be able to come to the Scythe with him to help work on the treatment for their mother. As he walked back though the empty Hall of Heroes, he made the decision that he would avoid her for the rest of the day. He didn't want to answer the questions she was bound to have. She'd want to know exactly what Falk had said and he didn't want to tell her. He would lay low. He would keep his head down. Once he had found out what Falk had planned for him at the Scythe, he would tell her. Until then, she could wait in the dark. It was her fault for being stubborn. As he left, the giant frescoes of the heroes and heroines of the great stories looked down on him. Slowly, Alice and King Peter, Pinocchio and Red Riding Hood looked at each other and shook their heads, each of them knowing that the path of least resistance was never the way to a happy ending, but each of them also knowing that academy apprentices had to discover such truths for themselves. Nobody could learn just by hearing a story. Apprentices only ever learned by being the hero of their own tale.

Chapter 21

In the Scythe

Grizelda screeched with glee.

'Her as well? It couldn't be better!'

She was peeking under a white sheet that covered a rigid body.

'Rest well, my dear,' she said, bending over to kiss the pale cheek of Miss Merrilore. The Deputy Headmistress showed no sign of movement, even at the old woman's stinking breath.

Grizelda straightened up and looked around the circular chamber. The walls were bare rock, cold and rough. She was in the Scythe, about half way up. There was only one small, pointed window in the chamber, giving the room a melancholy air. Fire torches burned in wrought-iron holders fastened to the walls, the rock above them blackened with soot. There were other rooms below and above just like this. The Synitorium was like a giant hive, housing the bodies of the sick.

Grizelda grinned. She was at the heart of the academy and nobody had challenged her presence there. Nobody had tried to force her to leave. She stretched and sighed contentedly, scanning the metal beds that circled the room. The head of each bed was against the outer wall, with its foot pointing towards the centre. Each was occupied by a body covered by a white sheet.

Other than Grizelda's movement, there was no activity in the room. No tubes administered medicine to the sick, no nurses checked their progress, no machines beeped, no research of any kind seemed to be taking place. The bodies just lay there, silent beneath their sheets. It was like a morgue rather than a hospital.

Grizelda was making an inspection of the patients with morbid glee, a mounting feeling of triumph as, one-by-one she saw who occupied each bed. It was better than she had expected;

so many of her old enemies were there – all those busy bodies, those tiresome do-gooders from the academy; those who had spurned and rejected her, all lying there incapacitated. She was almost beside herself with joy.

'So, it's going according to plan?' she said, turning to Victor who was standing by the door.

'Yes, Mother. It's going exactly as planned.'

'Good. Nobody questioned?'

'No. Mabel did an excellent job.'

The old woman cackled and then danced across the room to him. 'Oh Victor, me boy – yer old mum's so proud.' She put her hands on his arms and looked him up and down. 'My son in charge of Blotting's Academy – who'd have thought?'

'I'm not officially in charge, Mother.'

'No, not officially my dear, but you know as well as I do, that old sap, Grammatax is in your pocket. Seems he can't do enough for you. Might just as well hand you the keys to the headmaster's office now.'

'Yes. But it's better this way, Mother. I can stay below the radar while still having...influence.'

'Of course. You're a clever boy, Victor, a man after me own heart. It's always better to stay in the shadows.' She licked her lips greedily. 'That's where the real power is.'

Victor nodded, and Grizelda turned back to the beds. 'So, who do we have here?' She moved to the person lying beside Miss Merrilore.

'It's...'

'Stop!' the old woman held up her hand. 'Let me guess. That's half the fun. Oh Victor, I haven't had this much fun in years.' She studied the shape under the sheet. 'Let me see.' She sucked air between her teeth. 'It's a man. Portly.' She leaned forward and sniffed the body. 'More than a slight odour of whiskey.' Straightening up, she grinned. 'I know exactly who this is. It's so lovely to see you Mr...' she whipped the sheet away to reveal a moustached, jowly face, '...Mr Bumbler.' She roared with laughter. 'I was right! I was right!'

Victor stepped forward.

'Mother.'

'Yes, dear?'

Grizelda pinched one of Mr Bumbler's cheeks and wobbled his face. 'So lovely to see you, you old fool!'

Victor spoke hesitantly. 'There's something I need to talk to you about.'

'What is it, dear?' She walked to the next bed. 'Now, who do we have here?'

'It's about the children.'

'Children? What children?' She examined the form under the sheet. 'This one's a woman.'

'The Princess's children – the Apprentice Adventurers – Fletcher and Scoop.'

Grizelda spun round, her face twisting, 'Don't speak their names in my presence. Do you understand?'

'But, Mother...'

Grizelda let out a frustrated squeal and stamped her foot. 'Why did you have to mention 'em, Victor? Are you trying to spoil me fun?'

'No, Mother. It's just...one of them came to see me.'

'Came to see you? Why? What about?'

'It was the boy. He wanted to know how his mother's and the Storyteller's treatment were going.'

Grizelda snarled. 'Did he now? Poor little thing. Must be worried out of his mind.'

'He was rather concerned.'

'Didums.'

'But that's not what I needed to tell you.'

'Well? What do you need to tell me? Get to it, 'cause this is putting a right dampener on me mood!'

'The children know about the cave.'

'The Threshold?'

'Yes, apparently they've been told they need to journey to it – to go through it in order to heal their mother.'

'Damn and blast,' Grizelda yelled, thumping one of the metal beds. It scraped across the floor, the sheet shifting to reveal the fiery red hair of the person beneath it. 'Can't things ever be easy?' She lowered her head, breathing heavily. After a moment, she looked up again. 'Well, at least we know about it. It's better than not knowing, I suppose. Now we can do something to put a stop to it. We mustn't underestimate them though, Victor, those little runts. You need to deal with them, and you need to deal with them quickly.'

'I will, Mother. The boy's coming here tonight. He thinks he's coming to help. Instead, he may "accidentally" fall under the curse of the sickness. I don't think he'll be leaving here for a long time.'

'Good,' Grizelda purred. 'And the girl?'

'I'll take care of her too.'

'You better had. There's too much at stake for something to go wrong now.'

Victor looked irritated. 'I said I'd take care of her and I will.'

'Don't you cheek me, boy! You'd better not forget who's in charge here. I gave you life and I can take it away like this.' She snapped her fingers. 'Understand?'

'I understand,' he replied coldly.

Grizelda relaxed and gave a simpering smile. 'Aw, Victor, me boy, let's not argue. I'm only looking out for you – you know that, don't you?'

'Yes, Mother.'

'I know what they're capable of, that's all. Just make sure you deal with 'em quickly. Make sure you cut 'em out of the equation for good. Okay?'

'I will, Mother.'

'Good.'

As if forgetting the conversation, Grizelda turned to the bed she'd knocked and grinned. 'I know exactly who this is. Look at that lovely red hair.' She walked to the head of the bed and leaned over to stroke it, twirling it around her bony fingers. 'Such a shame to see someone so young, so talented, so passionate come to such an untimely end.' Gently, she pulled the sheet back. Underneath, Rufina's face stared up. Her skin looked particularly pale against her red hair. Grizelda moved closer, her lips almost touching the girl's cheek. For a moment, Victor thought he saw Rufina's toe move. But then it fell still. Grizelda breathed in, inhaling the girl's scent. 'Well,' she leered, 'it doesn't look like you're going to be spoiling any more of my plans for a while, does it, Miss Reed? Seems like we've put a stop to that little habit. You just lie back and enjoy my hospitality now. Might as well make yourself comfortable, eh? You're going to be here for a good long time, a good long time.'

* * *

As Grizelda was making her inspection of the Synitorium, Fletcher returned to Scribbler's House. He'd succeeded in avoiding Scoop all through their lessons. As the day faded to evening, he stared out of his bedroom window, looking at the flickering lights of the Scythe. How was Victor Falk healing the sick? What had he done to bring Mabel back from that living death?

I'll find out soon, he thought. *And then it won't be long before mother is awake again, and it will all be me down to me – just me.*

* * *

Scoop was in her room too. She sat on her bed feeling heavy with sadness and frustration.

What's the point? She thought. Fletcher had blanked her all afternoon. Every time she'd tried to talk to him about Falk, he'd made an excuse and walked away.

What on earth can I do on my own? I'm just an apprentice. Why is it always down to me to do something?

She let out a frustrated groan and lay back on her bed. She wanted to shut the world out, to pull the covers over her head and just sleep. She closed her eyes and rolled onto her side.

As she did, something crunched, crumpling beneath her head.

She propped herself up, looking down at her pillow. Lying on it were four small envelopes.

What's this…? For a moment she was thrown. Why were there envelopes on her pillow?

And then she remembered. *The talking animals!*

She sat up, her heart lifting, and spread the envelopes across the bed. Each was addressed to her and Fletcher – to the Shadow Stealers. Each was written in a different hand, but all were written with similar, small, spindly writing.

Scoop picked up the first envelope.

Should I wait for Fletcher? Maybe I should go and get him?

She held the letter for a moment, uncertain of what to do.

No, she decided. *He ignored me all afternoon. It was my idea to ask the talking animals for help, after all.*

She ripped open the envelope. The letter inside was smeared with something sticky. As she lifted it, she could smell what it was.

Honey. I know who this is from, then.

Thank you for the honey, it was very yummy. It was very kind of you to leave it. I have tried my best to find an answer to your question. I flew on my balloon - my red balloon - over the fields of Posyshire. I went to look for the Guardian of the Forests. Perhaps, I thought, he will know where the Yarnbard is. But I found his tree house empty. It looked as if it had been empty for many days. I spoke to some of the other talking animals from the east. They said the Green Guardian is missing too - the one who tends the Fields and Plains. I don't like to bear bad news, even though I am a bear. But this is bad news. No sign of the Yarnbard to the east. No sign of any Guardians in that direction.

Scoop looked up. *The Green Guardian is missing too?*

She picked up the next envelope and tore it open.

Horray! What jolly good luck. What spiffing fun! A splendid, shiny car just for me! And an adventure into the mix - to find a Guardian. What jolly antics! What larks! I drove my shiny new car north to see my cousin. Poop poop! Nothing like the open road to clear the head. The old boy has a beautiful house on the banks of the Puddles of Plot - doesn't come close to my hall, of course, but who could boast that? Over a bite to eat and a rather generous tipple, I asked the old fellow if he'd heard hide or hair of the old man. Sad to say he hadn't. Apparently, they haven't seen any Guardians up there for weeks. The Guardians of the High Places and of the Dark Places have vanished - thrown the Puddle People into turmoil. An awful mess, a terrible scene. But there you are. These things happen. Anyway, better dash - places to go, people to see. Awfully spiffing to have a shiny new car. Jolly good fellow for leaving it, I must say. Poop poop!

Scoop lowered the letter and stared out of the window. The

Green Guardian and the Guardians of the Forest, of the High Places and of the Dark Places hadn't been heard from. With the Yarnbard, that would mean five of the twelve Guardians hadn't been seen for weeks. How could that be? The Guardians protected the island. They kept it safe. How could they disappear without anyone noticing?

She thought for a moment. *Perhaps it's possible, though. After all, they don't like to take centre stage. They work quietly.*

The Guardians of Fullstop Island were mysterious. They governed gently, guiding and holding the island, never using force, never wielding power. They were servants of the land, partnering with it to maintain its balance, nurturing its ability to grow and to heal. It *was* possible they could vanish without raising concerns.

Scoop had a bad feeling.

Quickly, she opened the last two letters. They confirmed her fear. A talking bird had flown west to the house of Lady Wisdom, the Guardian of Hidden Treasure. The birds there said she hadn't been seen for three weeks.

Three weeks? Scoop thought. *Just like the Yarnbard. It can't be a coincidence.*

The birds also reported that the Guardian of the Highways and the Guardian of Cloud and Light had not been seen either. The final letter recounted that nobody to the south had seen or heard from the Yarnbard either. Neither had they seen the Guardian of the Sea or the Guardian of the Desert Sands.

The Storyteller himself was the final Guardian, and he was sick and incapacitated. That meant nothing had been seen of any of the twelve Guardians for almost a month.

Scoop felt her skin prickle.

All of a sudden, she remembered what she'd seen at the Yarnbard's office while touching the Yarn. She pictured it again – the darkness; the faint glimmer of light spilling down from above; the body curled up on the floor, bleeding and unconscious.

'The Yarnbard,' she said, standing up.

Now she felt sick.

She and Fletcher had been so angry with the old man for not returning, for not telling them what to do. It hadn't even crossed their mind that something could be wrong. The Yarnbard often wandered off, returning later with far-fetched stories and strange gifts. But this time he was in trouble, she was sure of it. She'd *had* seen something from his future. And now it had come to pass. It explained why the Yarnbard was missing, why they hadn't heard from him. He had been injured, he was in danger.

All the Guardians were in danger. Scoop was sure of it.

'I must tell Fletcher,' she said, forgetting her irritation with him. This was too important to let a squabble get in the way. They needed to do something. They had to tell someone.

But who?

Everyone she trusted was either sick or had vanished.

Scoop picked up the letters and headed out of her room. She and Fletcher needed each other now more than ever. Perhaps he would have an idea of what to do. She should never have let him ignore her. They should have sorted things out.

She headed down the stairs to the boys' corridor. Since the sickness, the house had been so quiet. People barely left their rooms. She could hear the floor of the old house creek beneath her feet.

She reached Fletcher's door and tapped on it.

'Fletcher,' she whispered. 'Fletcher, it's me.'

There was no reply.

Is he still angry with me?

She knocked again.

'Fletcher, we need to talk.'

She put her ear to the door and listened. There was no sound, no sign of movement.

Slowly, she twisted the handle.

'Fletcher,' she whispered, poking her head around the frame.

The room was dark. She pushed the door open farther, allowing light to spill in from the corridor.

Fletcher's chest and knapsack sat in the corner of the room. His sheets were piled in a mess on the bed. But Fletcher was nowhere to be seen. He had gone.

Chapter 22

Taken

To the east of Fullstop Island, deep in the heart of Tall Tale Tree Forest, an ancient oak stood. Its name was Huggard. Although the woodsman believed it to be the sacred heart of the forest, the tree hadn't spoken for nearly a hundred years. According to legend, Huggard's last word was, 'Radish', which has led many of the wood's folk to carry radishes in their pockets as talismans against the gossiping trees. Many, however, think that the tree was misheard and actually said, 'I've had it,' and then never spoke again.

Tonight, there was an eerie silence around the old oak. It was making Huggard twitchy. He was so accustomed to the endless yabbering of the forest he couldn't cope with the silence. Against their very nature, the Tall Tale Trees had promised to hush their noise out of respect. For tonight there was a visitor to the woods. There weren't many on the island, even throughout the whole of the Oceans of Rhyme, who could say they held the respect of the Tall Tale Trees. But this visitor was one of the few. That night, not a leaf rustled, not a branch creaked. The stillness was haunting.

The visitor in question had no home, a statement he always vigorously denied.

'I have many homes!' he would say. 'I am a rich man! Wherever foxes have holes and badgers dens, there is my home.'

This night, however, the visitor had chosen to make his home in Huggard's hollow trunk. Or rather, a home had been made for him there, for the visitor was currently in no state to be able to choose anything for himself. The only sign of his presence was a faint, glimmering light, shining through a gap in Huggard's roots, a gap just big enough to be used as a doorway.

Above this doorway, a squirrel perched on one of Huggard's

low boughs. It could tell the old tree was ill at ease. The squirrel was jittery too. It sat upright and alert, its tiny eyes darting, and its paws clenched. It had been given an important job. It had been tasked with guarding the visitor. It was to look out, ready to alert the talking animals, of which it was one, if there was any sign of trouble. The tree's inhabitant was a great friend of the talking animals, and there was distress in the undergrowth over his current predicament. All feared the visitor was in great peril.

A little way from the oak, an owl call punctuated the hush of the forest.

The squirrel spun round, its tail whipping the air.

Without warning, a gloved hand shot out of the darkness. Thick fingers closed around the squirrel, covering its mouth. The creature struggled, its tail flailing, but the hand tightened its grip.

A masked face drew close.

'Shh!'

The little animal could smell rum on his assailant's breath.

A pirate, it thought, the hair on the end of its tail bristling.

The creature thrashed again, biting the gloved hand that held it, but it had no effect. The pirate lifted his prey and peered at it. Then, grunting, he pulled a white handkerchief from his pocket. Carefully, he held the handkerchief over the creature's nose and mouth. The squirrel struggled with all its might, trying to escape. But after a moment, it fell still.

'Something to help you rest until we've finished,' the pirate said, his voice low, 'A little Chapter Break fluid.'

He laid the squirrel gently on the ground and then, rising, signalled towards a dense clump of trees.

There was a great cracking sound and a huge man dressed entirely in black emerged from the shadows. He was elephant-like.

The pirate pointed towards the roots of the old oak.

'What?' the gigantic man asked.

'In the tree!' the pirate whispered.

'Oh…okay.'

The giant lumbered forward, twigs snapping loudly beneath his feet.

The pirate raised a finger to his lips, 'Shh!' and the giant slowed. Lifting his great bulk, he tiptoed across to the oak. Reaching the trunk, he placed a hand either side of the opening and ducked his head inside. The gap was too small for his shoulders. He looked like a bear trying to steal honey.

'He's here.'

'Good. Grab him. We need to get out of here.'

The giant pulled his head from the trunk and reached inside. He stepped away. Dangling over his arm was the limp body of an old man. He looked no heavier than a feather in the giant's great hands. The old man's head lolled to one side, his mouth falling open. A cloth hat fell to the floor, revealing dried blood smeared across his forehead. He looked all but dead.

The pirate stepped forward and picked up the hat. He stared at the old man for a moment and then threw the cloth cap onto his languid body.

The forest was beginning to stir. The trees were waking up to the situation, and they weren't happy.

'Thieves,' the breeze breathed, beginning to rustle the leaves.

'Thieves! Stop thieves!'

'Stealing the treasure'

'Stealing the bard.'

The pirate looked up at the swaying treetops. 'Come. We need to leave – and quickly.'

Turning, he began to run through the trees, leaping across fallen logs, zigzagging through the woods. The Giant followed, crashing through the undergrowth, the old man in his arms.

From deep within his self-imposed solitude, Huggard watched mournfully as the body snatchers fled.

It's a sad day, he creaked to himself, *a sad day when a Guardian of Fullstop Island is snatched from the sacred heart of the forest.*

As the squirrel started to stir again, he thought he heard the faintest of whispers from the old oak's branches; no more than a breath, but a word none-the-less. It was the first word Huggard had spoken in a hundred years.

'Thieves,' the old tree whispered. 'Thieves!'

* * *

Libby awoke with a start. It was the middle of the night. Moonlight seeped through the thin floral curtains of her bedroom. A film of sweat covered her forehead. Her hot, damp sheets had been flung to one side, and Alphabet lay on them in a neat arc, purring contentedly.

After a moment of staring into the darkness, Libby reached down and pulled her laptop from under her bed. She flipped the lid open and pressed the power button. The glow of the screen lit the room with cold light. She leaned forward and typed her password.

F1R3B1RD

The screen sprang to life, the first note of the startup jingle ringing out. Flinching, Libby hit the mute button. The last thing she wanted to do was wake her dad, who was asleep in the next room.

Libby clicked the link that brought up her blog. It was a private blog, a secret, the place where she downloaded her thoughts, often late at night like this.

Her fingers hovered over the keypad, wondering how to start.

`"Just woke up."`

The keys clicked loudly.

`"I've seen his face in a dream – The Yarnbard's. He's the first person I've seen from the island for weeks."`

Libby looked at the clock.

`"It's 3.30am."`

She closed her eyes and focused on the image from the dream, not wanting to lose it.

`"His eyes are sunken and tired. He stares at me and then begins to reach out."`

Libby winced.

`"It looks as if he's in pain. There's blood on his head. As he's straining towards me, he opens his mouth. He wants to say something. There's something wrong - I can see it in his eyes. But just as he's about to speak, just as the words are about to leave his mouth...I wake up."`

Libby stared into the darkness.

`"It's a horrible feeling. I'm practically shaking. He's hurt. He needs me. But I can't help.`

`I don't know what to do. I can't get back to the island. I keep trying but something's blocking my way. And now this? I think he's trying to reach me. But the connection's too weak. If only I could talk to him. If only I could find out what's happening - what's happening to Fletcher and Scoop - what's happening at the academy."`

Libby stopped and scanned what she'd written. Then she shook her head, agitated.

`"Listen to me! I think I'm going crazy. I'm worried for one of my characters! I'm worried for myself more like.`

`I've had that thought again - it keeps coming to me...`

`I'm turning into her.`

`I know that's what people would say. 'They have the same weakness - confusing fiction and`

reality.'
  Maybe we do.
  Maybe I am.
  **I don't know anymore. I don't know what to do.
I've started not to trust myself."**
  Libby rubbed her eyes. She was exhausted.
  "God, I hope nobody ever reads this!"

Outside, there was a clatter. It sounded like something running across a dustbin lid.

Cats again, Libby thought. She looked at Alphabet. He shifted lazily on the sheets.

You understand me, don't you, boy? You listen to me.

A screech, like a wailing baby, suddenly echoed down the street. Alphabet opened his eyes and looked towards the window, alert.

'It's a fox – just a fox,' Libby said, running her hand over his soft fur, soothing him. After a moment, the sound stopped and Alphabet buried his head back into the sheets and closed his eyes again.

'That's what I need to do,' Libby whispered. 'Or I'll be fit for nothing in the morning.'

Saving the entry, she shut down her laptop. Closing the screen, she stowed it beneath her bed again. Then, lying down, she pulled her sheets back up, dragging the cat with them. She could feel him, warm against her legs. It was comforting.

You don't have to worry about these things, do you, boy? You just eat and sleep, eat and sleep, eat and sleep...

Before she knew it, Libby had drifted into the darkness. In her dreams, cats and foxes ran through cities...stalked though fields...crept under dark skies.

* * *

Fletcher was creeping along the narrow, winding street that led from the outskirts of the village to the Three Towers of the academy. Mindful of what Victor Falk had told him about not letting anyone know where he was going, he'd decided to stick to the back roads and alley ways. Lines of clothes hung between the houses, casting misshapen shadows across the cobbles. As they swayed in the moonlight, sinister figures spread their arms, as if trying to catch Fletcher, before vanishing into the darkness.

A cat suddenly dashed along a high stone wall, pursued by a ginger tom. The first cat jumped onto a dustbin lid, making it clatter. It disappeared down a gap between two houses. Fletcher pushed himself back into a doorway, not wanting to be seen. He waited for a moment, watching to see if there was movement in any of the houses, but the street was silent. And so quietly, he edged back onto the cobbles and continued his journey towards the Scythe.

* * *

Scoop was still in Fletcher's room. She was looking for a clue as to where he might have gone. She'd made a hesitant search of his bed and was now gingerly looking through the objects on his desk, lifting and returning things without making it obvious they'd been moved.

She'd just picked up a book called "Common Threats" when, without warning, something was pushed over her head. It covered her face. She stumbled backward, knocking the book to the floor. Someone was behind her. She lashed out, unable to see, but her attacker was big, and her struggles made no impact. Something tightened around her neck and Scoop choked, thick fabric pulling against her mouth. It tasted sickly sweet. She tried to pull it off, but it was being held in place.

A bag – someone's put a bag over my head! she thought, terrified.

The smell was thickening, becoming rotten and acrid.

Gagging, she struggled, but whatever the bag was doused in was making her feel woozy. Her limbs began to feel heavy and weak. Gulping another big breath of acrid air, she teetered, trying to focus, but her head was swimming. Her muscles wouldn't respond. Another breath and the room around her muffled, her hearing becoming faint. Next moment, her legs buckled.

Scoop was vaguely aware that she was falling. She toppled into the darkness.

As if watching from afar, she felt her body impact the floor.

And then she lost consciousness.

* * *

Fletcher had just turned a corner to see the lights of the Scythe flicker into view ahead of him. He began to stride quickly towards the tower when, out of nowhere, a hand grabbed his shoulder. Letting out a cry of shock, he spun round. For an instant, he caught sight of someone standing in front of him – a gigantic man. But before he had time to think, a bag was thrust over his head and his vision robbed from him.

Like Scoop, Fletcher struggled in vein.

His body was bundled onto an old cart, a hessian cloth flung over him to keep him from view. The next moment, the cart was rolling down the street away from the Three Towers, away from Scribbler's House, away from the village itself.

Fletcher and Scoop had been taken.

Chapter 23

The Black Horizon

Scoop gasped as water hit her face. It stung. Icy liquid ran down her hair, over her eyes and soaked into her clothes. She shook her head, a cloud of droplets flying from her hair. She could taste salt on her lips.

Sea water?

There was creaking and clanking.

Her stomach suddenly turned as the floor beneath her sank.

What? Instinctively, she gripped what was in her hands.

Rope?

The floor stabilized and then began to rise.

She blinked.

The bag was no longer over her head, but it was dark.

She tried to stand, but her hands were tied, held behind her back. The rope was rough and burnt her skin. She stopped struggling and tried to focus. Where was she?

I'm outdoors, she thought, shivering, a cold breeze biting her skin.

She could feel wood behind her.

She looked up. Above, the night swirled, dark and starless.

The clouds shifted and a mast appeared directly overhead, it's rigging stretching out like a dream catcher, silhouetted against the charcoal sky.

A ship?

She became aware of the sound of waves washing against wood.

I'm tied to the mast!

She glanced to her side. The outline of cliffs came into view, mist-shrouded in the darkness. The headlands looked like grey sentinels guarding the land. As the clouds shifted again, she could see fallen stacks of rock. They reached crookedly from the ocean.

Dead Man's Fingers!

As soon as Scoop saw them, she knew exactly where she was. These were the waters beyond Tall Tale Tree Forest, beyond the Cliffs of Uncertainty; this was the sea to the east of Fullstop Island. She'd been brought a long way.

These were dangerous waters.

'What the...?' a breathy exclamation came, as to her right there was a slosh and a shocked cry. 'That's cold!'

Recognising the voice, Scoop shot round.

'What do you think you're doing?' The sound of the voice was loud in the night.

It was Fletcher.

Scoop could see four other figures hunched next to him. They were circling the mast, facing outwards. It was too dark to see who the others were, but standing over them, a bucket in his hand, was someone Scoop would have recognised anywhere, even on the darkest night. He was elephant-like, his head large and misshapen. In the past he had worked against them, but that had changed at the Great Banquet of Alethea. Or she thought it had. She thought *he* had changed. Since then, he'd been one of the Storyteller's most loyal servants. He'd helped Fletcher and Scoop on numerous occasions, carrying things for them on their journeys, protecting them at night. Scoop had developed quite a soft spot for him.

'Knot?' she whispered.

The giant grunted.

'What are you doing, you oaf?' Fletcher yelled. 'I'm drenched. That water's freezing! Was it you who put that bag over my head? Untie me immediately! This is kidnap! I demand to know who's in charge here!'

The giant ignored him, pulling the bag off the next figure's head. He swung the bucket back and there was another slosh.

'Knot,' Scoop said, urgently, 'what's happening? Why are we here?'

The person who had just been drenched shook themselves, waking. 'Where am I?' said a groggy voice.

Scoop recognised it. 'Nib?'

'Scoop?'

'What are you doing here?'

There was a pause. 'I don't know...' Nib tried to remember. 'I was packing the swords at the Wordsmith's yard. Something covered my face. I struggled. I don't know what happened...'

'It was him!' Fletcher shouted. 'He knocked us out! He brought us here! He's gone crazy!'

'Knot?' Nib said, seeing the giant.

Again, Knot ignored them. Reaching down, he pulled the hoods off the next two figures. They were smaller than the others. SLOSH! The giant threw the seawater.

The spray hit Scoop.

'Watch what you're doing, you idiot!' Fletcher cried. 'That's freezing! When I get out of here...'

There was a squeal.

'Alfa?'

The squeal stopped. 'Sparks – is that you?'

'Yes. Thank heavens. You're here too! I thought...I didn't know what happened...'

Fletcher groaned. 'Oh, that's *all* we need.'

'Fletcher?' the Apprentice Spell-Shakers said together.

'Yes, it's me.'

The two girls squealed loudly.

'Will you *stop* that!'

'Who else is here? Is it just us and you?'

'I'm here too.'

'Scoop?'

'And me,' Nib said.

Alfa squealed again. 'We've got caught in an adventure!'

Sparks didn't sound so sure. 'That's good...I suppose.'

'Of course it's good. We're in a story – a proper story – with Fletcher and Scoop and everything.'

As they'd been talking, Knot had pulled the bag off the last figure's head. The water sloshed again and there was a noise like a horse whinnying.

'What's happening?' a frail voice croaked. 'This is irregular, highly irregular.'

'Mr Snooze?' the five apprentices said together.

'Who's that?' The old man sounded scared. 'Who's there?'

'It's me,' Scoop whispered.

'Scoop?'

'Yes. Fletcher's here too. And Nib, and Alfa, and Sparks.'

'What are we doing here? Where are we?'

'I think we're on a ship, somewhere to the east of the island.'

Nib leaned towards Scoop. 'How do you know that?'

'Dead Man's Fingers – over there. I saw them when the mist shifted.'

'Dead Man's Fingers? But that can't be. We've been told never to sail those waters.'

'I know.'

'They're dangerous. Nobody in their right mind would try to navigate them.'

'Some might,' Scoop said, darkly. 'Some have.'

Nib thought for a moment. 'Pirates?' he whispered.

'Exactly.'

Fletcher had heard enough. 'Knot, will you tell us what we're doing here?'

The giant didn't reply. His silence infuriated Fletcher. 'Why won't you speak to us? We trusted you, you oaf! We thought you'd changed! Untie me! This isn't funny!'

He continued to hurl abuse at Knot, demanding answers to his questions.

Alfa and Sparks began to whisper to one another, comparing

stories, trying to find out how they'd got to the ship.

Mr Snooze muttered to himself. 'Highly irregular, highly irregular.'

Scoop leaned towards Nib. 'Where's Rufina?' she whispered.

'Gone,' Nib replied.

'Gone? Gone where?'

'They took her – to the Synitorium.'

'What?'

'The sickness got her.'

Scoop felt a stabbing pain in her chest. Rufina was sick?

'I didn't want them to take her,' Nib continued, 'but Cadmus insisted.'

'Cadmus? I thought he of all people wouldn't trust Falk.'

'I know – me too. But he said we didn't have any choice. He said it was for the best. Red Hawks came to the Wordsmith's yard. They took her in a truck.'

Fletcher was railing at Knot. 'I knew we couldn't trust you, you lumbering fool! I said it all along – a leopard never changes its spots. Who are you working for – that Grizelda woman? Is she behind this? Are you working for her again?'

Knot covered his ears and began to moan. 'Ooargh Ooargh!'

The sound of shouting and moaning rose from the ship, swirling with the clouds, rising with the crashing waves.

Alfa squealed. 'So they put a bag over *your* head too?'

'We trusted you! You betrayed us!'

'Irregular, highly irregular.'

'Ooargh Ooarghaaa!'

Suddenly a shot split the air.

CRACK!

Everyone froze.

With the crack, a spark flashed and a figure came momentarily into view. He was standing a few feet from the mast, his black-gloved hand raised. In it, a pistol pointed skywards. His tricorn hat was wreathed in smoke where the gun had been fired.

A mask covered his face. In the night, he looked wraithlike.

He vanished into the darkness again.

I was right, Scoop thought, *a pirate!* Her heart was pounding. *And not just any pirate – a Dark Pirate.*

She'd heard stories of such buccaneers; those who had abandoned themselves to the sea, those who had left everything to face the shadows that lingered over the deep.

She could still see the pirate's outline, shadowy on the deck. The company around her held their breath, waiting. How had they found themselves on the ship of a Dark Pirate? Why were they there? What was he going to do to them?

Through the darkness, the pirate spoke. 'Welcome to the Black Horizon.' His voice was low. 'You are my guests. I bid you welcome.'

For a moment, he seemed to dissolve, disappearing into the night, swallowed by a swirl of cloud.

The little company waited.

The wind moaned through the rigging, as if trying to get closer, as if hungry to listen.

After a moment, Fletcher's voice cut through the silence. 'Funny way to treat guests...' He sounded scared. Scoop felt the company tense. '...attacked and tied up...'

They waited again. The sea slapped the hull and the ship creaked.

'My sincere apologies for the method of your summons...'

Scoop shot round. The pirate was closer now.

'...But time is short. I did not have the luxury of being able to convince you to accompany me. But you need to be here – all of you. You will soon know why. Much rests on how we act in the next few hours.'

'How *we* act?' Fletcher said. 'If you think I'll be doing anything with you, you're mistaken.'

'We shall see,' the pirate replied.

Before Fletcher could respond, the pirate turned to Knot.

'Bring out our final guest.'

Without hesitation, Knot turned and clumped across the deck. Scoop listened as he disappeared below.

Fletcher's confidence was growing. 'Untie us! This is outrageous. Who are you? Why have you brought us here?'

'You will have answers soon. When I am confident I have everyone's cooperation, you will be untied. You have my word.'

'Your word? I wouldn't trust your word if you were sent by the Storyteller himself.'

'Me neither,' Alfa added defiantly.

'Which is exactly why your hands are tied, young apprentices. As I have said, there is no time to debate or discuss. I do not have time to win your favour. But you *will* see that we need to work together. Sometimes we have to be confined for a short time in order to realise what needs to be done to bring true freedom.'

As he finished speaking, the sound of Knot's heavy footsteps rose again, and the giant returned to the deck.

'I believe you know our final guest,' the pirate said. A match struck, and a fire torch flared to life, bathing the deck in orange light. Scoop had to close her eyes for a moment, the light too bright. When she opened them again, she let out a gasp.

'Yarnbard!' Nib whispered.

The old man was lying limply in Knot's arms. He didn't move.

'What have you done to him?' Fletcher shouted. 'Have you hurt him?'

Sparks began to sob.

The old man hung motionless over the giant's arms, his mouth open, dried blood on his head. His skin looked as thin as moth wings, blue swollen veins running across the back of his hands.

'Is he…is he dead?' Alfa asked, quietly.

'No,' the pirate replied, 'he's not dead. But he is very ill.' Scoop thought she could hear a note of sadness in his voice.

'The sickness?' Nib asked.

'That's no sickness,' Fletcher said. 'He's been attacked – anyone can see that. They've attacked him – almost killed him by the look of things. You're monsters, the pair of you!'

'WE...DID...NOT...ATTACK...HIM,' Knot's voice boomed, slow and resonant. Everyone looked at him. It was the first time the giant had spoken.

The pirate laid a hand on the giant's arm. Knot lowered his head. 'We did not attack him,' he repeated, quietly.

'My friend is right,' the pirate growled. 'We did not attack the old man. In fact, we rescued him.'

Fletcher snorted. 'Rescued him? Why should we believe you?'

'There is no need to believe me. The Yarnbard himself will show you.'

'The Yarnbard?' Scoop asked. 'How? He's in no state to show us anything.'

Behind her, Mr Snooze stirred. 'That is why I'm here, isn't it?' The head of the Department of Dreams spoke slowly, his earlier confusion seeming to have left him.

'It is,' the pirate answered. 'I need you to take us into a dream. We need to see the last hour of the Yarnbard's memory, the hour before he was attacked. Can you do that?'

'I can.'

'Good. Then there is no time to lose. Everybody here needs to know the truth. Then, perhaps, we will be able to get down to business. What do you need?'

'Nothing more than a lock of my friend's hair and the fire you carry.'

In one swift movement, the pirate pulled a cutlass from his belt and lifted it to the Yarnbard's neck. It looked as though he was going to cut the old man's throat. Instinctively, Scoop turned away.

There was a slicing sound and the blade rang.

Nervously, Scoop turned back. There was no blood. The

Yarnbard's throat was still intact. The pirate held up a clump of grey hair.

Scoop looked at the Yarnbard. His usually pointed beard was now square at the bottom.

Mr Snooze spoke again. 'I need to be untied.'

The pirate nodded and Knot moved to the mast to untie the moon-faced man.

Mr Snooze's bones creaked as he pushed himself to his feet. 'Now, bring me the fire.'

The pirate took the torch to him.

Fletcher tensed. 'How do we know you're not going to cut our throats while we're in the dream?'

'If I had wanted to kill you, I would have done it by now.'

The company was silent.

'You know it to be true, young apprentice. Could you have stopped me?'

Fletcher didn't reply.

Silently, Mr Snooze reached into his nightgown pocket and pulled something out. Before anyone could ask what he was doing, he threw a fine powder into the torch flame. The fire leapt up, turning blue, bathing the whole ship in ghostly light.

'Moonshine,' Mr Snooze said, 'a dream accelerator. I prefer to draw my charges gently into their dreams, to lull them to sleep. But it seems that today we do not have time for such niceties.' With that, he threw the clump of beard into the flames. A plume of smoke poured from the fire, swirling around the company. In moments, it had covered the ship in a thick sooty cloud.

Fletcher coughed, the smoke filling his nose. He tried to breathe through his mouth, but the ashy cloud dissolved on his tongue.

Before he knew it, the dream had taken hold of him. There was no escaping it, no resisting its pull. It was violent, seizing his thoughts.

Fletcher was falling.

Then the darkness opened out. He took a gulp of air, opened his eyes and blinked.

He was in a forest clearing. The sun was low, sending shards of light glinting through the trees. The sound of a river filled the glade. It bubbled and splashed and leapt, echoing through the forest. It was as peaceful as a trickle and yet, at the same time, as powerful as a waterfall. The sound gave Fletcher a strange feeling, as if there were patterns in the water, as if the river was speaking.

As the thought crossed his mind, Fletcher knew that was exactly what the sound was. The river was calling. He tried to catch it, to hold it, to make sense of it, but it dispersed in eddies, swirling away in an ever-moving current.

It was disorientating. It was as if the river was inside him. He could feel it flowing through his body, welling up from deep within. He could feel its power – a swirling, churning power, the source dammed until it was released, rushing, tumbling and gushing from his lips.

It's coming from my mouth, Fletcher thought with a start. And then, *No, not my mouth.* He looked down. He was wearing yellow fabric that shimmered and glistened, sunset colours flowing through its threads.

The Yarnbard's kaftan, Fletcher realised. *I'm in the body of the Yarnbard. The sound of the river's coming from his mouth. The Guardian of the River Word is calling.*

Chapter 24

The Guardian's Gathering

The sound of the river intensified. Everything seemed to vibrate with its lapping, trickling, swirl.

Fletcher, or rather the Yarnbard, looked around. The colours of the glade were vivid: rich greens, earthy browns and, here and there, flashes of violet, yellow, purple and white. The light shooting through the trees was clear and bright. Somehow it felt...

Magical, Fletcher thought, *pure.*

A shard of light hit his eyes, a bright orb radiating through the branches. Fletcher blinked. For a moment, he thought there was a figure in the light – a woman. Her dress sparkled. The flush of her cheeks reminded him of spring, her lips of roses. But the feeling was fleeting. Almost instantly, her warmth darkened, a thundercloud passing over her face. Fletcher lifted a hand to shield his eyes. When he lowered it again, she had gone.

What was that?

He stood, not moving, the sound of water still bubbling through the trees.

Composing himself, Fletcher continued to scan the clearing. A small tree caught his eye. There was something strange about it. It stood alone, alive with summer greens, but as he stared at it, it seemed to change colour, becoming autumnal. *And yet*, Fletcher thought, *the branches are as stark as winter boughs.*

Confused, he turned away.

To the left of the tree was a boulder covered with snow. From its cold surface, he thought he could hear wind whistling through mountains, and the sound of travellers scrambling across ridges.

The snow formed an icy cloak that melted away into a patch

of lush grass. In the centre of the grass was a pool, its water was as still as a mirror. Fletcher stared into it. There was a flash of silver, just below the surface.

A fish, he thought, dreamily.

Behind the pool, the trees darkened, becoming dense. The thicket felt at odds with the light of the clearing. Fletcher peered into the shade. The branches were moving. Was there something in the trees? As his eyes adjusted, he saw that there was.

A horse.

He smiled.

The beast was large and brown. It was pulling leaves from the twigs. It raised its head and stared at Fletcher.

I know you, Fletcher thought.

The horse lowered its head, as if in recognition.

Suddenly, a voice startled Fletcher.

'See how overgrown it is.'

He looked round. Two people were entering the clearing. The first was a wiry man with dark, windswept hair and sun-stained skin. The second was a grandmotherly woman.

'It's ancient, this pathway,' the man was saying. 'Sadly, few travel it nowadays.' His manner was direct. 'See?' he said, crouching down. 'Poison Ivy. It grows over these old pathways – sucks the life from the soil.' He was carrying a large backpack on his shoulders. Under it, his shirt was grimy with sweat.

Standing, he shook his head. 'This pathway needs tending. And there –' he pointed into the thicket – 'Bittersweet Nightshade.'

His companion knelt down to examine the Poisoned Ivy.

'Careful. Don't touch it. It can bring you out an awful rash that can.'

The woman smiled and waved her hands. They were protected by green gardening gloves. 'But I have these,' she said.

'Ah, course. Should've known you'd be prepared for such things.'

The woman seemed to be dressed for gardening. She was wearing green wellies and had an apron tied over a floral dress. The pockets of the apron bulged with gardening tools: pincers, clippers and a trowel. As Fletcher watched her, he relaxed. She had a homely feel about her.

She turned back to the Poisoned Ivy. Reaching down, she extended a finger and touched the vine. As she did, the ground began to change. Green spilled from her finger, colouring the clearing around her with a pool of lush colour. The Ivy retreated, leaving the pathway clear.

'Ha!' The man laughed. 'I should bring you out for a walk more often!'

'It would be my pleasure, Christopher,' the woman replied, standing up again. 'We should help each other more often. What has it been now?' She paused, thinking.

He scratched his head. 'Must be...nigh on five hundred years.'

'Why yes,' she said, laughing, 'I think you might be right. Only feels like yesterday.'

'It does, doesn't it?'

The noise of the river intensified and the woman looked up. 'This is the place,' she said.

'Are you sure?'

'Yes. He's here somewhere. I can sense him.'

'I can see him! I can see him!' A voice called from above them. Fletcher looked up. A young girl was sitting on a high branch of one of the trees, swinging her legs. He recognised her instantly.

Lady Wisdom!

Dressed in green, she was camouflaged by the forest canopy. 'He's over there,' she said, mischievously, and pointed directly at Fletcher.

The sound of flowing water stopped, abruptly.

The man with the backpack and the grandmotherly woman looked in Fletcher's direction, as if seeing him for the first time.

'Yarnbard,' the woman said, beaming. The man nodded a greeting.

Fletcher felt his head nod and then look up at Lady Wisdom again. 'Very good, my dear, very good,' he heard the Yarnbard say. It was strange to hear the old man's voice coming from his own mouth. 'You were always skilled at Hide and Seek.'

'You mean you're always so bad at hiding, old man.'

'Well, there's no need to be rude.'

'Not rude – just telling the truth.' She poked her tongue out at him.

'Yes, well anyway…I think we're all here now.'

'We are!' Wisdom said, leaping down a few branches of the tree. '*They're* as bad at hiding as you!'

'I take offence at that, young lady,' a deep voice boomed. Fletcher looked across to see the snowy boulder suddenly grow larger. Like a discus player uncurling for his throw, it twisted upwards, transforming into a large, statuesque man. The man looked up at Wisdom. He had a Yeti-like mop of white-grey hair and a long fur coat that seemed to swirl like a blizzard as Fletcher watched.

Fletcher recognised him, although it took him a moment to remember where from.

Of course – it's the Auracle – the wind messenger who bought news of the Great Wedding Banquet last year.

A gust of wind blew through the clearing. 'I thought that was a good hiding place,' the Auracle said.

Lady Wisdom laughed. 'Noooo – you were the first I had sussed. The snow was a dead giveaway. I mean, it's not even winter.'

The Auracle looked disappointed.

'I can see the rest of you too,' Wisdom said, leaping down from the tree. With an acrobatic landing, she sprang across to the little tree. Reaching up, she began to tickle its branches.

There was a gravelly laugh. 'Stop it! Stop it!' The tree shook its branches, and before Fletcher could see how, it had transformed into a jolly looking fellow. His skin was as dark as tree bark and his smile as bright as summer. 'Stop it!' he laughed, wriggling away from Wisdom's hands. The birds in the trees around the clearing chirruped and chirped, as if the forest was giggling with him. 'Aw drat,' he said. 'I thought me had a good hidin' place there.'

'Sorry.' Wisdom grinned.

'Next time, eh?'

'We'll see.'

Reaching into her pocket, Wisdom pulled out a handful of small pebbles.

'Come out, come out, wherever you are,' she sang.

Turning, she began to throw the pebbles. One hit the pool, causing the water to ripple, the second she threw into the thicket. It hit a tree.

One by one they appeared. A mermaid with seaweed hair poked her head out of the pool. A hooded figure, his face covered by a dark cloak, became visible among the trees of the thicket. Moving past him, another person stepped into the light. Fletcher recognised him at once.

The hermit! he thought. And then something clicked. *Of course, the horse. I knew I recognised you.* The hermit looked at him, his dark brown eyes deep and thoughtful. He nodded, as if he knew what Fletcher was thinking.

'And finally...' Wisdom said. Spinning round she hurled a stone towards the setting sun.

The woman in the light shimmered into view again.

'There,' Wisdom said, 'none of you are *any* good at hiding.' She turned to the Yarnbard and grinned. 'All here – present and correct. And now, old man, it's time for you to speak.'

There was silence. The birds stopped singing, the trees stopped sighing. It was as if the whole forest was listening.

'Thank you, my dear,' the Yarnbard said. He turned to the

assembly, 'Friends. You know that a meeting of the Guardians is something that happens very rarely, and must only be called at times of dire need...'

A meeting of the Guardians, Fletcher thought. He looked around at the strange assembly. He knew the Yarnbard and Lady Wisdom were Guardians, of course. Although he'd met the Auracle and the Hermit before, he'd no idea they were too. He hadn't seen any of the others before, and he realised that although he knew the names of the Guardians, he had no idea what they looked like. They were a mysterious group. To see them all in one place...

There's something special about it, Fletcher thought.

He scanned the gathering. There was a sense of balance in that clearing; a feeling of quiet, gentle power.

The tree-man clicked his teeth. 'That's right, brother. In times of dire need...'

He must be the Guardian of the Forests, Fletcher thought.

'Must be...what...centuries since we last had a gathering like this.'

'Five hundred and seventy-three years,' the mermaid said. 'Not that I'm counting.' She blushed.

'You kiddin' me. It's been that long? Well, I'll be damned.'

The grandmotherly lady smiled. 'It's lovely to see everyone looking so well, isn't it?'

And she must be the Green Guardian.

'Sure is, sister, sure is.'

The Yarnbard cleared his throat.

'Sorry, brother, you carry on. Don't let me interrupt you now.'

'Thank you, Elder.'

''s all right, man, 's all right.'

The Yarnbard took a breath. 'Well, I believe this is such a time – a time when the island is under a grave threat. There is a sickness that flows through the sea...'

'That's true,' the Mermaid interrupted. 'The Fable Fish have told me of it – a blackness silently moving through the waters. Many of their shoals have been affected.'

A murmur of disquiet rose from the Guardians.

'Indeed, my dear. It is a terrible thing. With my connection to the academy, I stay closer to the village than many of you, and I'm sad to say that a great number of Bardbridge's inhabitants have been taken by the sickness too. They now lie in a sleep, from which they cannot be woken.'

'Excuse me for sayin' this, brother,' the Guardian of the Forest said. 'I realise this is all bad, bad news, but threats they come and threats they go, that's the way of things, you know what I'm sayin'? We've all been here an awfully long time. We've seen many things pass, have we not, brothers and sisters?'

A few of the Guardians nodded their heads.

'So what about this particular threat do you think warrants our gathering?'

'Because,' the Yarnbard said, 'this time the Storyteller himself has fallen under the spell of the sickness!'

This was obviously news to many of the Guardians, and it caused a commotion.

'No,' boomed the Auracle. 'It cannot be!'

'He cannot be woken?' The Green Guardian asked.

There was a hissing sound from the thicket that chilled Fletcher's bones. He realised it was coming from the hooded figure. It sounded like some sort of language, a dark language. *The Guardian of the Dark Places,* Fletcher thought.

'I tell the truth, friends,' the Yarnbard said, trying to quieten the crowd. 'He is sick and he cannot be woken. But worse than this—'

'Worse?' the Green Guardian interrupted. 'Can it be any worse?'

'I'm afraid it can. Into this tragedy, a man has arrived, a man who claims to be our saviour. He goes by the name of Falk. He claims that he is able to cure the sickness. He is using this apparent gift to win power to himself. He has all but taken control of the academy. He has his own private army.'

'Army?' a number of the Guardians said at once.

'I've heard of him,' the man with the backpack said. 'There is much talk of him on the pathways.'

He's the Guardian of the Highways, Fletcher thought.

'They say he's a miracle worker. They say he can bring people back from the dead.'

Another murmur spilled through the clearing.

'I believe his claims to be bogus,' the Yarnbard said. 'Of greater concern is that he has taken guard of the Storyteller. He is allowing nobody access to his body. He claims that *he* alone is able to communicate with the Storyteller. Only he is able to carry his words. In effect, he has taken the Storyteller's place.'

At this, there was uproar.

Deep in the forest beasts began to howl. Wind rushed through the canopy and flocks of birds leapt into the sky.

Suddenly, a bright light shot through the trees. At once, everything fell still, each of the Guardians raising their hands to cover their eyes.

The woman in the light spoke. 'I have heard enough,' she said, her voice strong and clear.

The Guardian of Cloud and Light, Fletcher thought, in awe.

'I believe the course of action we must take is clear. We must stand against this man. We must come out against his power.'

'I agree,' the Yarnbard said, lowering his hand.

'And I,' the Auracle boomed.

'And I,' the Guardian of the Dark Places hissed.

And I, the hermit whispered without moving his lips.

One by one, each of the Guardians gave their ascent.

'Then it is decided,' the Yarnbard said. 'The Guardians of Fullstop Island will stand together to bring an end to—'

'Blah, blah, blah, blah, blah,' a harsh voice interrupted. 'Yada, yada, yada.' Suddenly, a little rock that had been unnoticed in the centre of the circle began to transform.

'Grizelda?' the Auracle said.

Lady Wisdom stepped forward. 'Sister?'

'That's right,' the old woman chuckled. 'Surprise!' She stretched out her arms theatrically and bowed. 'Pleased to see me?'

'You're here? But what are...' the Yarnbard trailed off.

'Yes, I'm here,' the old woman spat. 'What of it? Thought you could have this little party without me, did yer? Well, I'm sorry to disappoint you. But, if you hadn't forgotten, there are twelve Guardians on this 'ere island.' She began to count, pointing a spindly finger at each of the Guardians. 'One, two three,' she spoke slowly, obviously enjoying the moment. 'Four, five, six...' She grinned wickedly at each in turn. 'Seven, eight, nine and ten... Add the Storyteller, that's eleven. Oh, but there's one missing, isn't there? Now who could that be?' She raised a finger to her lips, as if thinking. 'Oh yes, I remember.' She jabbed her thumb into her chest. 'That'll be...me! Guardian of Grit, Guardian of Base Materials, Guardian of fire, stone and ash, Guardian of Pain in the Bleedin' Butt, reporting for duty, sir!' She saluted.

The Guardian of the Forests spoke up. 'But you've never taken your seat on the council of Guardians. Since the beginning, you've rejected the place set for you.'

'Well, I'm taking it now, me dear. Problem?'

Nobody replied.

'You know, I've been listening to your little meeting and you know what I hear?' She waited for a response. When none came, she shook her head. 'Yada, yada, yada, blah, blah, blah – a load of hot air being made by a boring old bunch of has-beens...'

'How dare you!' the Auracle interrupted.

'Shut it, fatty! It's my turn now. You've had your go. I've got something to say, and you'd better all listen up. It's over, this is. This whole Guardian thing – you've had yer day. I'm here to declare this meeting closed!'

Grizelda raised her fingers to her lips, puckered her mouth and let out a shrill whistle.

From the trees stepped a squadron of Red Hawk soldiers. They circled the clearing, their coats blazing in the sunset, their swords glinting.

For a moment, nobody moved.

Then, the Guardian of the Forests began to laugh. 'Have you forgotten who we are? We have the power to squash your little friends like ants. We have the power of the sky in our control. The rains pour at our command. The sky blazes at our word. We could command a stampede of wild animals to crush your friends beneath their hooves. We could command swarms of bees to dispatch them with a thousand swords. We could cover their world in darkness, sweep them away in the river's flow, bury their bodies under boulders. We could command the vines to wrap themselves around them and squeeze out their last breaths. We could command their paths to twist and the lakes to receive their corpses. We have this world at our fingertips. We hold it gently, yes, but make no mistake – nobody will take us captive.'

Grizelda paused, and then lifting her hands, began to clap, slowly. The sound echoed through the trees. 'Well now, that were a pretty speech, weren't it? You should think about a career on the stage.' She turned to the Red Hawks. 'Did you like it, my little birds of prey?' They stood, unflinching, surrounding the Guardians, their faces stony. 'I can tell you did,' she said, turning back to the Guardians. 'You know what they say, don't you – about pride and a fall? Have you forgotten that you're supposed to spread your power? You're not supposed to have big shows of strength, are you now? You're not really supposed to gather, are you?'

'Only in times of dire need,' the Yarnbard said.

'Oh yes, I forgot,' Grizelda said. She studied her fingernails, disinterestedly. 'Well, whatever. I was hoping you might gather.

Makes my job a whole lot easier, don't it?' She looked up. 'See the only problem with your little speech, mister, is you forgot to add a little word – *did*. Funny how such a little word can have so much power. You *did* have the power to make the rains fall from the sky. You *did* have the power to make wild animals...yada, yada, yada. Whatever. But that's when you had the Storyteller on your side. Unfortunately for you, he seems to be taking a little nap at the moment. Ain't that sweet? I've given him a teddy bear and everything. Point is, you don't have that power now. But I do.'

The Guardians exchanged glances.

Grizelda cackled. 'Aw, don't you believe me? Try it. You –' she pointed at the Guardian of Cloud and Light – 'make lightning streak from the sky.'

The Guardian raised her arms, a fierce look on her face.

Nothing happened.

'Aw, shame now, ain't it?'

Grizelda turned to the commander of the Red Hawk squadron. 'Seize them,' she hissed.

The Red Hawks raised their weapons and marched forwards.

Other Guardians raised their hands, trying to use their power, but as with the Guardian of Cloud and Light, nothing happened.

Fletcher felt a wave of panic sweep through the Yarnbard's body. His heart rate increased, his breathing becoming laboured. For the first time, the old man felt weak, vulnerable.

Run, he thought.

Turning, he made for the trees.

Behind, there were cries and shouts of outrage.

His kaftan got caught under his feet and he stumbled.

When he looked up, there was a soldier in front of him, the butt of his gun raised.

The gun came crashing down towards him. He jumped sideways, but was too slow. The gun caught the side of his forehead, glancing from it.

The pain was excruciating. It pulsed through his body. The old man cried out.

Somehow he kept moving. There was blood on his forehead. It trickled over his eye, blurring his vision. The soldier in front of him had been distracted by another Guardian.

The Yarnbard took his opportunity and staggered forward, slipping into the thicket.

For a moment, he turned back. Three Red Hawks were pushing the Auracle down to the ground. Behind, a soldier was threatening the Green Guardian, the barrel of his musket inches from her face. She looked terrified. The clearing was a blur of red coats and friends being seized, struck and bundled to the ground.

Run!

The Yarnbard turned and ran.

Our power gone? He couldn't take it in. *It can't be!*

The forest was dark. He stumbled again.

Must keep going...must get message to them...they must find him...

He pressed on, pushing one foot in front of the other, moving away from the shouts and cries. He didn't know where he was going. He just knew he had to get away.

There was a sound behind him. Footsteps. Someone was following him.

He re-doubled his efforts.

The trees seemed to leer at him, reaching down as if to catch him.

Must get away...anywhere...

A gunshot.

They've opened fire!

His head was throbbing. He couldn't think.

Only he can help now...must get them to his ship...

He was dizzy. His leg buckled, but he pushed himself up, aware of the sound of footsteps behind him again.

Must tell Fletcher...Scoop...find the Dark Pirate...ask for help...

And then the Yarnbard collapsed.

Through the blood and pain he looked up. There was a flash of colour.

Red.

A red coat?

No.

He closed his eyes.

'You'll be all right,' a voice said.

He felt someone lift him.

'I have you now. I'll keep you safe.'

He was aware they were running through the forest.

Must find the pirate...he's the only hope...

And then his world went black.

Chapter 25

Releasing the Patients

At the bottom of the Scythe, a small group of villagers waited in the dark. They stood in a dishevelled queue, their shoulders hunched. They looked grey and worn. Every so often, their eyes darted nervously, expectantly, up the narrow steps that spiralled up the tower.

Next to the queue, a mottled green wagon sheltered a squadron of Red Hawks. Four soldiers stood by the van guarding the steps. One carried a clipboard in his hands.

Peering up the tower, the villagers could see other Red Hawks stationed at doorways and positioned at lookout posts, their weapons lowered, ready to defend the Scythe. Now and then, a white-coated nurse wearing a surgeon's mask would bustle out of one of the doorways and hurry up the stairs to the next level, where they would disappear.

Fire torches dotted along the stairway threw grimy, flickering light around the tower, the jagged rocks casting long, monstrous shadows into the night.

Suddenly, one of the doors a few floors up opened. Two nurses appeared, flanking a portly figure. The three of them made their way methodically down the stairs, keeping in perfect time, as though marching. On reaching the bottom, one of the nurses handed the portly fellow over to the Red Hawk with the clipboard. The nurse pointed to a name written on the sheet.

'Bumbler,' the soldier called.

There was a scuffle in the queue as someone pushed their way to the front. The man was wrapped in a long coat, a hat pulled low over his head, as though he were hiding. But from his frame, it was clear the man was Mr Grammatax.

'Yes, yes...thank you,' he muttered to the soldier. 'I'm here to collect Mr Bumbler.'

'Sign here,' the soldier said, holding out the clipboard.

Mr Grammatax took the pen and signed.

He leaned close to the soldier and said, 'Thank Mr Falk for granting my request and, you know, speeding up the process for this particular patient will you, my good man?'

'Mr Falk is very busy, sir,' the solider replied, not lowering his voice. 'He doesn't like to be disturbed.'

Mr Grammatax looked sad. 'Yes, of course, of course... wouldn't want to interrupt. But still, when he sees who I am...'

'Move along now, sir,' the soldier interrupted. 'Other people are waiting to pick up their loved ones.'

'Yes, of course...sorry to inconvenience you.'

Grammatax turned to Mr Bumbler and took him by the arm. The island's historian stared straight ahead, a blank look in his eyes.

'Come on now, old friend. It's good to see you up and about again, restored to full health. Let's get you home. It looks like you need to rest.'

'We have Mr Falk to thank for my recovery,' Mr Bumbler said, his voice flat and emotionless.

'Yes,' Mr Grammatax agreed. 'He's a remarkable man, isn't he? I will pass on our thanks when I see him.'

'He has saved me.'

Mr Grammatax nodded and began to lead Mr Bumbler away. 'Yes, well, let's get you a nice cup of tea. Or a whiskey maybe – I bought your favourite blend, especially.'

Mr Bumbler didn't reply. He shuffled away, staring straight ahead, following his friend obediently.

Behind him, the door on the third floor of the Scythe had opened again and another patient was being led down the steps by the nurses. They moved in the same mechanical, methodical way. Like Mr Bumbler, they stared straight ahead.

Reaching the bottom, the soldier called out, 'Miss Dotty', and her sister pushed forward to collect her.

'We have Mr Falk to thank for my recovery,' Mr Grammatax heard her say, as he and Mr Bumbler shuffled away into the darkness.

Chapter 26

Back on the Ship

Fletcher retched, coughing.

With the same violence that the dream had grabbed him, he found himself back on the ship.

The smoke had cleared. Above, the clouds had cleared too. The sky was speckled with a thousand, thousand stars. They were so bright and clear against the blackness that for a moment Fletcher felt his spirits lift.

One by one, those around him woke from the dream with a cough and a splutter. Nib was the last to wake. 'The Guardians taken?' he said, his voice hoarse.

For a moment, nobody said anything.

Then Scoop turned to the pirate. 'So, you're him?' she said, slowly. 'The pirate the Yarnbard was thinking about when he...when he...' She broke off. The old man still hung lifelessly in Knot's arms. It was too much to bear.

'I am,' the pirate said.

'Our only hope,' Nib added.

'Yes, I believe so.'

'Why?' Fletcher asked, curtly. Now he had adjusted to being back on the ship, there was a battle raging in his head. Part of him thought the pirate had done the right thing, bringing them here. He'd done what was needed. Part of Fletcher even respected him for it. Things were far worse than he'd realised. The Guardians had been ambushed, the Yarnbard was unconscious, the Storyteller was sick, and the academy had all but been taken over by Falk. They had nobody to turn to. The pirate had taken charge. Perhaps he was their best hope. But the other part of Fletcher raged and railed:

He drugged me! He put a bag over my head! He brought me here without my say so!

At the moment, it wasn't clear to Fletcher which of these voices would win through.

'Why?' he asked again. 'Why are you our best hope?'

'Because,' the pirate growled, 'I've been there.'

Been there? Fletcher thought. *What's he talking about? Been where?*

And then something clicked.

Oh, he thought.

He looked at Scoop and knew instantly that she was thinking the same.

'Been where?' Alfa piped up. 'Will someone tell us what's going on?'

'Ask your friends,' the pirate said. 'They know what I'm talking about.'

Alfa turned to Scoop. 'Scoop? Fletcher? What does he mean? Where has he been?'

'Well,' Scoop said, slowly, 'if I've understood rightly, I think he's been to a cave.' She looked at the pirate and saw a smile flick across his lips.

'A cave? What? What's this about?'

'There's a cave,' Fletcher interrupted. 'It's a doorway. We have to cross through it.'

Scoop continued, 'Whatever's through that cave will help us cure the sickness.'

'What do you mean you have to cross through a cave?' Nib asked.

'It's called a Threshold,' Scoop answered.

Nib looked thoughtful. 'I've heard of them, but...'

'But I thought Falk had found a cure for the sickness?' Sparks interrupted.

'Think about what you've just seen,' the pirate growled. 'A man who raises an army, who attacks and imprisons the Guardians, who sets upon a man like the Yarnbard...' He pointed to the old man lying in Knot's arms. 'Does such a man seem like a healer to you?'

'But we saw him bring Molly Quill back. You saw it too,' Sparks said, turning to Fletcher and Scoop.

'Yes,' Scoop said. 'That's what it looked like. But there was something wrong. Did you see Molly's eyes?'

'Blank,' Nib said. 'There was no life in them.'

'Exactly.'

The pirate stepped forward. 'Whatever he's doing, he isn't healing those people.'

'He's right,' Fletcher said in a low voice. 'I thought Falk had healed her too. Our mother...' his voice cracked. 'Our mother is sick and I'd hoped...I wanted to believe he could do it. But I know it's not the truth. I think I knew it all along. I just hoped...' Fletcher paused. 'I was on my way to see him. I'm sorry.'

The pirate laid a hand on Fletcher's shoulder. 'Don't be,' he said. 'You were doing what you thought was right.'

Fletcher looked up at him. 'That's why you had to move so quickly, isn't it? Because I was on my way to see Falk.'

'Yes. The Yarnbard asked me to keep an eye on you and Scoop. I've been watching, keeping my distance, but watching. When I realised you were on your way to see him, I had to act. Had you reached the Scythe, I fear you would not have escaped.'

Fletcher had made up his mind. He'd been a fool. He'd been headstrong, and it had blinded him. He hadn't listened to Scoop, hadn't paid attention to her doubts. He'd put them both at risk. However he felt about the way the pirate had brought them there, he had to admit, he was glad he had. The pirate had saved them. He'd saved Fletcher from himself.

'So you can take us there?' Fletcher said, slowly. 'To the cave?'

'I can.'

'Then it appears we will be working together after all. Thank you.'

'There is no need to thank me.' The pirate looked down at the apprentices' bonds. 'I said once I knew I had your cooperation you would be free. I am a man of my word.'

Reaching down, he began to untie them. One by one, they stood up and stretched. Scoop rubbed her wrists. It was good to be able to move again.

However, something had been troubling Nib. 'But I remember learning about Thresholds. From what I remember, they say that once you cross a Threshold, there is no return. That's what the legends say, isn't it?'

He stared at Fletcher and Scoop, hoping that one of them would correct him. Neither did.

'But, we can't let you...'

'It's the only way,' Fletcher said. 'I allowed myself to think for a while that there might be another way. I thought Falk's promises might mean we didn't have to cross the boundary. But look where that's got us. I'm not going to make that mistake again. There is no other way. We have to go through that cave. We have to be strong.'

Nib shook his head.

'We already made the decision, Nib,' Scoop said, gently. 'In the desert, we already made our choice. That's where we were when the Yarnbard called us away at the festival. And we know it's what we have to do.'

Nib stared at his friends. He'd seen that look in their eyes before, and he knew there was no point trying to change their minds.

'Okay,' he said. 'But I'm coming too.'

'And me,' Alfa added.

'And me,' Sparks agreed.

Fletcher and Scoop looked at each other. 'Thank you for being here for us,' Scoop said, 'but this is something we have to do on our—'

'They're coming,' the pirate interrupted. 'This is my ship and I choose the crew. This is the company I have chosen to travel to the Threshold. Who actually crosses through – well, that's a discussion for another day.'

Fletcher and Scoop looked at the pirate and nodded. Inside, Scoop had to admit that she was pleased. They would have company for the journey. They would be with friends.

'For now,' the pirate said, 'we have other things to deal with.'

'Like the fact we can't leave the Storyteller and our mother with Falk while we sail away,' Fletcher said.

'Nor Rufina,' Nib added.

'Precisely. We must rescue them. Tonight. Once they are aboard, we will set sail.'

Alfa squealed. 'A rescue mission? Fantastic!'

'Tonight?' Scoop said.

'Yes. Falk was expecting Fletcher to visit him this evening. When he doesn't arrive, he'll know something's wrong. We cannot delay. We must act now.'

Fletcher lowered his head. His choice to go and see Falk had forced them into what would be a risky situation. Scoop laid her hand on his back. 'It's okay,' she whispered. 'You were doing it for Mother.'

The pirate stepped forward. 'We need to get a closer look at the Scythe so that we can plan the mission. But we need to remain hidden.'

'You can use the Wordsmith's Yard,' Nib said. 'There's an old lookout post there, with a clear view of the Three Towers. And Cadmus would welcome us and keep us safe.'

'How will we get there without being seen?' Scoop asked. 'There are guards posted at all the village gates.'

Nib smiled. 'Through the Story Caves,' he said. 'There's a tunnel that leads from the Cliffs of Uncertainty to the village. From the caves, there's a doorway that opens directly into the Wordsmith's Yard.'

The pirate nodded. 'Good. Then there is no time to lose. Fletcher, Scoop, Alfa, Sparks and Nib will come with me to the village. Knot, you can row us ashore and wait in the boat for our return. Mr Snooze, you stay aboard the ship as night watchman. I will show you how to use the signal to bring us back safely.'

The moon-faced man nodded.

'Then let's go. We have a princess to rescue.'

Chapter 27

Arnwolf's Secret

Arnwolf was wearing the mottled green tunic that signalled his position as son of the King of the Basillica Isles. He was leaning on a large wooden desk, his palms flat on the table.

'What? You've had twenty squadrons of our best men already. You want more? We can't leave the Archipelago unprotected. There are raiders from the Furnace Islands to think about, and the Grand Committee of the Storyless States has doubled their armament production in the last year.'

The desk stood in the middle of a room on the second floor of the Scythe. The room was square, its mahogany panelling hiding the bare rock wall behind. Large maps, lit by glass lanterns, filled the panels: maps of Fullstop Island, maps of the Oceans of Rhyme, maps of trade routes and territorial control. The desk, and the large leather chair that stood behind it, were the only pieces of furniture in the room.

Victor Falk sat on the chair, his red hawk-feather cloak around his shoulders.

'I understand your father's concerns,' he said, 'but if he provides me with the manpower I've asked for, I will double his army – triple it!'

Arnwolf shook his head, part in frustration and part in awe. 'How are you doing it?'

Falk smiled, his teeth sparkling. 'Well, it wouldn't be prudent to give away all my secrets now, would it? But rest assured, the alliance between Fullstop Island and the Basillica Isles will stand strong. I will provide what I have promised – a doubling of his army.'

'You better had. My father won't be pleased if you fail.'

Victor stood, and moved around the table. He laid a hand on

the boy's shoulder. 'Your loyalty to your father does him credit, Arnwolf. He should be proud.' The corners of Arnwolf's lips twitched. 'But you can take the message back to him that the multiplication of the Red Hawk Army is proceeding as planned. You've seen it with your own eyes, after all. Where there were only twenty squadrons, there are now thirty.' Arnwolf nodded. He looked up at Victor, his eyes shining. The two looked almost like father and son. 'And I have agreed to all your demands, have I not: a position as commander of your own squadron, a seat at my table, access to the Scythe?' Arnwolf nodded again. 'We are allies, Arnwolf. Together we will bring order to this island, which for too long has been allowed to degenerate into anarchy.'

Arnwolf's face hardened. 'I will tell Father you need more men. He will send them at my request.'

Victor gave him a firm pat on the shoulder. 'Good boy. He will not be disappointed.' Breaking away, he moved back round the desk. 'Now, if you will excuse me, I have some business to attend to.' He pulled a sheaf of papers from a drawer and sat down to study them. 'Close the door on your way out,' he said, not looking up.

* * *

Arnwolf headed up the steps of the Scythe. He felt important. He felt that, for the first time, things were as they should be. He was the son of a king; he *should* have soldiers at his command, he *should* be party to negotiations, he *should* be addressed with respect. The Red Hawk soldier guarding the third floor door saluted him.

Rounding the corner, Arnwolf stopped. Someone was coming towards him down the stairs. He recognised her. She was dressed in the standard issue, plain green pyjama-like uniform of a patient, but her fiery red hair made her stand out from the other inmates. Arnwolf would recognise that hair anywhere. It was Rufina. She was a friend of Fletcher and Scoop's. Arnwolf felt his hands becoming clammy as she walked towards him. She was attractive in her way; he had thought that before. She had a sort of rustic beauty, unspoilt, pure.

And that fiery temper, Arnwolf thought, straightening his jacket.

'Stop,' he said as she drew level with him.

Rufina stopped instantly. She looked directly ahead, her eyes blank.

'Oh,' Arnwolf's lips curled up into a thin smile. 'You've been done, haven't you?'

Rufina didn't reply. She stood perfectly still, staring ahead, the breeze blowing her loose clothing.

Arnwolf stepped closer to her. Still she didn't move. Slowly, he moved his face towards her until he could feel her hair brushing his cheek.

'I have Mr Falk to thank for my recovery,' Rufina said, her voice emotionless.

'Yes, you do,' Arnwolf said, moving back. 'And I'm working with Mr Falk. What do you say about that?'

'Mr Falk is a great man.'

The reply irritated Arnwolf. 'I'm sure he is,' he said, 'but I have provided Red Hawks soldiers for him. Without them, he would be nothing. And I am in command of my own squadron.'

There was a pause. 'Then you are a great man too.'

'I am, yes.' Arnwolf leered. 'What do you plan to do now that you've been cured from the sickness?'

Without hesitation, Rufina replied, 'I would like to serve Mr Falk.'

'Indeed.' Arnwolf thought for a moment. He looked Rufina up and down, studying her, taking in her freckled skin, the way her arms hung by her side.

'It could be fun having you around,' he said, half to himself.

'I am here to serve,' Rufina replied.

Arnwolf was feeling more confident now. He considered the situation. 'You would do exactly as you were told, wouldn't you?'

'I would.'

'Come,' Arnwolf said, making a decision. 'You will work for me.'

'It would be an honour to work for an ally of Mr Falk.'

'Good,' Arnwolf replied, drawing out the word. 'You have chosen the right side this time.' He leaned forward, speaking quietly, 'They say Mr Falk cannot be killed.'

Rufina stared into the darkness.

He moved closer still. 'But I know a secret,' he whispered. 'They say the only way he *can* die is by seeing his own face. You see,' he smiled, 'I know things. Stay with me and serve me and I will protect you.'

Rufina waited.

Arnwolf laid a hand on the small of her back. 'Come,' he purred, 'follow me.' With that, he began to walk up the stairs. Slowly, mechanically, Rufina turned and followed her new master up the steps of the Scythe.

Chapter 28

The Wordsmith's Yard

The Wordsmith's Yard was an enclosure, surrounded by a high wooden fence made from logs driven into the ground. It was like a fortress. Inside was the courtyard, used by apprentices to train in the arts of fencing and swashbuckling. There was also a scattering of outbuildings, including the stables and smithy. Inside the smithy, a furnace blazed, ready to receive the spikes of burnished bronze. Once hammered into weapons and tools, these were thrust into the great water butt that hissed and steamed as the metal cooled.

Fletcher, Scoop, Alfa and Sparks emerged through a trap door into the armoury that stood next to the smithy. They were followed by the pirate, who carried a fire torch. Nib led the company.

As stable boy, the Wordsmith's Yard was like a second home to Nib. He had met Rufina there. She was the daughter of Cadmus, the Wordsmith, and Cadmus now treated Nib like a son.

'Shh, follow me,' Nib said, as Sparks pushed herself up from the ladder that led from the Story Caves. As she entered the armoury, she looked around. The walls were lined with shelves, piled high with helmets and breastplates, shields and armour. Racks of pikes and broadswords waited in the darkness.

'Look,' Alfa whispered, pointing to an arrangement of crossbows, harpoons, grappling hooks and wire that hung from the wall. 'They look fun!'

It was all a little overwhelming, but Sparks nodded in agreement.

'Okay,' Nib said, as the pirate emerged, closing the hatch behind him. 'You wait here. I'll go and find Cadmus – let him know what's happening.'

He lifted a latch and pushed a wide, wooden door ajar. He peeked out and then, after a moment, slipped out into the darkness.

The little company waited nervously, nobody speaking. The fire torch crackled, making the swords and armour glint.

Before long, Nib returned and beckoned the others into the courtyard.

'I've told Cadmus we're here. He'll make sure we're not disturbed. Follow me, this way.'

He led the little group across the courtyard and through another door in the corner of the enclosure. 'This is the old lookout post,' he said, as they entered.

A rickety wooden staircase led upwards. Sparks looked down as she climbed, careful not to lose her footing. At the end of the stairs, a narrow ladder led up to a small, square room, barely big enough for the six of them to stand in. The ceiling was low and, towards the top of the walls, were a series of narrow, horizontal windows, from which a watch could be made.

'If you look out there,' Nib said, 'you can see the Three Towers.'

The pirate pulled a telescope from his belt. 'Good work. Hold this.' He handed the fire torch to Nib. Raising the telescope, he looked out through one of the windows. 'This is excellent – exactly what we need. I have a clear view of the Scythe. It's dark, but the tower's lit and I can see it well enough.' He looked round. 'I'll describe what I can see. Listen well. We'll need to plan our approach carefully.' Looking back, he focused on the base of the tower. 'There are four guards stationed at the bottom,' he said slowly. 'There's a squadron wagon too.'

'It's well fortified,' Nib whispered.

'Yes. Falk isn't taking any chances.' The pirate scanned upwards. 'There are guards stationed on each level. I count ten levels and one, two, three...four snipers positioned at stations along the length of the staircase.' The pirate lowered his telescope. 'You know the academy better than I. Is there only one way up the Scythe?'

'Yes,' Fletcher said, 'just the one staircase. And it's a precarious climb too. Students aren't allowed up there without permission. It's too dangerous.'

The pirate sniffed and turned back. 'What else can we see?' He paused. 'Hang on, there's movement on the third floor. There are two...they look like nurses...wearing white coats and masks. They're escorting somebody down the tower.'

There was a creaking noise below them and the sound of footsteps climbing the ladder. Instantly, the pirate spun round, putting his hand to his cutlass.

'It's okay,' Nib whispered. 'It's only Cadmus.'

The Wordsmith poked his head into the room.

Hesitantly, the pirate released his grip of the weapon.

'I heard you talking,' Cadmus said. 'That'll be a patient they're escorting back to their family. Falk has started releasing the healed – Mr Bumbler was the first. If you look to the left of the guards at the bottom of the steps, you'll see a queue of people waiting for their loved ones.'

The pirate looked. 'Yes, I see it.'

'Any news of Rufina,' Nib asked, quietly.

'None.' Cadmus sounded tired. 'They're summoning the families of the patients they're intending to release at the start of each day. I haven't heard anything yet.'

'What's the smoke?' the pirate said.

'Smoke?' Fletcher asked.

'Yes, there's a steady stream of ashy smoke rising from the window on the eighth floor.'

'Nobody knows,' Cadmus said. 'It started a few days ago. Most people think it's from a fire that's being used to heat the wards of the hospital.'

'Hmm,' the pirate said. 'And I assume the Storyteller and Princess are being kept at the very top?'

'That's right. Nobody's allowed access except Falk and a handful of guards who've been specially trained for that duty.'

The pirate focused on the room at the top of the Scythe. 'One window,' he said. 'No others on the far side?'

'No, only that one.'

'The rock face is sheer. There's definitely no way to climb it.' The pirate focused in closer. 'I can see a guard inside the room. I assume the door's locked from the inside. There's another soldier outside. The fourth sniper's position is just below the ninth floor. Hang on, what's this?' The pirate paused. 'Two Red Hawks are climbing the stairs to the top chamber...past the sniper...salute. The guard who was inside looks like he's coming out...salute again...I can't see... Wait! Looks like they're talking. They're on the steps, just outside the door. No, hang on. One of the new guards is entering the room. I can't see the other one... There he is. I can just see his coat now. He's taken up position outside the door. And the old guards are descending the stairs.'

'They must be changing guards,' Nib said.

'Yes, that's what it looks like. And now things return to how they were. All done in a matter of seconds. They're slick.' The pirate lowered the telescope. 'I wonder how often they change guards.'

'From what I've seen,' Cadmus said, 'it's on the hour, every hour.'

'I see. And you're sure there's no other way up the tower apart from the staircase?'

'I'm sure,' Nib said. 'That's the only way.'

'So, we have to negotiate the four guards at the bottom, possibly nine doorway guards, the four snipers and the specially-trained Red Hawks protecting the top chamber. Then, we have to rescue the Storyteller and Princess, carry them down a precarious staircase, bring them here and smuggle them back to the ship – all before first light.'

Nobody spoke. It felt as though they'd failed before they'd

even begun. Falk knew exactly what he was doing. He held all the cards.

Alfa broke the silence. 'May I have a look through the telescope?'

'Be my guest.' The pirate handed it over.

Alfa climbed onto a small crate in the corner of the room and lifted the telescope to her eye.

'We have plenty of weapons here,' Nib said, 'swords and armour. The six of us could storm the tower, take them by surprise.'

'We'd have no chance,' the pirate replied. 'Even if we managed to get past the guards at the bottom, they'd have the advantage of being higher than us at every level. No, we have to find another...'

'I have an idea,' Alfa interrupted. She jumped down from the crate and handed the telescope back.

'You do?'

'Yes. Come here, I'll whisper it to you.'

What? Fletcher thought, irritably. *This is hardly the time for games.*

Nevertheless, the pirate leaned down. Alfa was so small he had to crouch so that she could reach his ear.

The company waited, watching the pirate's expression.

All at once, his face broke out into a wide toothy grin. It was the first time Scoop had seen him smile.

'You think you can do it?' he said.

Alfa paused for a moment and then nodded, resolutely.

The pirate winked at her. 'Well, my friends,' he said, standing again, 'it seems we have ourselves a plan, thanks to the smallest member of our crew.'

Fletcher and Scoop looked at each other. What had Alfa seen? What was her idea?

'We're going to need to use some equipment from the armoury.'

'No problem,' Cadmus said. 'Take whatever you need.'

'Thank you. Then let's move back downstairs. We'll outline the plan from there. May we have some food and drink as we talk?'

'I've already prepared it. It's waiting in the armoury.'

'Good. Let's go, then. Time is against us.'

As they filed back down the stairs, Sparks prodded Alfa. 'What have you got us into?' she whispered.

Alfa grinned, mischievously. 'You're going to love it,' she said. 'This is going to be the best adventure ever!'

Chapter 29

The Seventh Level

Rufina was in the round, rock room that occupied the seventh level of the Scythe. She waited, expressionless, passive, her hands hanging by her sides. Arnwolf was at the centre of the room, standing over a single metal bed that dominated it. On the bed, a body lay, naked, but covered to its chest with a standard issue green sheet. To one side of the room, a pair of long desks curved around the wall. At them sat Mr Snip and Mr Splice in white coats, their faces covered with masks. They were working. Mr Snip was holding a test tube up to a plain, white light bulb that hung down over him. Inside the tube, an inky material was suspended, cloud-like, in liquid. Lowering the test tube, he picked up a pair of thin tweezers, inserted them into the tube, and extracted a fine, black thread. He discarded the thread into a dish and then handed the test tube to Mr Splice. Picking up a vial of reddish liquid, Mr Splice filled a teat pipette with it and then squirted its contents into the test tube. The inky material swirled, turning a maroon colour.

The men ignored Arnwolf and Rufina completely.

'This is our next specimen,' Arnwolf said, spreading his arms above the body on the bed, 'the next in line to undergo Mr Falk's treatment. Look here,' he pointed to black wires that were attached by sticky pads to the patient's temples. The wires trailed across the room to a tall, metallic grey machine. It beeped.

Knobs, dials and leavers covered the top part of the machine. Under the dials, a spindly needle moved back and forth across a continuously moving sheet of paper.

'Come here,' Arnwolf said. 'I want to show you.'

Rufina did as she was told, moving mechanically to Arnwolf's side. The boy put his arm around her waist, running his fingers across her skin. He was enjoying showing off for his new girlfriend.

Girlfriend – I like the sound of that, he thought.

'See here.' He pointed at the paper as it fed steadily through the machine. As the needle moved across the sheet, words appeared.

'That's his life, right there in ink, being extracted from his mind while he's asleep. And here,' Arnwolf pointed lower down to where a comb moved across the paper. A fine black thread was being caught in the teeth of the comb. Below, the paper was blank again.

'The comb collects the words,' Arnwolf said, 'and then they are sucked through a tube –' he traced his finger across the machine to where a vial bubbled with black liquid – 'to here. Here, the thread is mixed to become the person's Life Draught. And then here,' Arnwolf was getting excited. He took Rufina by the arm and pulled her across to where Mr Snip was extracting a fine black thread from another test tube. 'Here is where the "problematic" parts of their stories are removed – disobedient thoughts, troublesome characteristics, heretical ideas. We call it editing. It's like smoothing out their story, ironing out the peaks and troughs. And here –' he pulled her across to Mr Splice – 'this is where their stories are strengthened.'

'Strengthened?' Rufina asked.

'Yes.' Arnwolf grinned. He pointed to a rack of vials containing the reddish liquid. 'They are filled with Mr Falk's story. It's brilliant, isn't it? He's taken his own blood, his own life, and is infusing a little into each of the patients, strengthening them with Falcon blood. I think that's what's healing them.'

'You think?'

Arnwolf looked uncomfortable. 'Well, from here the edited Life Draughts are taken upstairs to the Fire Room. I don't really know what happens to them there, but...' He looked irritated. 'Look, you're asking way too many questions.'

'I'm sorry,' Rufina said, blankly. 'I will do better next time. I want to be a good servant.'

Arnwolf's face softened and he put his arm around her again. 'I will let you off this once. But just remember who's in charge. You're lucky to be here.'

'I am,' Rufina replied. 'I am lucky.' As she said it, she moved as if to hug him, but her foot got caught on the leg of the desk. It scrapped across the floor, knocking the rack of red vials over. They toppled down, crashing to the ground, many of them shattering. Falk blood splattered the floor.

'Be careful!' Arnwolf yelled.

Mr Snip and Mr Splice stumbled to their feet and began, awkwardly, to tidy up. Even then, they didn't acknowledge Arnwolf or Rufina's presence. They wore blank expressions, their eyes empty. Six of the vials were still intact. Carefully, they picked them up.

Rufina knelt down to help.

'Leave them to it!' Arnwolf said, harshly. He grabbed her sleeve, pulling her up. 'Come on, you've done enough damage here already!' He looked round at the glass-strewn floor. 'We need to get out of here. If they find out we've been in here…' He pulled Rufina roughly towards the door.

As they exited, Rufina looked back. Mr Snip and Mr Splice had finished clearing the mess and were taking their seats again.

Five vials of Falk blood rested in the rack on the table.

A smile flicked across Rufina's face.

Chapter 30

The Rescue

'Shh!' Sparks said, pulling Alfa back into a narrow doorway. She could hear footsteps above them. The sound was getting closer. Both girls were dressed in black and disappeared into the shadows. They had been climbing for fifteen minutes now and were half way up the academy's tower.

'They're coming this way,' Sparks whispered.

Alfa nodded and reached back to try the handle of the door behind them. At first it didn't budge, but then, with a scrape, it turned and the door creaked open. Alfa tapped Sparks on the shoulder and, lifting a finger to her lips, beckoned her to follow. The two of them slipped through the doorway and found themselves in a dingy little room. It looked like a storeroom and smelt dank. Alfa carefully pushed the door closed.

The only light in the room seeped through a grimy little window that overlooked the steps. Alfa rushed over to it and peered out.

Sparks paused and then took a few steps into the room. She squinted into the gloom.

'Urgh!' she cried, stepping back. In front of her, a row of shelves was lined with jars and boxes. From the jars, eyeballs stared out. The boxes seemed to be piled high with body parts. One was full of severed hands, another contained fingernails, a foot poked out of a third at an awkward angle. They looked real. It was horrible.

'Look,' Sparks said, moving closer to her friend.

Alfa glanced over her shoulder. 'Oh yes,' she said, unfazed. 'This is the Frankenstein room – spare body parts. I saw it on the sign outside. She turned back to the window.

Suddenly, she grabbed Sparks' sleeve and tugged it. 'Duck!'

she whispered.

As the girls bobbed down, a thin man in a black suit and top hat walked passed. Alfa peaked over the window frame.

'It's Romulus Twain.'

As he disappeared around the tower, the girls straightened up.

'Come on,' Alfa said, 'he's gone now. We need to get up there quickly.'

Sparks pointed at a large black bag that Alfa was carrying over her shoulder. 'Do you want me to take it for a while?'

'Oh, yes please, if you wouldn't mind? It's pretty heavy. We can swap back in a bit.'

Taking the bag from Alfa, Sparks pulled it over her shoulder. Then the two girls slipped back out onto the stairs. They looked both ways to check that the coast was clear and, seeing that it was, continued their journey upwards.

* * *

Fletcher and Scoop had just slipped out of the back door of Scribbler's House. The cart from the Wordsmith's Yard that Nib had brought them in waited in the narrow backstreet. They walked quickly, not running, not wanting to draw attention to themselves. Reaching the cart, they jumped onto the back, sat down and pulled a large hessian cloth that covered the cart over their heads. The pirate was waiting for them underneath.

'Got them,' Scoop whispered, as the cart jolted forwards. 'I was right – the zombies used them for the School of Horrors Christmas Ball last year.' She handed a white nurse's coat and a mask to the pirate. She and Fletcher had their own coat and mask too.

As the cart bounced along the cobbled street towards the Three Towers, they put their costumes on.

'Remember,' the pirate said, 'it's all about confidence. Look like you should be there. There's nothing as effective as hiding in plain sight.'

We're actually going to do this, Scoop thought. She shivered with excitement and fear. *We're actually going to walk straight into the lair of the beast.*

They finished putting their costumes on and stared at each other. There was something unnerving about not being able to see someone's face clearly.

'Next stop,' the pirate said, 'the Scythe.' As he said it, Fletcher felt the hairs on the back of his neck bristle.

* * *

Alfa and Sparks had finished the long climb up the tower. They stood outside the final doorway. Its knocker was made out of a pair of crossed knitting needles. Beside the door, the sign read, "The Eye of the Needle: Office of the Yarnbard, Ambassador of the Storyteller, Head of the Department of Quests, Guardian of the River Word".

Sparks looked across to the Scythe, its fire torches flickering in the night. It looked smaller from here. The Needle was the tallest of the Three Towers, so that she looked down at the glassless window of the Scythe's top chamber. Now she was at the top, the gap between the two towers looked immense. It was like an abyss. She felt sick.

Let's hope this works. Just a few seconds, she said to herself. *Just a few seconds and we'll be there.*

Alfa pulled a key from her pocket and unlocked the Yarnbard's door.

Lucky the old man had these on him, she thought.

The door swung open and the two girls entered. They stared up at the Yarn that twisted above their heads, a web of knots and threads. It looked spooky in the dark. Sparks could almost picture a giant spider sitting at the top of the room, waiting to pounce. The old man's office was lonely without him.

Alfa walked to the window that overlooked the Scythe. 'Okay, bring that here,' she said.

Sparks took the black bag from her shoulder and placed it carefully on the floor.

'Right,' Alfa said, nervously. 'Let's get set up. Then, we wait.'

* * *

Fletcher, Scoop and the pirate walked towards the steps of the Scythe. They could see the four soldiers posted at the bottom. They were talking. The one with the clipboard was pointing at a villager, beckoning them.

Scoop's heart was pounding. Her hands were hot and she couldn't keep her mind from imagining disaster. It leapt from scenes of them being discovered, to looking down at her feet as she ran, to the jolt as a hand seized her, to pictures of them tied up and captured.

As she approached the steps, she took deep breaths, focusing on the sound of the air entering her lungs.

Hold it together, she said to herself. *Be confident. Act as if you should be here.*

The soldiers were just in front of them now. One of them stepped out towards them. He stood right in front of the steps.

He's going to stop us. He's going to stop us, she thought, her mind racing with the impulse to run, to get out of there while she could. But her legs kept moving forward.

As they reached the soldier, the pirate nodded. It was a nod that said, "We're supposed to be here. We've done this a thousand times." Despite the fact the soldier was directly ahead, he didn't slow his pace. The soldier looked as if he was going to raise his hand. For a second, she thought the pirate and soldier would collide, but just at the last moment, the soldier sidestepped away, returning the pirate's nod as he did. Scoop felt herself step onto the first stair.

We're here. We've done it. We're in!

Buoyed by the triumph, she relaxed. But the respite was only momentary. A few steps up and another soldier came into view, guarding the first floor door.

They made the same approach: confident, not slowing their pace. The nod came again. This soldier didn't respond, but he didn't try to stop them either.

Scoop pressed on, following Fletcher, watching his feet as he climbed ahead of her. They were above the surrounding houses now. Scoop could see over the rooftops. There were lights in the streets and smoke rose from some of the chimneys. It was a hard climb. The steps were uneven, worn in places, so that they sloped precariously to the side. Scoop pressed against the rock as she passed a place where part of the tower had crumbled, leaving only half the staircase intact. There was a sheer drop to the side.

Don't look down, she thought.

She glanced away. She was level with a window. Through it, she caught a glimpse of a room full of patients. They were lying, motionless, on beds that circled the room. They were covered with sheets up to their shoulders. She blinked. She recognised one of them. It was Mr Bumbler.

No it can't be, she thought. *Cadmus said Mr Bumber had been released.*

She looked again. It definitely looked like Mr Bumbler.

Perhaps he's sick again.

She passed the window and the room vanished from view.

He must have been mistaken.

Her breathing was laboured now but she knew they couldn't slow their pace. They had to maintain a purposeful stride.

Just ahead of them, the first sniper post came into view. A Red Hawk knelt behind a ledge of rock that jutted out from the tower. He held his musket, the flint cocked, its barrel resting on a prop. There were sandbags around him.

They marched on, moving behind him. He barely glanced at them, focused on the streets below.

'So far so good,' Fletcher whispered.

'Shh,' Scoop said. She didn't want to talk. She didn't want to think. She just wanted to focus on moving one foot in front of the other, knowing that, however slowly, they were getting closer to their goal and farther away from the threats that were already behind them.

They marched passed another soldier, guarding a doorway. And another. The second sniper returned the pirate's nod. They were half way up the tower now.

Nobody's stopping us, Scoop thought. *We're going to get there. We're going to make it.*

Just as they passed the guard stationed on the sixth floor, there was a commotion ahead of them, out of sight.

The pirate glanced round. 'Keep going,' he growled.

Scoop bit her lip. It had all been going too well. Something was bound to go to go wrong, she was sure of it. She knew their luck couldn't last.

As they rounded a bend and saw who was ahead, she lost her footing and almost fell. Emerging from the doorway on the seventh floor was Arnwolf Falcon.

Arnwolf? Scoop thought, panicking. *Couldn't it have been anyone but Arnwolf? What's he doing here? He'll recognise us. He's bound to.* She paused for a moment to steady herself.

Ahead, the pirate kept climbing. Fletcher had seen who it was too. Scoop watched his body stiffen. But he continued as if nothing was wrong.

I have to carry on. There's no other option. Scoop willed her feet to keep moving. Somehow they did.

Arnwolf wasn't alone. There was a girl with him. He was gripping her arm.

He's hurting her, Scoop thought.

The girl, who was obviously a patient, was facing away from

them, her face hidden. She seemed to be following Arnwolf obediently.

'Come on,' he was saying, 'we have to get out of here. If they see what you've done...' He turned towards Fletcher and Scoop and stopped speaking.

That's it. We're done for, Scoop thought. Arnwolf looked directly at her. But Scoop didn't see recognition in his eyes, only...

Fear, she thought. *He's frightened about something.*

Clearly frustrated, Arnwolf turned away and began to drag the girl up the stairs.

'Quickly,' Scoop heard him say, 'we have to get out of here – now!'

'I live to serve Mr Falk,' the girl replied. 'Mr Falk and you.'

I recognise that voice, Scoop thought.

And then, just for an instant, the girl turned and Scoop caught a glimpse of her face.

'Rufina!' she said aloud.

Not hearing her, Arnwolf continued to climb. He reached the eighth floor door and, barging past the guard, disappeared inside, dragging Rufina after him. The door slammed shut. A few moments later, the pirate, Fletcher and Scoop passed it.

Scoop's mind was racing. That was Rufina. But somehow she looked different.

She was awake though, healed. That was good news, surely.

I live to serve Mr Falk, the words repeated in her mind. What had happened? Had Rufina switched sides? Had she betrayed them?

No! She fought the idea. Rufina was the most loyal, the most courageous ally of the Storyteller she knew. Rufina was her hero.

But I heard it with my own ears. I live to serve Mr Falk. Mr Falk and you.

As soon as they were out of sight of the eighth floor guard, she stopped. 'Wait!' she hissed.

Fletcher turned to look at her.

'What are you doing?' the pirate said.

'We have to go back.'

'Back? What are you talking about? Come on!' He stepped up another couple of stairs.

'No,' Scoop hissed. 'I'm not going!'

The pirate's face flushed with anger. 'If we don't go now, we will be caught – the mission will be over, the Storyteller will not be rescued, you will not get to the Threshold and hundreds of people on this island will be trapped in a sleep from which they cannot be woken.'

Scoop stared at him. This was worse than being discovered, worse than being captured. She couldn't leave her friend behind, could she? She looked at Fletcher.

'He's right,' he said. 'We have to keep going. If we try to go back, we won't help Rufina. She's with Arnwolf. He would sound the alarm, and we won't succeed in rescuing the Storyteller either – or Mother. We'd fail at everything. We have to go on. It's the only choice.'

Scoop looked back. There was ashy smoke spilling from the window of the room that Rufina had disappeared into. A bit of grit blew into her eye, making it water.

'We have to trust,' Fletcher said. 'We have to trust that if we rescue the Storyteller, things will work out. Rufina will be all right. She's a fighter.'

'But did you see her? Did you hear what she said?'

Fletcher looked at her. What could he say? He had heard. He had felt it too, the stab of betrayal. There were no easy answers here. All he knew was that they had to press on.

'Come on,' he whispered. 'We're nearly there.'

Scoop took one more look back and then nodded. 'Okay,' she said. And with that, the three of them continued their ascent of the Scythe.

* * *

Alfa was looking out of the window of the Yarnbard's office. Next to her, stood the contraption that she and Sparks had carried up the tower, which was now constructed. It was a crossbow mounted on a tripod. Loaded into the crossbow was a silver arrow with a grappling hook on the end. A coil of wire attached to the arrow waited on the floor beside it, the other end fastened to the solid circular table in the centre of the room. Sparks was looking through a small black tube, mounted on the crossbow. The cross in the telescopic sight was perfectly lined up with the window in the top chamber of the Scythe.

'You're sure it's set up right,' she said.

'As sure as I can be,' Alfa replied. 'We used these in our castle-scaling sessions during Overcoming the Monster lessons. Don't you remember?'

'Yes,' Sparks said, thinking that she hadn't realised at the time she'd be using one in a real adventure quite so soon.

'That's it!' Alfa suddenly said. She sounded excited. 'Come and look. It's the signal.'

Sparks moved around the crossbow and peered out of the window.

There was a bright flash of light.

It came from the staircase of the Scythe just below the ninth floor doorway.

'That's them, isn't it?' Alfa said.

'I think so,' Sparks replied. She was long past the feeling of sickness. She just felt numb now. This was happening. There was no way out. She had to play her part.

'Right then,' Alfa said. 'Move out of the way.'

Sparks stepped back. Crouching, she picked up two short lengths of rope with handles on either end. There was a pulley wheel in the centre of each.

'Two flashes in quick succession. That's our signal to go.

There isn't much time, remember.'

'I know – just the time it takes to change the guard.'

'Exactly.' She looked at her friend, nervously. 'Ready?'

'As I'll ever be.'

Just as she said it, there were two quick flashes of light from the Scythe.

Alfa took a deep breath. 'Three, two, one...' She fired the crossbow.

ZIP!

The arrow shot out, the coil of wire unwinding with a whizz. Both girls ran to the window.

'Yes!' Alfa said, punching the air. The arrow had hit its target – a wrought iron bar at the top of the chamber window in the Scythe. Alfa pulled the cable back and felt the hook catch. She tugged it.

'Feels good to me,' she said, tying off the excess cable. 'We have to go. We have to be there when the guard comes in.'

Sparks nodded, handing Alfa one of the short ropes.

Alfa fastened the pulley wheel to the wire, pulled herself up onto the window ledge and jumped. She shot away into the darkness.

There was no time to think. Sparks fastened her pulley wheel to the wire, stepped up to the ledge, and then...

The tower fell away. Sparks was flying. She felt as if she were walking on air.

The wheel whirred as the zip-wire carried her towards the Scythe. It looked beautiful, its torches flickering in the night. Her arms hurt, but she held on tight.

Ahead, Alfa lifted her legs and then, reaching the tower, she let go of the handles and jumped through the window.

Before she knew it, Sparks was lifting her legs too. And...

Jump!

She let go of the handles and flew into the chamber. Tumbling to the floor, she scrambled to her feet. 'We did it!' she said.

'Shh!' Alfa raised her finger to her lips. She was already to the side of the door, pressed back against the wall.

There was talking outside.

And then, the handle began to turn.

Sparks sprang across the room, pushing herself against the rock next to Alfa.

The door opened, concealing them behind it. A Red Hawk soldier entered. Closing the door behind him, he locked it.

Before he had turned round, the two girls set upon him. He was totally unprepared.

Alfa sprang up, wrapping her arms around his neck. Before he could cry out, she pressed a fabric rag over his mouth and nose. At the same time, Sparks ran headlong into his legs. They buckled and the soldier fell to his knees.

Alfa held the rag in place. The soldier struggled, but the fabric had been doused in Chapter Break Fluid. Before he knew what was happening, the room began to spin. He tried to lash out, to shake the little scoundrel from his shoulders, but his muscles had turned to jelly. They wouldn't respond.

The Red Hawk teetered on his knees and then fell forward.

Alfa held the cloth over his mouth a moment longer and then she released it. The soldier lay awkwardly on the ground, his eyes staring up, wide with shock. He was out cold.

'Quick, let's move him,' Alfa whispered. Together, they grabbed his coat and began to drag him across the floor. He was heavy, but Alfa and Sparks were determined. Before long, he lay behind the door, sprawled at the side of the room.

Alfa stood up, panting. 'We did it.' She grinned.

Sparks grinned back. She never thought she'd be able to do anything like that. It made her feel somehow bigger, more confident.

They stepped away, and for the first time, the two girls looked around the room. It was bare, apart from the guard's chair and two beds, pushed against the rock wall. On the beds, pale and still, were two bodies. It was the Storyteller and his princess.

'Wow, it's them,' Sparks whispered, taking in the scale of what she was involved with.

'Yes,' Alfa said.

They both stared at the bodies for a moment. These two people held the keys to their world. They created it. And yet here they were, looking so fragile, so weak. With a wave of realisation, Sparks became aware of the power she had in that place. It was an awesome feeling, and yet at the same time she felt unprepared for it. She felt unworthy.

'Come on,' Alfa whispered, turning away. 'We need to deal with the next guard – the one outside.'

Sparks nodded.

'Same again?'

'Yes. It worked that time. Let's keep in simple.'

'My thoughts exactly.'

Sparks took her position behind the door. She looked down at the Red Hawk they had knocked out. He stared at her, his face fixed with shock.

'Sorry,' she whispered.

Alfa had moved to the door. Slowly, quietly, she turned the key. The lock clicked. Then, turning the handle, she pulled the door ajar.

Joining Sparks against the wall, they waited. She could hear her own breathing, it sounded so loud, too loud. She tried to quieten it. Her skin was prickling. It wouldn't be long before the guard noticed the door was open and realised something was wrong. And then...

'Hello.' She heard a voice from outside. 'Aldrich?'

Alfa and Sparks looked at each other.

A hand appeared around the door. It creaked open. A shiny black shoe stepped into the room. The Red Hawk appeared, his coat pristine, his buttons shining. He looked around, wondering what was happening.

As he saw the girls, they jumped at him.

He stumbled back, bemused,

One of them leapt up. Before he knew it, her arms were around his neck.

He struggled, but she pushed a rag into his mouth. It tasted sweet and acrid.

The second girl barged into his legs.

Ouch! He fell to his knees.

What on earth...

The room was spinning.

Behind the door, he caught sight of Aldrich, slumped on the floor, his face frozen with surprise.

Taken out by two girls, the soldier thought as his face hit the ground. *I'll never live this down.*

* * *

Alfa and Sparks waited, their hair sticking to their faces, their hands sweaty and shaking. After dragging the second soldier across the floor, they locked the door again. Now their adrenalin levels were dropping, tiredness was beginning to kick in. They'd just zip-wired across a forty foot gap with a fatal drop below them and taken out two fully grown, fully armed soldiers. The reality of the situation was hitting them hard.

Must stay focused, Alfa said to herself. *We're not out of this yet.*

There was a tap at the door.

Rat-a-tat... Rat-a-tat...

The girls froze and looked at each other. They waited. They had agreed a secret pattern with the pirate. If it was them, it would be repeated.

Rat-a-tat...Rat-a-tat... The knock came again,

'It's them,' Alfa said. Rushing to the door, she unlocked it. Fletcher and Scoop pushed their way in, the pirate following. Scoop looked at Alfa and Sparks with a mix of anxiety and sheer relief. As the pirate locked the door, she ran to them and scooped them up in a huge hug.

'You did it!' she said. 'You did it, girls! That's amazing. I can't believe we're all here!'

'Neither can we,' Sparks said, her pent-up energy dissolving into a fit of giggles. Alfa and Scoop joined her. Together, the three girls laughed until their faces turned red.

Fletcher looked at the two Red Hawks lying in a heap behind the door. Even he had to admit the Apprentice Spell-Shakers had exceeded expectations.

Meanwhile, the pirate was busying himself. He laid two large, black body bags on the floor and unzipped them, folding back their covers.

He turned to the Storyteller and princess. 'Help me with them,' he said to Fletcher.

Fletcher headed across to the beds. He looked down at his mother's face. She was ghostly pale. It was strange to see her in such a deep sleep, to see her so vulnerable. He leaned down and kissed her gently on the forehead.

'We're going to get you out of here,' he whispered. 'It's going to be okay.'

The pirate moved to the foot of the bed. 'You take her arms, I'll take her legs,' he said.

Fletcher stepped back and slipped his arms under his mother's shoulders.

The pirate took hold of her feet. 'One...two...three...' They lifted the princess off the bed. She was light. It didn't take much effort to move her to the body bag.

Fletcher watched as the pirate folded the cover over her face and she disappeared.

It was harder to move the Storyteller. Fletcher had to ask for Scoop's help. But before long, he too had been lifted from the bed and placed into a body bag.

Once they had zipped up both bags and secured the bodies,

the pirate moved to the window. The zip-wire still stretched out towards the Needle. He pulled a thin coil of rope from his belt and threaded the end through the bottom of a double pulley wheel. Reaching up, the pirate fixed the top wheel to the zip wire, the rope hanging down from it. He slid it along the wire to check that it moved freely. When he was satisfied, he took the end of the rope, threaded it through a loop on one of the body bags and then tied it to the second.

'Give me a hand with this,' he said, taking the other end of the rope, which ran up to the zip-wire.

It's a crane, Scoop thought.

The pirate began to pull. Fletcher and Scoop ran to help him. Together, they hoisted the bags up towards the zip wire, Alfa and Sparks guiding the bodies as they left the floor, making sure they didn't bump into the rock by the window. When they had finished hoisting, the body bags hung, framed in the opening. Alfa and Sparks moved to help hold the rope.

'Have you got the weight?' the pirate asked.

The four apprentices nodded.

Letting go of the rope, the pirate pulled a metal stick from his belt. He tugged the end and it began to extend.

'Telescopic,' he said to Sparks, who was watching with her mouth open. 'Here, hold this,' He handed her the end of the stick. She took it, one hand still holding the rope. Slowly, the pirate extended the stick towards the window, until it was a metal pole that stretched across the room. Then he took a forked piece of metal from his pocket and attached it to the end. Lifting the pole to the zip wire, he positioned the fork so that the pulley wheel slotted into it.

'Ready?' he asked.

'Ready,' each of the apprentices replied.

Using the pole, the pirate began to push the pulley wheel out along the zip-wire. It was hard work, the bodies were heavy and the pirate huffed and strained as he pushed them out and up towards the Needle. But slowly, the body bags moved away from the Scythe. They hung, swinging from the rope, suspended from the zip-wire. Fletcher, Scoop, Alfa and Sparks allowed the rope to feed through their hands as the Storyteller and princess moved out into the darkness between the two towers.

Gradually, the bags disappeared into the night. When they were far enough away from the Scythe to be camouflaged against the dark rock of the Needle, the pirate stopped pushing.

'Okay,' he said. 'Now we lower them.'

Steadily, smoothly, the apprentices, now with the help of the pirate, began to release the rope. It reminded Scoop of lowering the sails on the Firebird, building a rhythm, acting as one. The rope ran along the zip wire and slid through the pulley, extending downwards. The Storyteller and princess descended into the darkness. The apprentices worked together, aware of the value of the treasure they held. One wrong move, one slip, and the Storyteller and princess would plummet down to the ground and it would be over.

Slowly does it, Scoop thought, moving her hands to release more rope through the window. *Steady and sure.*

They continued to lower the bodies for what seemed like an age, all the time alert, sensing each movement, each sway, each jerk of the rope, until finally, it began to slacken.

They stopped moving.

'I think we're there,' Fletcher said.

'Yes.'

They could feel the rope moving below as Nib received the bodies. He had positioned his cart directly below, close to the Needle, hidden from the view of the guards at the bottom of the Scythe and the snipers, who looked out across the island, rather into the gap between the Three Towers.

There was a tug on the rope to signal that the bodies had been untied, and quickly, pulling in time, they hauled it back up. It was weightless now and, freed from its cargo, they had soon hoisted it back up to the zip-wire. They left it there, the other end of the rope in a heap on the floor in the room where they all stood. Then, Fletcher and Scoop both pulled folded white coats and masks from their pockets. They handed them to Alfa and Sparks, who shook them out and put them on. Scoop, Fletcher and the pirate pulled up their masks, which had been around their necks.

'Right,' the pirate said. 'We can't go altogether. Scoop and Sparks, you go first. After a few minutes, Alfa and Fletcher will go and then I'll bring up the rear. Remember, don't run – a steady, moderate pace. Off you go.'

Scoop and Sparks took a deep breath and left the top chamber of the Scythe, beginning their decent along the stairs.

At the bottom of the Scythe, Nib had finished laying the Storyteller and Princess out in the back of the cart. He covered the body bags with the hessian cloth, climbed onto the front of the cart and gave the reigns a shake. The wheels creaked and the cart set off towards the pickup point, where he would meet the others.

* * *

Grizelda had just left Victor's office on the second floor of the Scythe. The old woman was fuming.

'You said you'd sort it, Victor. You said you had it in hand!' She walked up the steps two at a time.

'I did, Mother. The boy hasn't turned up yet, but he may still...'

'He won't come now! It's too late. You're a fool, Victor. Something's wrong, I can feel it.'

They passed two nurses coming down the stairs. One was very small to be a nurse, but Grizelda was too furious to pay attention to anything apart from her anger.

'We need to get up there and check on that meddling fool and his priggish strumpet.'

Victor panted as he followed her. 'The door is locked from the inside, Mother. There are two guards, one inside the room, one outside. There's only one way up the tower, past four snipers and thirteen fully trained, armed Red Hawks. I think we can be fairly confident they are not going anywhere.'

'You are a moron, Victor – a monstrous hulking dullard. Your complacency makes me sick! Fairly confident? Fairly confident? If they've gone, I'll have you strung up by your feet and have my crows peck out your eyes while I laugh.'

'Do you have to be so...' Victor searched for the word, '...so rude, Mother? So, quite frankly, unpleasant?'

Another two nurses passed, making their way down the tower at quite a pace.

Grizelda stopped outside the sixth floor door. She turned to Victor, pointing a scrawny finger into his face. 'Unpleasant? Unpleasant? Do you want to rule this island or not? Do you want to be the greatest king the Oceans of Rhyme has ever seen? Because at the moment you sound like a scrawny, snivelling little maggot!' she spat the last word.

'I do, Mother, you know I do.'

'Then man up!' She poked him in the shoulder. 'You don't know these people like I do. You haven't had to deal with them year after year after year. They are...' her face turned red. 'They are...'

'Breathe, Mother. You'll do yourself an injury.'

'Argh!' the old woman screamed in frustration. 'Come on, we need to get up there and check on them.'

Turning, she continued up the stairs, pushing past a lone nurse, who nodded at her.

* * *

Nib helped Scoop and Sparks to climb onto the back of the cart.

'She knows,' Scoop said, breathlessly, 'Grizelda knows there's something wrong. We haven't much time. We have to get out of here.'

Nib looked back towards the Scythe. 'I can see Fletcher and Alfa. They're on their way. Get under the cloth.'

Scoop ducked under, joining Sparks.

* * *

As soon as they'd passed the four guards at the bottom of the steps, Fletcher and Alfa broke into a run.

Alfa was white. 'Did you see her face? She's livid. I hate to think what will happen if she catches us.'

'Then don't think about it,' Fletcher said, panting, 'because it's not going to happen.'

Nib patted Fletcher on the back as he jumped onto the cart. 'Almost there,' he said. 'Went like clockwork.'

Just as Fletcher ducked under the cover, a distant cry punctuated the air. Grizelda had reached the top of the Scythe. The cry came from above. It seemed to echo unnaturally along the village streets. It was rasping and guttural. It was dangerous. As it sounded, a sheet of black rose from Bardbridge, as thousands upon thousands of crows leapt from rooftops and took to the sky. Their cawing and crying joined the scream, until the whole village rang with the discordant, raucous din. The alarm had been sounded. The crows amassed around the Scythe in a dark, circling cloud. Red Hawks spilled from the side streets, running and shouting towards the Three Towers.

A figure pelted towards the cart. 'Let's get out of here,' the pirate yelled. Nib flicked the reigns and the horse lurched forward, pulling the cart away, as the pirate jumped onto the back.

From the top of the Scythe, Grizelda bawled, 'They've gone! Find them! Find them! Find them!'

Chapter 31

The Search

Starlight brushed the side of Mr Snooze's cheek, making his face look like a new moon. He shivered. He'd been standing on the forecastle deck, at the prow of the ship, watching the coastline since the apprentices and the pirate had left. The night was now in its third quarter, and the head of the Department of Dreams was worried. He'd been expecting their return since midnight. He scanned the cliffs again, his eyes moving slowly along the rocks; rocks that guarded an island that was now under threat from within its own borders.

Suddenly, along the cliff, there was a distant flash of a light.

Mr Snooze paused, blinking.

What was that?

He peered into the darkness.

Had he imagined it?

The light flashed again, just for an instant, a faint twinkle in the mist. Then it disappeared. No, he wasn't seeing things. This was it – the signal.

He lifted an iron storm-lantern with a long spout. There was a shutter over the end of it. Pointing the lantern towards the glimmer, he opened the shutter. A thin beam of light reached through the misty air, signalling the way to the ship.

In the light, a small boat came into view. It rose and plunged on the black waves. Mr Snooze thought he could see Knot straining at the oars, and silhouetted, standing on the bow, was the pirate.

It's them, Mr Snooze thought.

He closed the shutter again and the boat disappeared into darkness.

* * *

From above, Grizelda could see the fire torches of the Red Hawk soldiers spreading through the village. They looked like a swarm of fireflies in the night. She imagined picking them off, one by one, squashing them between her thumb and finger. The sound of bloodhounds rose like the cries of a hellish choir. The lights of the cottages below slowly flickered to life, in a pattern fanning out from the tower.

Victor had descended the Scythe to take charge of the hunt on the ground, but Grizelda had chosen to stay at the top. It was easier to think there, and she trusted her own intellect, her own intuition, more than all the soldiers in the world.

Suddenly, a crack echoed upwards, reverberating through the village like thunder. For a split second, the hounds fell still.

Gunfire, Grizelda thought. She peered down to see if she could make out where the sound came from, but the noise had sent her crows spiralling around the Scythe, blocking her view. From the ground, the tower looked like a volcano about to erupt.

Muttering, she turned back to the chamber. She studied the rope on the floor and the zip-wire running out from the window.

Clever, she thought, *very clever.*

Out of the corner of her eye, she noticed one of the incapacitated guards move his foot. He was still lying in a heap with his comrade behind the door. Anger suddenly surged through the old woman. She ran across the room and landed a kick square on the jaw of the waking guard. He groaned and slumped back.

'That'll teach you to fail me,' she spat.

Reaching down, she rummaged through his jacket pocket and pulled out a pair of binoculars.

'They know about the Threshold,' she said to herself, repeating what Victor had told her earlier. 'They've been told they need to cross it to cure the sickness.' She walked to the eastern most window and looked out. Her crows had settled again and she had a clear view.

Only one place they're heading, she thought, *and that's out there.* She scanned the ribbon of black between the island and the dim horizon. It looked as if the world fell away into nothing.

The sea, she thought, *that's where we'll find 'em, not in the village. They'll be preparing to sail for Skull Rock – to the Threshold.*

Suddenly, she stopped. Out in the black, there was a brief flash of light, no bigger than a pin prick.

She paused, holding the binoculars still.

*Come on, come on…*she willed the light to flash again.

Yes, there it came.

She lowered the binoculars. *Got ya!* she thought, with a smile.

* * *

Victor strode through the village. All around him was the baying of bloodhounds, the thumping of doors and the shouts of soldiers summoning villagers. He walked past a lady in curlers and a nightgown, who was screeching at a Red Hawk.

'All houses have to be searched, ma'am,' the soldier was saying. 'We're just following orders.'

'I don't care what you're following,' the woman yelled back. 'This is my house and you've got no right to come in!'

A large dog growled at her, straining on its lead, trying to push its nose past her. In the end, the Red Hawk shoved her to the side and barged past. He shut the door, locking her out. She was left banging on her own front door, red with rage.

Sounds of houses being ransacked, furniture being scraped across floors, and plates and pots being smashed, echoed through Bardbridge.

Victor was being led by a Red Hawk sergeant with a purposeful stride. 'Almost there, sir,' he said over his shoulder.

Good, Victor thought, *we need to find these traitors quickly or there won't be a village left for me to rule.*

Crossing the bridge, they drew up in front of a high, wooden fence. Its large gates stood open. Victor could see a courtyard inside, surrounded by a number of outbuildings. As he entered, he noticed that part of the gate had been destroyed by gunfire.

The sergeant nodded at the shattered wood. 'That's when we realised there was something here worth finding.'

He led Falk through the courtyard to one of the outbuildings. Inside, a large, muscular man, wearing a dirty leather apron, had been tied to a chair, his mouth gagged. The building seemed to be some sort of armoury, with swords, helmets and shields lining the walls. Victor scanned the room, taking it in.

In the centre of the floor was an open trap door. Victor peered into it. A ladder led down into the darkness.

'We found these next to the hatch,' a soldier said, handing over five discarded white coats and masks.

'Good work, sergeant,' Falk said.

He crossed to the man who was tied to the chair and pulled off his gag. 'Where does this tunnel lead?'

The man craned his neck as if he was going to speak. Victor leaned down to listen, but as he did, the man pushed his head upwards. He spat, sending a great gob of phlegm flying through the air. It landed on Victor's cheek.

Turning, Victor wiped it away.

Behind him, he heard a groan, as the sergeant struck the man with the butt of his musket.

Victor turned back. 'Now, we can do this the easy way or the hard way. But rest assured, we will find out where this tunnel leads.'

'Don't waste yer time on this scum,' a voice said. 'I already know where it leads.'

Victor turned round to see Grizelda framed in the doorway.

'Hello, Mother,' he said.

She glared at him and then wandered over to the man tied to the chair. 'Lovely to see you, Cadmus,' she said, nodding at him.

She lowered her face to his. He pushed away, turning his head. 'Hoping to keep yer little friends safe were yer? Well, I'm sorry to disappoint you, old friend, but I know where they are. I've seen the ship.' Cadmus looked back, fear in his eyes. 'Ah yes,' she laughed, 'I know exactly where they are and where they're going. That's nice, ain't it? And right now, a whole fleet of Red Hawks are being dispatched to meet 'em. In a couple of hours we'll have 'em back here, where we can look after 'em.' She looked up at Victor. 'We'd better be going,' she spat. 'Don't want to miss all the fun now, do we?' Turning to Cadmus, she patted him on the cheek. 'See yer later now. Keep safe, won't yer?' She winked at him.

As they left the armoury, she said to the sergeant, 'Keep him tied up, lock him in and leave him in the darkness. Give him time to imagine his little friends being captured, eh?'

'Yes, ma'am,' the solder said, as he closed the door.

* * *

Rufina was watching Arnwolf. He was speaking to one of the soldiers from his squadron.

'Put this man on the wagon,' he said, handing over a tall, broad-shouldered man with a hessian sack over his head. The man's hands were tied behind his back, but he made no struggle.

'Yes, sir,' the soldier replied. He led the man to the back of the wagon and, helping him climb up, sat him on a bench at the end of a row of Red Hawks.

'We will sit in the front,' Arnwolf said to Rufina.

Walking around the wagon, he allowed her to climb up first.

'Take us to the port,' he said to the driver, as he pulled himself up into the seat next to her. 'We're joining the fleet of Red Hawks in pursuit of the traitors.'

'Yes, sir,' the driver replied.

The engine started, and the vehicle rumbled away from the

Three Towers towards the Port of Beginnings and Endings, leaving a cloud of dust in its wake.

Chapter 32

Nemesis

The small boat rose and fell on the waves, as it drew close to the Black Horizon. The movement made Scoop nauseous. Alfa and Sparks, who had stopped talking, looked pale too. The ride out to the pirate's galleon had been choppy. Even Knot was looking a little green. The body bags with the Storyteller and princess in them, lay in the centre of the boat.

They drew alongside the ship. The boat looked tiny next to it. The Black Horizon was smaller than the Firebird, having only one mast, but Fletcher could tell it was fast.

And painted black, he thought. *Good for making an escape!*

A face appeared above them, looking down over the side of the ship.

'Boatswain?' Scoop said, surprised.

'Yes,' the pirate answered. 'I've taken on some of the Firebird's crew. They wanted to help, and there aren't any sailors on the Oceans of Rhyme I'd trust more.'

The boatswain grinned. 'Hello, maties,' he bellowed down.

Fletcher and Scoop waved up at him. It was comforting to see a familiar face. He disappeared for a moment and then reappeared with a ladder, which he unwound down the side of the ship.

Alfa and Sparks were the first to climb up to the galleon, with Fletcher and Scoop following. When all but the pirate were aboard, the boatswain lowered a rope. The pirate tied it to the body bags, and they carefully hoisted the Storyteller and princess onto the Black Horizon.

'Take them to the captain's quarters and make them comfortable,' the pirate said when he was aboard.

Knot picked up the bodies, one in each arm, and carried them carefully to the captain's cabin.

'Strictly speaking,' the pirate said, 'we don't have a captain on the Horizon. We are a crew of equals. But unless anyone has an objection, I will take a lead.'

The apprentices nodded.

'Good, then we need to begin the necessary preparations. We sail before dawn.'

Just as he finished speaking, there was a cry from the other side of the ship. Everyone looked round.

Mr Snooze appeared on the quarterdeck. He looked dishevelled, his eyes wild. He pointed out to sea. 'Look,' he stammered.

The crew of the Black Horizon rushed to the side of the deck and stared out. There on the dark waters, lit by fiery lanterns, was a fleet of longboats. There must have been thirty of them, twenty men on each, and they were coming towards them.

'Red Hawks,' Scoop cried, dismayed. 'They've found us!'

* * *

'What do we do?' Sparks said, fear in her voice. 'Can we sail? Can we outrun them?'

'There isn't time,' Fletcher answered. 'It will take an hour to make this ship ready to sail. They'll be here in ten minutes, less perhaps – there's twenty men rowing each boat.'

'There's only one option,' the boatswain said, grimly. 'We fight. There is no other way.'

'But there must be hundreds of them,' Sparks said. 'Thirty boats, that's…'

'Six hundred soldiers,' Fletcher whispered.

'And how many of us are there?'

'Twelve,' the boatswain answered. 'Fourteen, including the Storyteller and princess. We must arm ourselves,'

The pirate stepped forward. 'No. That is not the way. The Storyteller would not want us to lead a group of children into a battle that will surely bring about their deaths.'

'Then what?' the boatswain asked.

The pirate paused. 'We hoist the white flag.'

'Surrender?' The boatswain sounded horrified.

The pirate turned to him. 'Many years ago I abandoned the land, gave up all its certainty and placed myself into the hands of the sea. It is a way of life I have committed to, and it has never failed me. Dark Pirates know the truth – we are powerless against the elements, and many of the rocks we cling to for protection, are illusions. Once you give yourself to that truth, you are free. And when you are free, the story can turn in surprising directions. We cannot protect ourselves against this assault, but that does not mean we will not *be* protected.' He pointed towards the captain's quarters. 'Although the man in there is asleep, although it feels as if we are abandoned, he is our Storyteller – our captain. I believe this would be his way – to harness the elements and not to fight them – and I choose to trust it. We will surrender. Hoist the flag.'

* * *

'Lay your weapons down,' the sergeant of the Red Hawks called to the crew of the Black Horizon. Victor Falk's army had by now surrounded the ship. His boats fanned out around it in a perfect circle, their lanterns blazing, casting pools of light onto the inky water. The sergeant stood on the prow of one of the boats to port of the galleon.

'Lay your weapons down,' he shouted again. 'Put them on the forecastle, and retreat to the main deck.'

The pirate, the boatswain and two of the other sailors climbed up to the forecastle. One by one they lifted up their swords and pistols, showing their arms, before lowering them to the deck. Stepping away from the small pile of weapons, they climbed back down to the main deck.

'Put your hands in the air,' the sergeant shouted.

The little crew stood in a huddle just in front of the mast. They raised their hands.

From different points around the galleon, ropes appeared, thrown up from the boats below. Six soldiers emerged, climbing quickly onto the deck. Without pausing, they turned and lowered ladders down the side of the ship. Then, the Red Hawk army began to board the Black Horizon. They spilled over its sides, climbing onto the deck, circling the pirate and apprentices, their muskets raised. As the last of them took ship, the sound of boots pounding the deck quietened.

Fletcher and Scoop stared out at the sea of Red Hawks, the barrels of their muskets only feet from their faces, a hundred dark eyes boring into them. Fletcher was conscious of the weight of his arms, raised above his head, exposing his sides. Never before had he had the sense of absolute defeat that now filled him. It was over.

In front of him, the soldiers parted, creating a corridor through the Red Hawk circle. At the end of the corridor stood Grizelda and Victor Falk. A grin flicked across the old woman's face as she saw her captives. The two of them, mother and son, walked forward, toward the Black Horizon's crew. They stopped in front of them.

'Well, well, well,' Grizelda purred. 'What have we here, then? A little band of rebels. Is this the best you could do?' She spat on the floor in front of them. 'Pathetic.'

'You,' she pointed at the pirate, 'on yer knees.' Slowly, the pirate did as he was told. He knelt just behind the gob of spit.

Grizelda waved at one of the Red Hawks. 'Go and get his pistol from up there.' The soldier obeyed, climbing up to the forecastle and returning with the pirate's weapon. Grizelda grabbed it from him and sauntered over to where the pirate knelt. 'They say Dark Pirates aren't afraid of death, that you've already given yerselves over to it – that yer fearless. Well, let's just see how true that is.' She paused. 'Put yer hands behind yer head.' The pirate did as instructed, his face inscrutable. Grizelda stepped forward. She cocked the flint of the pistol.

Click!

'No,' Scoop shouted. 'Leave him alone!' Grizelda whirled round, swinging the pistol towards her. 'Shut it, or you'll be next, little Miss perfect.'

'Leave it,' Fletcher whispered.

'You should listen to that little runt of a brother of yours! Now, where was I? Ah, yeah…' She turned back to the pirate and wandered behind him. She raised the pistol to his head, her finger on the trigger.

'Say goodbye,' she said.

'STOP!' There was a cry, behind her.

The voice was strong and clear. Some of the soldiers looked round, a few of them swinging their weapons to change aim. Grizelda turned. Standing on the quarterdeck, overlooking the circle of Red Hawks and the crew of the Black Horizon, was Rufina. She stood proud, her hair blowing in the wind. To one side of her, stood a tall, broad-shouldered man. His face was covered with a hessian sack. Rufina was holding his arm. To the other side of her, Arnwolf waited passively, his eyes blank, staring straight ahead.

'Rufina?' Nib blurted. 'How…?'

'Arnwolf?' Victor called, surprised. The boy didn't reply.

Grizelda let out a cry, half-yelping, half-screaming. She stamped her foot and then, as if trying to crack the deck, stamped again. 'Argh!' Phlegm gurgled in her throat as she pushed the noise from her lungs. 'Why?' She shook a clenched fist at the sky. 'Why? Why? Why! Why do I always have to put up with these do-gooders, with these bothersome, stinking, self-proclaimed heroes?' She pointed at Rufina. 'I thought I'd seen the last of you. Why can't you just stay out of the way – just for once? Why do you have to keep poking your nose in where it's not wanted?'

'The Storyteller and his princess breathed life into this island, Grizelda. There are things written into its story that you can't simply stamp out in a few short weeks. But, I'm not here to see you, old woman,' Rufina called down. 'I'm here to see Mr Falk.'

'I don't care who you're here to see,' Grizelda bawled. She lifted the pistol, aiming it at Rufina. 'I'm going to blow yer bleedin' brains out, yer meddlin' little...'

'No!' Nib shouted.

It was as if the world suddenly slowed. He watched the old woman's finger pull back on the trigger, releasing the hammer. 'No!'

CRACK!

The sound shook the galleon. Fletcher felt it vibrate through his body.

Scoop screamed and ran forward.

Red Hawks grabbed her and Nib, pulling them back.

Scoop spun round, looking up to where Rufina had been standing, her heart thumping. She fell backwards, collapsing into the arms of the Red Hawk who held her.

Rufina still stood on the quarterdeck, her eyes like fire, staring down at the scene below. She was unharmed. She glared down at Grizelda.

Victor, who was next to the old woman, was holding her arm in the air. He'd grabbed it, sending the bullet upwards, to where it had lodged itself in the mast.

'What are you doing, you cretin?' Grizelda yelled, pulling her arm from his grip. Turning on him, she struck him with the gun.

Victor ignored her. He had been focused on the disguised figure that stood next to Rufina. There was a power that drew Victor to him. He could feel the space between them. The ship became a blur, fading into the background. He was spellbound. Whoever the figure was, he needed to see him. And whatever it was that Rufina wanted to say, he wanted – no needed – to hear it.

In the background, he could hear the old woman yelling at him, but he didn't care. The figure on the deck above pushed everything else from his mind.

Grizelda hit him again. Not taking his eyes from the disguised figure, he reached down and wrapped his arms around the old woman, restraining her. 'I want to hear what Miss Reed has to say,' he said quietly. 'Take my mother away,' he commanded two of the Red Hawk soldiers. 'Take her down to one of the boats.'

They looked hesitant.

'Do it,' Victor growled.

Nervously, they grabbed the old woman, one taking each arm. Victor released her.

'What are you doing?' she railed, as they dragged her across the deck. 'Victor, don't do this! Victor, I'm yer mother. Victor, we're nearly there. We're nearly the rulers of this stinkin' island.' She wriggled and kicked, but the soldiers held her tight, half-dragging her, half-lifting her to the side of the ship. 'You'll regret this,' she yelled at them. 'I'll have yer tongues cut out. I'll have yer feet cast in iron. I'll have yer children boiled alive! Let me go! Let me go!' But they held firm. Just as she was disappearing over the side of the ship, down one of the ladders, she looked at Falk. Fletcher had never seen such a look of malice. 'You've failed me, you have,' she hissed. 'You're no son of mine. You're a weak-willed disappointment and you'll get yer comeuppance.' And then, dragged down by the guards, she disappeared, her cries still echoing from the boat below.

Victor turned to Rufina. 'Well?' he said. 'Let's hear what you have to say for yourself, Miss Reed.'

'I don't want to *say* anything, Mr Falk,' Rufina shouted down, her voice cutting through the night. 'I want to show you something.'

Before Victor had a chance to reply, she turned to the man

next to her and pulled the hessian sack from his head.

As those aboard the Black Horizon saw the face that had been hidden by the sack, chaos broke out. Red Hawks dropped their muskets, stepping back, their tight formation degenerating. They tripped over one another's feet, pointing up at the man on the quarterdeck, a cloud of mutterings and exclamations rising into the night.

Victor Falk stepped forward. He stared, open-mouthed at the man who Rufina had just revealed.

Standing on the deck above him, the man stared back.

He stared with Victor's face.

He stood with Victor's body.

He was Victor.

'Doubles,' Rufina said. The crowd fell still. 'They've been creating doubles. That's what's been happening in the Scythe. They haven't been healing people from the sickness at all. They're all still there, still locked away, asleep. The Scythe has become a factory for creating doppelgangers. They're stealing the stories of the sick – taking their Life Draughts and altering them – "editing" they call it. They are removing the souls of their patients – the parts of them that question, the parts of them that might challenge their rule, the parts of them that dream, that love, that hope – gone, cut out. They are like surgeons cutting out hearts, cutting away minds. And then, to these anaemic Life Draughts, they add some of Falk's own blood. This diluted half-person, this monstrous concoction, is then thrown into a pool. You have all seen the smoke issuing from the Scythe. Well, that smoke rises from the pool into which the doctored Life Draughts are thrown. It is a pool of lava. And from this lava, the doppelgangers are born. To the eye, they are alike in every way to the ones from whom they have been extracted. But the real person is still locked away inside that death factory, still asleep.'

As Rufina spoke, Scoop remembered that she had glimpsed Mr Bumbler's body, still lying asleep in the Scythe.

It was his double that was released, she realised. *That's why everyone Falk has healed looks blank – it's not really them at all!*

Rufina's voice was clear in the night. 'Look, here's one I made myself.' She pointed at Arnwolf. He didn't respond. 'That's right, this isn't really Arnwolf at all. It might look like him, but the real Arnwolf Falcon is back at the Scythe. This is a fake apprentice.'

The Red Hawk soldiers glanced at one another, unsure of what to do, unable to act.

Rufina continued, 'Like all the people you have seen "healed", he can walk, he can speak, he can even follow orders, but to all intents and purposes, *he is dead.*' She paused and looked directly at Victor. 'Mr Falk, I stole one of the vials of your blood from the lab at the Scythe, and look here at what I have created.' She pointed at the second Victor, 'This is *your* double, Mr Falk. Come and look at him. Come and stare into his eyes.'

Victor felt strange. He was attracted by the man who stood on the forecastle deck. He couldn't take his eyes from him. It was as if an invisible force was pulling him towards his double. But at the same time he was repelled. In a deep, guttural way, he feared him, he loathed him.

Slowly, he walked forward, not taking his eyes from the second Victor, his mirror image. He climbed the forecastle steps. The Red Hawks and the crew of the Black Horizon looked from one man to the other. Apart from the red cloak Victor wore, they were indistinguishable. The fiery lanterns flickered across their faces as Victor reached the top of the steps and turned to face his Nemesis.

Gradually, the two men walked towards each other. The way they moved was spellbinding, each holding the other's gaze. It was as if they were dancing – an intimate and dreadful dance. They circled one another, their feet sidestepping, their shoulders square, both locked into the same orbit, both pulled by the same magnetic force.

And then they stopped. They faced each other, only a sword's length between them.

Slowly, the two men began to raise their hands. They mirrored one another exactly. They reached forward, moving to touch each other's faces, hungry to feel the skin of their rival, extending their fingers, almost tenderly.

The entire crew of the Black Horizon, the mass of Red Hawks, all held their breath, caught in the moment.

Rufina gazed at the two men. This was the moment of truth. Had Arnwolf been right? Could Victor really only be destroyed by seeing his own face, by being confronted by what he really was? Her body was tense. This was what she'd worked towards since tracking down the Yarnbard the day after Victor had arrived at the Wild Guffaw. She'd known something was wrong from the presence of Mr Snip and Mr Splice in the village. Using the Yarn in the old man's office, she'd followed his trail to the meeting of the Guardians. She spied on them from the trees. And she was glad she had, for if she hadn't been there, Falk would now have the Yarnbard captive with the rest of the Guardians. She would never forget carrying the old man, bleeding and unconscious, to the safety of Tall Tale Tree Forest. And she would never give up on the commitment she'd made, then and there, to stop Falk. That commitment had led her to go undercover in the Scythe, to pretend to be sick. And it had kept her going in that foul place day upon day, as she was starved and manhandled. She needed to know exactly what Falk was up to. She *would* find a way to bring an end to his tyranny; she had to.

This moment was the culmination of her plan.

She watched, holding her breath, as the two Victors reached out to touch one another's faces.

As Victor touched the cheek of his double, he didn't know where he began and the man facing him, ended. It was as if they were one, as if they were inseparable.

Victor looked into Victor's eyes. And in that moment he knew the truth. He saw himself as he really was.

He knew.

All pretence was stripped away; all thought of ruling, of commanding armies, building his kingdom, acquiring honour, glory, wealth and power. In that moment, they all dissolved. They were nothing.

Victor saw who he was, and he knew his own emptiness.

The golden mask that had protected his face began to crack like lava. Clumps of ash fell to the ground, revealing charcoal skin below. And then, all at once, the mask crumbled, flaking to dust. Wisps of it blew away in the wind, leaving parts of the creature's face bare. Victor looked at his naked face, his real flesh. And then, as one, the two men began to sob. The sound was chilling and lonely, a thin, high whine. Victor saw it all, from his beginnings as a monster created from the lava pool with undead blood. He knew the story he had believed about himself was a lie. He was not who he thought he was. He had believed himself to be a respectable member of the Falcon Household. He had believed himself to be a man of standing. He had believed Grizelda was his mother. And although he was repelled by the old woman, part of him almost loved her. Now he saw the truth. He was not a son. He was not even a man. He was unnaturally born. Grizelda was not a mother – she had created him to do her bidding and gain power. She was the monster and he hated her. He hated her from the very core of his being.

Victor's shoulders began to shake. The sob grew, rising unstoppably from his guts, forcing itself upwards, becoming a howl that echoed across the waters, one with the wind.

Fletcher would never forget that howl. It was as if it rose from the earth itself. It was heartrending, and he knew it would live in his memory for the rest of his life.

* * *

On the other side of the Un-Crossable Boundary, Ms Speller

collapsed to the floor, the pen still clutched in her hands. She couldn't do it. She couldn't keep them at bay. She had tried to keep them away, tried to stay in control, but it was no good. Somewhere in the depths of her being it rose up, a voice calling, a voice she couldn't suppress or ignore.

She found herself singing.

They're coming on the clouds of night.
They're coming from the shadow's reach.
They're coming where the dream wind blows.
They're coming where the time sands shift.
The Sandman comes, the Sandman sings,
And sleep's the gift the Sandman brings.

She thought of Libby as she sang. And as she thought of Libby, emptiness welled up in her.

I've failed. I've failed you. You wouldn't want me back even if I wished to return.

She got up and, scrambling across the floor, flung open the window.

She threw the pen out with a cry. There was a splash as it hit the sea, and she pulled the window closed. Then, running across to her bed, she fell on it, threw the covers over her head and began to sob.

* * *

Scoop watched as the two Victors froze. They looked like statues.

Gradually, they began to change colour. Rock grey crept down their heads, slowly seeping through their bodies. They stood, two monuments, frozen in the moment.

Nobody on the ship moved. It was as if, just for that instant, the world held its breath.

And then, like a great bird sweeping down from the sky, a gust of wind blew through the rigging. It swirled down, rushing across the deck. Scoop watched as it caught the two bodies, flinging them upwards. They broke apart, turning into a swirling cloud of dust. The dust cloud rose, and then, as the wind changed, what once was Victor Falk disintegrated fully and was swept out to sea, the dust disappearing into the night.

The deck was left empty.

One by one, around Fletcher and Scoop, the Red Hawk doubles, those soldiers that Falk had engineered to grow his army, also began to dissolve. Like Falk, they turned to stone, becoming statues, and then, quietly, the wind swept them away. They rose in ashy clouds, blowing through the rocks they call Dead Man's Fingers. Across Fullstop Island, all of Falk's doubles, all who shared his blood, began to disintegrate, leaving fireside chairs and comfortable beds empty.

Seeing their comrades disappear around them, the soldiers who were left on the ship retreated, their faces pale, moving as men who had just seen an army of ghosts. They didn't speak. In turn, they climbed over the side of the Black Horizon and disappeared into their boats.

Left alone, the crew of the Black Horizon slowly lowered their arms. Dazed, they walked to the side of the ship and watched as the depleted Red Hawk army retreated, their lanterns disappearing into the night.

From behind them, there was a cry. Reacting without thinking, they crossed to the other side of the ship and looked out to see where it had come from. In the darkness, Grizelda's boat could just be made out among the Dead Man's Fingers. The Red Hawks that had been manning her vessel had disintegrated. Now, she drifted, alone.

'I'll get yer!' she cried. 'I'll have my victory, you'll see. This isn't over yet!'

Then, as they watched, the mist swallowed her, and she was gone.

The pirate picked up his pistol again. 'She's right,' he growled. 'This isn't over.' He glanced at the cabin where the

Storyteller and his princess still lay sleeping. 'We have a journey to make.'

As he spoke the words, the same image filled both Fletcher and Scoop's mind – stepping into the wide black cave. The future was upon them.

The pirate raised his voice. 'Prepare the Black Horizon. We head south.' He looked at Fletcher and Scoop. 'We may have won this particular battle, but we still have a war to win. We sail for the Threshold.'

From the Author

Thank you for purchasing The Nemesis Charm. I hope you enjoyed reading it as much as I enjoyed creating it.

If you have a few moments, please feel free to add your review of the book at your favourite online site for feedback (Amazon, Apple iTunes Store, Goodreads, etc.)

Also, if you would like to connect with other books I have coming in the near future, or catch me at an event, please visit my website for news www.danielingrambrown.co.uk, follow me on Twitter @daningrambrown or like my Facebook page www.facebook.com/danielingrambrown

Thanks!

Daniel Ingram-Brown

An excerpt from

The Firebird Chronicles: Through the Uncrossable Boundary

Chapter 1

The Black Horizon

'Dead Man's Fingers!' the Dark Pirate cried. 'Hard to port!'

The outline of a flinty column emerged from the mist. It looked scaly, like the decaying claw of a fallen sea monster waiting to snare ships. The Boatswain swung the wheel hard to the side, sweat pouring from his bristly beard. The ship lurched, making the crew stumble. Knot, already unsteady on his feet due to his considerable bulk, grabbed a rope as the vessel tilted. He watched, wide-eyed, as the ship curved away from the wrecking rocks, sending a cloud of sea spray into the night.

* * *

At the prow of the ship, two young Apprentices, Alfa and Sparks, fought the buffeting wind. Their waterproof hoods were pulled tight, frizzy hair whipping their faces, as they pressed into the storm. Sea lanterns swung from their hands, the beams trying to pierce the night. But the mist twisted the torchlight into ghostly shapes and rain formed a curtain of jewelled light in front of them.

'I can't see a thing!' Sparks called, her voice shrill above the waves.

'Me neither,' Alfa replied, 'but we have to try. Dead Man's Fingers are notorious wrecking rocks. A little light could make all the difference.'

Sparks's hands were trembling. 'Do you think they'll come after us?' She glanced to her side, looking for the flicker of lights in the ocean. Moments ago, the crew of the Black Horizon had been captive, surrounded by an army of Red Hawk soldiers. But then, as their leader, Falk, had met his end, the soldiers had retreated. Sparks had barely had time to take in what had happened.

'I don't know,' Alfa replied. 'They'll probably regroup and come after us. Red Hawks aren't known for their mercy. That's why we must get out of here now, even though it's dangerous to sail these waters at night. I heard the Boatswain say we had to make it past Turnpoint Island by dawn.'

'We better had,' Sparks said, 'because you know who else is out there.'

Alfa knew exactly whom Sparks was talking about – Grizelda. The old woman was their deadliest enemy.

'She's not going to leave us alone, is she?'

Alfa shook her head. The old woman would probably be even more dangerous now Falk had been defeated.

'Watch out!' Spark shouted. 'Look!'

Alfa swung her lantern to reveal a second jagged needle puncturing the sea.

'Hard starboard!' the Dark Pirate called. Sparks felt the ship adjust its course. She gripped her lantern tightly, holding her breath as they narrowly cleared the rock.

* * *

At the other end of the galleon, Mr Snooze watched the coastline of Fullstop Island disappear into the darkness. The skin of his face was paper thin, his silver hair pale in the night. Tears stung his cheeks. He closed his eyes for a moment and imagined the calming candlelight of his little Bedtime Story Slumber Shop in the village of Bardbridge. This was the first time Mr Snooze had been away from home and he was scared. It felt as though a chasm had already opened between him and everything he was familiar with.

I wonder when I'll see my home again, he thought. *If I'll ever see it again.*

He opened his eyes and blinked back a tear.

You mustn't think in that way, he told himself. *Stay strong.*

Mr Snooze squinted, trying to make out the cliffs, but he couldn't see them anymore. There was nothing but inky blackness, smudged by cloud.

His home was in terrible danger.

That's why I'm here, he reminded himself. That's why we must leave.

Fullstop Island was under the curse of a strange sickness – a living death that had swallowed many of his friends. He pictured them: Mr Bumbler, the Quill sisters and Isaiah Scriven. Mr Snooze took a sharp intake of breath and wiped his eyes.

Be strong, he told himself again. *Be strong for them.*

OUR STREET
BOOKS

Our Street Books
JUVENILE FICTION, NON-FICTION, PARENTING

Our Street Books are for children of all ages, delivering a potent mix of fantastic, rip-roaring adventure and fantasy stories to excite the imagination; spiritual fiction to help the mind and the heart; humorous stories to make the funny bone grow; historical tales to evolve interest; and all manner of subjects that stretch imagination, grab attention, inform, inspire and keep the pages turning. Our subjects include Non-fiction and Fiction, Fantasy and Science Fiction, Religious, Spiritual, Historical, Adventure, Social Issues, Humour, Folk Tales and more.
If you have enjoyed this book, why not tell other readers by posting a review on your preferred book site.

Recent bestsellers from Our Street Books are:

Relax Kids: Aladdin's Magic Carpet
Marneta Viegas
Let Snow White, the Wizard of Oz and other fairytale
characters show you and your child how to meditate and relax.
Meditations for young children aged 5 and up.
Paperback: 978-1-78279-869-9 Hardcover: 978-1-90381-666-0

Wonderful Earth
An interactive book for hours of fun learning
Mick Inkpen, Nick Butterworth
An interactive Creation story: Lift the flap, turn the wheel, look
in the mirror, and more.
Hardcover: 978-1-84694-314-0

Boring Bible: Super Son Series 1
Andy Robb
Find out about angels, sin and the Super Son of God.
Paperback: 978-1-84694-386-7

Jonah and the Last Great Dragon
Legend of the Heart Eaters
M.E. Holley
When legendary creatures invade our world, only dragon-fire
can destroy them; and Jonah alone can control the Great
Dragon.
Paperback: 978-1-78099-541-0 ebook: 978-1-78099-542-7

Little Prayers Series: Classic Children's Prayers
Alan and Linda Parry
Traditional prayers told by your child's favourite creatures.
Hardcover: 978-1-84694-449-9

Magnificent Me, Magnificent You The Grand Canyon
Dawattie Basdeo, Angela Cutler
A treasure filled story of discovery with a range of inspiring fun
exercises, activities, songs and games for children aged 6 to 11.
Paperback: 978-1-78279-819-4

Q is for Question
An ABC of Philosophy
Tiffany Poirier
An illustrated non-fiction philosophy book to help children
aged 8 to 11 discover, debate and articulate thought-provoking,
open-ended questions about existence, free will and happiness.
Hardcover: 978-1-84694-183-2

Relax Kids: How to be Happy
52 positive activities for children
Marneta Viegas
Fun activities to bring the family together.
Paperback: 978-1-78279-162-1

Rise of the Shadow Stealers
The Firebird Chronicles
Daniel Ingram-Brown
Memories are going missing. Can Fletcher and Scoop unearth
their own lost history and save the Storyteller's treasure from
the shadows?
Paperback: 978-1-78099-694-3 ebook: 978-1-78099-693-6

Readers of ebooks can buy or view any of these bestsellers by clicking on the live link in the title. Most titles are published in paperback and as an ebook. Paperbacks are available in traditional bookshops. Both print and ebook formats are available online.

Find more titles and sign up to our readers' newsletter at
http://www.johnhuntpublishing.com/children-and-young-adult
Follow us on Facebook at
https://www.facebook.com/JHPChildren and Twitter at
https://twitter.com/JHPChildren

Printed and bound by PG in the USA